ASKING
for a
FRIEND

ALSO BY KARA H.L. CHEN

Love & Resistance

KARA H.L. CHEN

ASKING
for a
FRIEND

Quill Tree Books
An Imprint of HarperCollinsPublishers

Quill Tree Books is an imprint of HarperCollins Publishers.

Asking for a Friend
Copyright © 2024 by Kara H.L. Chen
Interior illustrations © 2024 by Debs Lim
 For information address HarperCollins
Children's Books, a division of HarperCollins Publishers, 195 Broadway,
New York, NY 10007.
www.epicreads.com

Library of Congress Control Number: 2023944147
ISBN 978-0-06-323788-9
Typography by Laura Mock
24 25 26 27 28 LBC 5 4 3 2 1
First Edition

For my brother, Charles,
and
Sophia and Ariana

This is a work of fiction. Any parental figures contained in this novel are fictitious. Any resemblance to actual parents, Taiwanese or otherwise, is purely coincidental.

1

HOW TO WIN COMPETITIONS AND INFLUENCE PEOPLE

THERE ARE MANY ways to crash and burn at a networking event for a competition you need to win. Getting people's names wrong. Being overly aggressive. Making inappropriate jokes. Then there's having everyone find out that you once barfed on the judge's father. That's just a category all by itself.

Oh, I wish I were kidding.

The day had started out so well, too: perfect outfit (suit in a responsible dark blue, sensible low-heeled shoes, hair pulled back in a stylish ponytail); practice questions written on notecards in my pocket; and extra copies of my résumé in my purse. All the reasons I was the best candidate to win the Asian Americans in Business Competition—aka the AABC—memorized and practiced under mock stressful conditions (i.e., my younger sister, Hattie, giving her best impression of our mom's Duck Cleaver Death Glare while I practiced). Text messages to my partner, Eric Lin, reminding him of the location and time of the event. Texts that he, of course, didn't answer.

Partnering with Eric had been my mom's idea. He perfectly fulfilled my mom's criteria: he, like me, was also Taiwanese and a senior in high school, was on the straight path to the Ivies and then to business school, and was Taiwanese.

Did I mention he's Taiwanese?

Plus, Eric's siblings had already gone to Yale and Wharton, respectively, and his family was firmly and benignly on top of the social tree. Unlike ours, which had suffered a spectacular fall due to my older sister, Bella.

Thus came Gèi Wéi, aka the Master Strategy. You know how the rising tide lifts all boats and all that? To my mom, latching myself to Eric's incandescent star was the first step toward our triumphant return back into society. My mom had been isolating herself from everyone—and their judgment—since Bella had gotten pregnant in medical school and had dropped out. I had seen how she had to sit on the couch by herself at parties, in the early days, her carefully pressed dress pooling around her. How the other parents would chat about their kids, and my mother would have to focus on her meal, her chopsticks slowly picking up small pieces of rice. It was bad enough that she was alone since my father's death. But there was a different kind of awkward after Bella. Silence may be a virtue in America, but it meant shame for my mom and her friends.

But my mom's self-imposed solitude didn't mean that she had stopped plotting. Like Napoleon in exile, she was constantly searching for a way back in.

The only problem with Gèi Wéi was that I, you know, had to work with Eric Lin. I had to go up to him at school, even though we were *not* friends, and ask him to partner with me. He had not responded at first, and I could almost see his calculations: on the one hand, he knew from our shared membership in the Student Business Association that I was smart and hardworking. A win in this competition—which was super prestigious—could help both of us with our college applications. On the other hand, his mom might give him grief about partnering with me since I was part of a family that already had one rebellious daughter. Mrs. Lin thought I could also be a loose cannon, firing into the sky of Failure. The silence between Eric and me stretched to downright awkwardness, but he had finally agreed before scuttling off with his friends.

But since then, even though I had been diligently researching all the past challenges and winners, he had not done a thing. I had seen his mom picking him up after school, and I had tried to wave at them both. She refused to make eye contact with me, then pulled Eric away.

I'm sure it would be fine. He would get his act together, then we could go and crush this thing. I looked for him as I walked into the chilly lobby of the Esher Convention Center. Today was the kickoff party for the AABC, before registration opened in two days and everything officially began. I remember when these networking events used to be held in the gym of our local high school or in a small room at the cultural center in Old Taipei. I was really young then, sneaking free snacks from the potluck tables and trying not to get in trouble along with

3

Bella and Hattie. I never could have imagined the competition would have grown to be so big and fancy by the time I was old enough to compete; winners now got a prize package that included a prestigious line on their college applications and—thanks to corporate sponsors—a full scholarship to the college of their choice. But as the AABC grew, so did the number of competitors.

I checked in my coat and then went over to a table with a silver-colored tablecloth, which had name tags neatly lined up on top. There were a lot of name tags. More than I had expected. I recognized some of the people, like Rhonda Naidu, who had started a nonprofit to provide medical services to countries devastated by natural disasters. She had given one of the student keynote speeches at the state Student Business Association conference last year. Crap. Was she also applying? I recognized some of the other names, people who had recently won the Mayfield and the Gillford competitions. Were they all here?

I scanned the letter L name tags, and Eric's was missing. At least he had showed up. Which was . . . something.

The ballroom was beautifully decorated with my dad's favorite colors, silver and green. Oh, the other thing about this competition? It had been started, years ago, by my father. He had the idea for it the year he died, when I was eleven. He had wanted to give back to the community and to encourage Asian Americans to enter the world of business. In his will, my father had left the administration of the AABC and some of his other business assets to his friend, Mr. Lee. Five years ago, it had been taken over by Mr. Lee's son, James.

I had seen the AABC since its conception, scribbled on a small napkin on a table over my father's hospital bed. He had written a broad outline with a leaky rollerball and had later detailed it more thoroughly in his will. As I grew up, I had gone to every award ceremony, stood on the side with my mom and my sisters, and watched teen after teen take the trophy emblazoned with my father's name. I had seen person after person intern at the Lee Corporation and go on to Harvard or Yale, where my father went. Where I needed to go.

By the door was the large plaque that they had made the first year of the competition. Every winner had their name engraved on it, along with the year of their victory. There was a blank new silver plate for this year. And a space. For my name.

If winning this thing meant I had to partner with Eric Lin, so be it.

I finally found Eric in a corner talking to Albert Goda, who was in the Student Business Association with us. Albert was a computing genius and also loved street art and graffiti. He had started an app where people could upload pictures of their favorite murals and add their own drawings. I wondered who his partner was. I didn't see anyone else from our school. Maybe he was pairing with someone from another city?

As I marched up to them, they abruptly stopped talking. Eric had the nerve to give me a small wave, like he hadn't been ghosting me for the past week.

"Did you get my texts?" I asked, then remembered my manners. "Hi, Albert."

He glanced at Eric but didn't say anything. Eric was the personification of uncomfortable.

"Juliana," he said. "You made it."

I wasn't the one who was ghosting here, *Eric*. Of course I had showed up.

I was about to ask Eric what his deal was when he suddenly straightened. I turned, and there was James Lee, our judge. A few feet behind him, talking to some of the other contestants, was his father.

Oh God. I had my résumé in my purse, right? Networking questions memorized?

I inhaled for exactly five seconds and pictured a large balloon filling, then deflating. This was going to be fine. Totally fine.

James (Harvard Class of 2001, Harvard Business School '04, CEO of the Lee Corporation, a tech company now worth millions) was in his forties and was legendary in the Taiwanese American community. He was basically who I wanted to be when I grew up. I didn't know him super well since he was much older than me, and my family hadn't seen many people since our social plummet, aka The Fall. There had been rumors of some kind of rift between our fathers a long time ago, but it must have all worked out since Dad had left Mr. Lee all of those things in his will.

James walked toward us, and I tried to figure out if he seemed more friendly to us than the others.

Aaaand . . . no.

"Juliana Zhao." His tone was formal. "Nice to see you again."

I tried to appear confident yet humble, a combination that, unfortunately, made my face spasm. We made small talk for a bit, then he said, "I'm not surprised to see you here. You, of course, want to go into business? Like your dad?"

Focus. I had practiced this. "Yes, I believe business is the ideal major for people who are self-starters and provides a perfect foundation for financial success."

James tilted his head. "But which part are you interested in? There are many aspects of business and many reasons why people want to pursue it. Why do you want to go to business school? Specifically?"

Specifically? I had already given him my whole answer. It was the sentence I had perfected over weeks of drafting. I specifically wanted to win this competition and go to Yale.

He waited. But when I didn't say anything further, he said, "I suggest you figure that out before you register, Ms. Zhao."

Eric stepped forward. "I am interested in venture capitalism, much like you are." He started a private conversation with James, but I didn't care. I was still thinking about what he had said. Why wasn't my answer good enough?

Next to us, James's father, Mr. Lee, was walking slowly, shaking everyone's hands. When he got to me, he smiled warmly.

"Juliana Zhao!" He was always so nice every time I saw him, even after The Fall.

Oh, wait.

Oh *no*.

Mr. Lee was always so nice, but he always told the same story whenever he saw me. The exact same story, which was innocuous enough when I was with my mother but not when I was in front of Eric Lin, Albert Goda, and our competitors.

"Juliana, I remember when you were a baby—"

Oh God.

"—you must have been only a few months old!"

Could I stop this somehow? Pull a fire alarm? Pretend to faint?

"You remember? And your dad let me pick you up, and you—"

Don't say it. Don't say it.

"—spit up right all over me! So much throw up! Do you remember?"

I smiled, weakly. Eric seemed like he wanted to step into a giant sinkhole and vanish.

Mr. Lee patted my arm. "So good to see you. Are you really old enough to compete now?"

"Yes, sir." I tried to project confidence instead of, you know, looking like a person who couldn't keep down baby solids.

"And are you doing well in school?"

I said yes with what was hopefully the proper amount of modesty.

"Good! Good." He leaned on his cane. "Your father would have been proud."

I knew he meant to be kind. He had no way of knowing I had spent the morning in my dad's office, going through his old books and photos. Didn't know that I had pictured this moment for so many years, but in my dream, my father was alive. *Good luck*, he would say. *Speak slowly but confidently. And remember . . .*

And remember? I would say.

He would hug me. *You'll do fine.*

The legacy of him in my imagined other life was as large as my memory of him in our real one. What could he have been, if he had lived? What else could he have created? What could our family have been? I had read the half-finished notes in his desk, full of mysterious ideas and charts, but they were indecipherable to me. That's why I needed to go to Yale, to follow in his footsteps. I could complete his legacy.

But the first step, the necessary stamp of my legitimacy, was winning his competition. He had left these white pebbles in the forest for me, and it was my job to pick them up and follow them.

The prickling came then, an unexpected grip of grief. I was used to it, these sudden waves of emotion, and knew what to do. I'd had a lot of practice crating my feelings—boxing them, weighing them down, and letting them sink into the dark water. But I didn't do it quickly enough.

Eric, horrified, stepped forward as I gathered myself together and focused on the competition. "It must be so nice to see your son take over things so successfully, Mr. Lee."

When Mr. Lee had been in charge of the AABC, it had been more in line with what my father had envisioned: a networking event and a competition that were more about teaching the contestants to navigate and succeed in the corporate world. He had challenges that helped contestants become more comfortable with promoting their own work and encouraged them to think creatively.

Since James had taken over, though, the AABC had become more results oriented. The hypotheticals began to focus more on how to make and launch products. James had started a savvy marketing campaign and had made the AABC into an influential component of college applications for undergrad business majors.

Mr. Lee was also Taiwanese, so he, like my own mother, seemed to be allergic to complimenting his own child. It was seen as boasting and, thus, a huge no-no.

"Jimmy tries so hard. But he could still make the challenges more educational," he said.

James was almost twice my age, but I could recognize all too well the suppressed eye roll. "Generating revenue is the most important thing in business. They should learn early, Dad. As I had to."

A silence fell between them, and it was downright awkward.

Mr. Lee said, in Taiwanese, "Enough. It's all in the past."

It didn't look like it was in the past. What was James talking about? Eric glanced at me, but I had no clue. I was going to ask, but Mr. Lee had already left to talk to the next bunch of contestants, and James left with him.

Two girls came up to us—Kelly Nguyen and her cousin Linda Tham. I had met them both at the state SBA conference. Kelly had helped me when I had gotten lost and we had all bonded over the difficulties women in leadership positions faced. They were a formidable duo. Kelly had a strong programming background and was into innovative tech solutions. Linda's father was an entrepreneur and had helped her to launch several micro start-ups in the fashion arena. I had bought one of her sweaters, and it was easily one of my favorites.

They said hi, and Eric acted uncomfortable, like I was fraternizing with the enemy. But Albert was staring at Linda like he had just seen the sun emerge from a cloud. Hmm. Linda's fashions had more of a free-form edge, and she might like Albert's art. Also, she was, as far as I knew, single.

I introduced them to each other with a proper hook and I saw them both brighten. I subtly pulled Kelly aside and took Eric with us.

Kelly stifled a laugh. "It's not only at the SBA," she said. "You do this all the time?"

At state conference, I had noticed Chad Brickowski and Wayne Porter eyeing each other and trying to arrive at the cafeteria at the same time for every meal. I finally arranged a big group lunch and made sure they sat next to each other. The rest I left up to Cupid.

(Or me. I also made sure they sat next to each other during the closing ceremony and had each other's contact information before the conference ended. I mean, Cupid is nice and all, but sometimes a girl's got to take matters into her own hands.)

"What?" I was the epitome of innocence. "I merely wanted to let them know what they had in common."

Kelly laughed, then carefully glanced around the room. She pulled me into an empty corner. Eric seemed nervous, but I motioned him over to join us.

"I heard something," she said.

"Oh?"

"I think the challenge is going to have something to do with a website."

I said, "What?" at the same time Eric blurted out, "How did you find out?"

Kelly looked at him curiously.

Wait. Eric didn't say, "How do you know?" He said, "How did you find out?" He also wasn't surprised at all. Had he somehow heard about this before and didn't tell me?

"Did you know about this?" I asked. Is this why he was ghosting me?

"What? No. No, why would I know?" Here's another thing Eric Lin could not do, in addition to returning texts: lie. His glance was guilty, sliding to the side of me.

Kelly glanced at me. *This guy is your partner?*

I know, Kelly. Really, I know.

I said to her, "Are you sure?"

Kelly leaned forward. "I overheard James and Mr. Lee talking to one of the organizers. They were making sure the servers had enough capacity to host a bunch of websites."

If Kelly was right, this was a serious problem. I knew less than nothing about programming or web pages, and I was pretty sure Eric didn't, either. Here was the extent of my computer knowledge: you turn on your laptop. It's supposed to work. End of story.

"Do you know anything about tech or design?" I hissed to Eric.

He glanced at Kelly, like he didn't want to talk in front of her. Which was totally rude, considering she had just given us a major hint. I smiled at Kelly, apologetically. I thanked her for her help and wished her luck on the competition. But by the time I had finished chatting with her, Eric had disappeared. And so had Albert.

2

EVERYTHING IS ALL GOOD! *ALL GOOD!*

ERIC LIN WASN'T going to hose me, was he? He wouldn't dare. He knew this competition required partners, so if he dropped me this late in the game—*two days before registration opened*—I would be totally and utterly screwed. Even Eric Lin wouldn't be that ruthless, would he?

But I thought about him in our SBA meetings, how he was always driven and particularly fixated on college admissions. I had once asked him which school he wanted to go to, and to my surprise, he said Dartmouth. When I asked why, he said, "It's an Ivy and it's the farthest away." I heard through the grapevine that if he didn't get into an Ivy, his parents were going to make him stay in the tri-state area, where they could keep an eye on him until grad school.

I thought my mother was . . . motivated. But Mrs. Lin was at a whole other level. Even when we were little kids, Eric was always in extra math or science classes or at sports competitions. He was also the first to disappear or skip out on where he was supposed to be. His grades were still stellar, since he was kind of a genius, but I recently had seen him refuse to go to tennis practice and other social events. Giving his parents an attitude in public. I knew it was agonizing for Mrs. Lin, because we children were basically report cards on how good of a job that our parents have done.

My non-Taiwanese classmates might never understand how much of a currency the Ivy League was to my mom and her friends, but it was the world she had to survive in. The rest of America was different and confusing, with fast language and slang and values that she didn't understand. So she had no choice but to swim in the Line gossip river, aka the Linevine. Hattie called it messed up, but that's just how things were.

And I, now that I had come of age, was finally eligible to enter the competition. But since my mom had boasted about the prestige of the AABC for years, I had no choice. I had to get on that award plaque or die trying. Because it was about more than me or my mom. It was my father's name on the line.

During our last dinner party, when I was fifteen, I remember one of the aunties had asked about Bella, right as the news of her unwed pregnancy was scorching up the Linevine. In other communities, this might have been a nonissue. But for my mom's group, where even divorces were gossiped about, this was scandalous. Bella had been Mom's ace, but now she was her biggest liability. Mom had offered a generic *Grandkids are such a blessing*, but the uncles and aunties knew. They all knew.

That was when my mom retreated. She put away her fancy clothes, wrapped up the last of her dignity, and hid. She couldn't bear to have the same conversation, to have to fall on her sword at every meal after humble bragging about Bella for years. There was schadenfreude, and then there was Linevine schadenfreude, which was basically the electricity the whole system ran on. We stopped going to events. No more parties, except for the huge ones.

Until this year, when we had attended one of our rare social functions, a big potluck. Mom and I had gone to the bathroom before it had started. We were both about to leave our stalls when an auntie's voice floated through the bathroom.

"There was another article about the AABC in the paper." She was speaking in Taiwanese. "It's starting soon."

Another auntie said, "It's so big now. So famous." I felt a happy warmth, like finding a dollar in your pocket. People still remembered my dad, remembered what he had done.

"Is your son in it?"

"*Ai-yo*, he wants to be a doctor, like his dad." The other auntie tried to sound like it was a burden.

"Oh, like Jùnhóng's older daughter. Such a shame about what happened to her."

Was she talking about Bella? In the stall next to me, my mom's shoe shifted ever so slightly. But she didn't say a word. Neither did I.

"And the youngest one, always wearing the wild clothes." The auntie tsked.

"Is the middle one going to try?"

There was the sound of water running. "Did you hear she tried to do early admission to Yale but didn't get in?"

The cold spikes of shame skewered me. I had gotten the letter in December. It was the other reason I needed to win the competition, the reason I couldn't talk about. I had been kicked to the general admission pile, so I had one last shot to get into Yale. A victory in the AABC could give me a huge advantage.

The auntie said, "I don't see how she can do well. She hasn't done any of the other competitions, either, or interned anywhere. Poor Jùnhóng. Sùyīn isn't paying enough attention to those kids. He would have been so upset. All of them, such—" There was more water running, then the aunties left.

It was silent for a long moment. Then I heard my mom's quick and precise footsteps walking toward the sink. When I got there, her hands were on the counter and her head was bowed. Then she unclasped the latch of her black Chanel purse, pulled out her reddest lipstick, and carefully applied it. She faced me, and we were in total agreement. It was *on*. She dusted off her fancy clothes and began to plot. And I started researching the competition in earnest and reading all of my dad's old business books.

After all that, I wasn't going to be derailed by a slacker partner. I searched around the ballroom, but Eric and Albert weren't there. Whatever. I spent the rest of the evening networking my little heart out, chatting with people I had seen at the SBA state conference or meeting new people who I had not talked to before. It was rather exciting to see all these Asian Americans in one place, all ready to break the ceilings of corporate America. Dad would have been proud.

I happened to be next to some of the competition organizers at the end of the event. They were quietly gossiping about the huge donation from Mrs. Lin and how it was helping them run the tech side of things. Is that how Eric had found out this year's challenge had something to do with a website?

I pulled out my phone and texted him: Where are you?

No answer.

3

WOULD WE CALL THIS BEING HOSED?

I WOKE UP and there was still nothing from Eric. I texted him one more time: We have to finalize the registration. Please send me your details ASAP.

I tried—and failed—to practice my meditative breathing as I dashed to my Saturday morning activity, Chinese class. One of the problems with a highly efficient schedule is that it doesn't allow much time for unplanned challenges. It would be okay, though. I was used to balancing a lot of things at once, and I hadn't dropped a plate.

Yet.

Unfortunately, the bad in my day got exponentially worse when Garrett Tsai entered the classroom. Garrett and I had grown up together and kind of hung out when we were little kids, before The Fall. We had both gone to Taiwanese culture camp in New Hampshire between our sophomore and junior years, when we were fifteen. But now I saw him only at Chinese class every week. Which was perfectly acceptable to me.

He strolled in as I was collecting homework packets from the younger kids. I had planned on sitting down before class and reviewing the past competition challenges, but our teacher, Anna Lǎoshī, had asked for my help and I would have felt bad about saying no.

Garrett had been growing his hair out since the summer, and it made him seem even more like a stranger. Today it was loose, brushing his neck and cheekbones. He strolled over as I was lining up all the little kids and asking them to put their homework in a basket.

"You know, there are teachers who can collect those," he said.

"Nice job, Amy!" I said, ignoring him.

All the little kids were cute, but Amy, who was super shy, might be my special favorite. She also happened to be Garrett's younger sister. How two people could be so opposite—one adorable and sunny and one off-the-charts prickly and cynical—was genetics at its most mysterious.

Fine, it was true that, when Garrett and I had gone to camp two summers ago, we had almost become . . . friends. But after he cut me off on the last day, I was forced to acknowledge that our time together had been this oasis away from reality. An outlier. Garrett and I were total opposites. And it was better to keep our interactions to a minimum.

Amy looked at the ground, her little pigtails swinging. I knelt down to give her a hug. "Is gymnastics going well?" I asked.

She nodded. I patted her head and sent her along with the other kids to the classroom next door. I understood her shyness. When I was younger, I had let Bella answer all my questions for me since she was almost eight years older and was everything I wanted to be: brave, brilliant, unstoppable. She had graduated from high school early, blazing a path so bright that her teachers still talked about her light, even today. She always spoke for Hattie and me and took care of us while our parents were at work. It wasn't until our father died, and Bella left in a fury of slammed doors and shouting, that I had to learn to speak up. Mom was too busy keeping the company together and Hattie was too young. I was the last one left, so it had to be me.

Garrett swung into his usual seat, the one behind mine, and pulled out his tablet. No *How is school going?* Or *Any news about college?* You know, the questions other people might be polite enough to ask.

I whirled away from him and grabbed the papers from the basket. I tapped them on the desk, straightening the edges. Suddenly there was a worksheet in my face.

"Amy forgot a page," Garrett said.

Oh, His Royal Crankiness deigned to speak to me. What an honor.

I plucked it from his hands, found her sheet, and stapled them together. "Thank you." I would take the high road. Model good behavior.

He was still standing there, watching me collect the last of the worksheets. "You know, the kids can turn those in by themselves."

"Some of us are helpful," I said, in Taiwanese.

"Some of us don't need to say yes to everything all the time," he muttered, also in Taiwanese.

Taiwanese is an entirely different language than Mandarin Chinese. Since it's not the official language of Taiwan, it's like a secret language spoken at home, passed down from parent to child. Some of our friends understood it pretty well from listening to their parents, but only a few of us spoke it. Garrett and I both had grandparents who had lived with us when we were younger, so we were both fairly fluent. He also spoke Mandarin annoyingly well and only took these classes to learn how to read and write.

What he was saying somehow sounded even worse in Taiwanese. Did he call me a *doormat*? Unbelievable. Just because Garrett Tsai refused to worry about college and academics didn't mean it wasn't important to the rest of us. He was into digital art and graphic design and had been working on a webtoon on the side. Things like the Ivy League weren't as vital to him as his digital art apps. His older brother, Patrick, was on track to achieve the mythical Harvard Hat Trick (undergraduate and joint law/business degree). Amy was also clearly an academic prodigy. So I guess the pressure was off Garrett. Must be nice. I allowed myself to think for a second about what it would be like to click any college application I wanted, to go anywhere I wanted. California, Washington, DC, maybe even London. What would it be like if I didn't have to stay home and pull our family together?

I couldn't even imagine; that wasn't the world I lived in.

Which is why I needed to pay attention, stat, since my Mandarin was spotty at best. Unlike Garrett. But all I could think about was the competition. Where was Eric?

I sneakily pulled out my phone and sent him a quick text: Hello, registration is tomorrow. Where are you? Nothing.

Anna Lǎoshī gave me the stink eye. I quickly shoved my phone under the desk.

"Zhuāxīn," Anna Lǎoshī said. *Pay attention.*

I waited until she turned around and then pulled out my phone again. No new messages.

During break, I was texting Eric again when I was pulled aside by my friend Emily Yao.

She flashed a quick smile at Lewis Guo, a fellow junior like her, then yanked me into the hall. "Juliana." She clutched my arm.

Emily and Lewis had been completely unaware they were perfect for each other. That is, until I had figuratively kicked Emily in the tush and convinced her to ask Lewis to a new restaurant in town. They were both major foodies and had separately mentioned how much they wanted to try it. What could be better than trying it *together*?

I mean, was it hard to be right all the time? Really, it was.

"What's up?" I glanced at the clock. Fifteen minutes left in break, and there was still so much to do: finish researching the other competitors, make a list of what I thought the challenge might be this year. Hunt down Eric Lin and roast his ghosting little entrails in the middle of the school parking lot.

23

I needed to get to work, but I loved Emily dearly and hated to let her down. I just hoped her question was quick.

Emily thrust her phone at me. On the screen was an emoji from Lewis—a brown heart.

"This is from Lewis? The Lewis who we saw two seconds ago?" I said.

"It's brown!" she wailed. "I thought he liked me."

"It's still a heart. Besides, you guys already did the kissy face last night, did you not?"

Emily's parents had forbidden her to date until college, but such a small technicality had never stopped her. Her parents thought she had joined every extracurricular under the sun. There was actually only one: Club Romance.

She shoved me. "Brown. With no other text. What does it mean?"

"Brown hearts are sometimes used in the social justice context? Were you talking about that?"

"No," she said. "He only said, 'see you soon.' Then brown heart."

"Does he like the color, maybe?" I asked.

"I don't think so."

"Oh! Maybe he was using it as a substitute for something brown? Like how people say, 'I orange heart' to mean they love oranges?"

"Okay, okay. What's brown?" She grabbed my arm. "Porcupines? Is he saying I'm prickly? Or *poop*? Poop is also brown. Is he sending me a poop heart? Is he trying to break up with me?"

I peeked into the classroom. Lewis immediately looked over,

then seemed disappointed it was only me. I ducked back into the hall. "Nope, he's still totally into you."

"THEN WHY THE POOP HEART, JULIANA?" Emily said.

A brown heart in this context was admittedly a little . . . unusual. I mean, yellow: friendship. Red: true love, obviously. Pink: cute, puppy love. This was a bit of a mystery, but there was only one way to find out what was going on.

I dragged Emily past Garrett, who was watching us, arms crossed. Whatever. He had never believed in love and romance, not like I did. Garrett had done his seventh-grade English project on death in eighteenth-century literature, was currently drawing a webtoon about betrayal and the end of the world, and had told me once, unironically, that "love is for fools and divorce attorneys." For him, the glass wasn't half empty. It was half empty and contained carcinogens that would directly cause a prolonged and painful death.

He was super fun at parties, Garrett.

I brought Emily toward Lewis. I swear, the guy turned into a walking heart-eye emoji at the sight of her.

"Lewis," I said.

"Hi, Juliana. *Emily.*" Lewis blushed, which was adorable. (Clearly Emily thought so, too, because she beamed.)

I had to get this train back on track because I had a competition to research and break was almost over.

"So, I have a quick favor to ask," I said to Lewis. "I am doing a word association project and I need your help."

"Okay?"

"Let's go." I glanced at the clock. Seven minutes left. "Shoe."

"Sneaker."

"Ice cream."

"Butter pecan."

"Oh, my favorite!" Emily said. They smiled at each other. Was this too much, even for me? Maybe.

"Brown," I said.

"Chocolate."

Emily made a noise. "Chocolate? Not . . . I mean . . . not . . ."

Lewis finally looked at her. "I sent you a— Maybe you didn't have a chance to see it yet? Remember we were talking about our favorite chocolate places? Last night?"

I practically saw Emily start to glow. "*Chocolate*," she said. "I do remember."

I discreetly nudged her in his direction and then dashed to an empty corner. Love preserved, yes! Time for research. But then Garrett came up to me.

"Another match successfully saved?" He made it seem like a crime.

"You're just jealous I can promote real human connections. Unlike you."

"Sure, they seem happy now," he said. "They'll probably have a few good weeks until their scarring breakup and months of recovery."

"What. Is. Wrong. With. You." I didn't understand how he could possibly be so negative all the time. Especially about love. My dad had always believed in it—the alchemy between people. Even after he died, whenever I saw people in love, it was like a reminder of him. He had that magic with my mom and had never wanted us to forget it. *Don't settle for less, girls.*

Garrett said, "You're just setting people up for inevitable pain. It's best to not even start." Someone else might say this as a joke. Had we been at camp, years ago, Garrett might have said it lightly, teasingly. But now he wasn't kidding.

My phone beeped. Finally! I turned away from Garrett without responding and checked my messages.

Eric: We need to talk.

We need to talk? Sometimes people said that before good news, right? Like, we need to talk—you won the lottery! We need to talk—you got into Yale!

Or not.

I checked the clock. Two minutes left before break ended. I rushed into the hall and called him.

I didn't want to hear it. I knew what he was going to say. But when the words actually came out, it was like a stab.

"I don't think we're going to work out." Eric didn't bother with the small talk, and I didn't want it. "We should find different partners."

"Are you kidding me right now? Are you, what—doing the competition with Albert?"

"I wish you the best of luck." He had the nerve to sound genuinely regretful.

"Are you ditching me for *Albert?*" I shouted.

There was a long pause. "Listen, my mom—"

"Don't try to blame this on *your mother.*"

"My mom's not the problem." There was no cruelty in his

27

voice, though there could have been. "It's yours."

"What's that supposed to mean?"

"My mom thinks . . ." He didn't have to say it. We were a bad influence. Her son shouldn't get close to me, due to our Fall. I was not a good enough partner to vault her precious Eric to victory.

I was hot with the peeling feeling of shame. It was like we were toxins and Mrs. Lin wanted to make sure we were as far away from Eric as possible.

He said, "Goodbye, Juliana." To his credit, he did sound regretful. But it was way outweighed by the fact that he still did a shitty thing.

I shoved my phone into my purse, then stood alone in the hall, stunned.

I was royally, epically screwed.

4

YES, WE WOULD CALL THIS BEING HOSED

IT WAS ABSOLUTELY, 100 percent not time to panic.

Okay, my dad's favorite book, *How to Be Your Best Entrepreneur*, would say to break each problem down into manageable components. Then create a clear strategy and execute it with small, clearly defined steps.

Inhale organization. Exhale organization. Ahhh.

There was no time to find someone who wanted to do this competition with me. I had already reviewed all the other potential candidates before I had talked to Eric, and everyone I knew either had no time or wasn't interested. Okay, maybe I should find someone who could partner with me in name only. Surely I could find *someone* and offer to help them with homework or something in exchange for registering with me. Yes. Yes! Okay, this was workable. I could take care of the rest of the competition on my own and still win. Or at least beat that weasel Eric Lin.

I quickly Googled "how long does it take to learn to design a professional website?" while Anna Lǎoshī was writing something on the whiteboard.

Google answers:

FIVE TO SIX MONTHS

TWENTY WEEKS

THREE HUNDRED HOURS??

I shoved my phone back into my purse. Wrapped my hand around the key chain Dad had given to me when I was a kid, a jade pig, since I was born during the Year of the Pig. I pictured my meditation balloon puffing and narrowing.

Maybe I could use one of those sites that had premade templates? You pay a fee, pick one and *voilà*! Website! I quickly pulled up the most famous company and scanned some examples. Perfect. It could work.

Anna Lǎoshī rapped on the whiteboard. "Juliana."

I smiled. Everything would be fine.

Everything was not fine.

When I got home, I did a deep dive on one of those builder sites as a kind of practice run. Dad always said that early preparation is the best preparation. So I signed up for a free trial on WeBuilder.com, picked out a template, and used a free graphic design program to create a logo. So far, so good!

I found a photo I liked, pasted, and then . . . huh. Why was it so large? How could I make it smaller? I tried clicking on a few buttons, but it somehow moved to a side column and I couldn't figure out how to move it back.

Argh!

This was a problem. My earlier idea to get someone in name only might not cut it. What I really needed to do was find someone who knew how to do web design. I went through my contacts again. Jonah from the Student Business Association dabbled in it, but his site was worse than mine. Mariah Jones might have the expertise, but she wasn't Asian American, so she couldn't compete. I was prohibited from hiring a professional designer, so that was out. I suppose I could partner with someone in name only and then sneakily hire someone on the sly, like some freelance high schooler, but I wanted to win this one square.

Unfortunately, I happened to know of one person who would exactly fit the bill. Someone who was writing his own webtoon, was a whiz with graphic design, and who had spare time since he couldn't care less about the Ivy League. The last person on earth I wanted to ask.

The truth is, I had forced myself to push Garrett out of my mind this past year. I didn't talk to him outside of class, not even when I heard he had gotten an early acceptance into RISD, which was his dream school. Not when Anna Lǎoshī held a whole class on Chinese opera, which the old us would have found hysterical. He had made it more than clear what he thought of me.

I scanned Dad's office as if some alternate solution would magically appear. My mom had kept it just as it was before he died; the only change she had made was that she had closed the heating vent so we wouldn't waste electricity. I snuck in here sometimes to study, and I knew Hattie did, too, because I occasionally found empty White Rabbit candy wrappers in his drawers. But we never talked about it.

I sat in Dad's desk chair now, swiveling in slow circles. When he was alive, I had never been able to touch the ground. Now I could, easily. I wondered what he had thought about when he sat here. His business? Us?

I remembered when we had gone to Taiwan for my grandmother's funeral, we had burned small packets of fake money, paper cars, letters. People believed the smoke from these talismans could cross the border between life and death. We could gift our relatives with these things they needed in the afterlife.

I knew what I would burn for my father—a single piece of paper with one message on it: *I won, Dad. I did it.*

I hadn't been old enough to really know him before he died, so I had collected as many fragments of him as I could over the years. I had shadowed his footsteps, each foot precisely within each outline, because I believed—I *knew*—if I took the same journey, I could come that much closer to understanding him. When I got to Yale, when I got to walk on the same paths he had, when I got to take the same classes with his old professors, I could decipher what mattered to him. Who he was.

For him, I could do this. To uphold his name and legacy so the gossiping uncles and aunties wouldn't drag it down, I would ask *Garrett Tsai* for a favor. I would swallow that pill.

I stared at the photo of Dad and his college buddies, then touched it for good luck. But I knew as well as anyone that luck wouldn't win me this competition. Luck—like everything else—could never be trusted to stay when you needed it.

5

INTERLUDE: SUMMER CAMP, NEW HAMPSHIRE

ONE OF THE favorite things my dad used to do every Sunday night was read the "Modern Love" column in the *New York Times*. Chance meetings, relationships surviving long distance, love at first sight—he adored them all. It was his favorite part of the newspaper.

I preferred the "Tiny Love Stories," entries of one hundred words or less that tell the story of a relationship. I loved seeing little windows into the profound connections that can happen between two people, even if the ending is bittersweet.

I had read them every week since Garrett and I had our time together in New Hampshire, and I had often wondered if one hundred words could ever capture the birth and death of a friendship.

If they could, they would be these.

(1)

You were the only other person I knew in our small group. We had grown up together but had not been close. You laughed at my joke about fried squid snacks. We were the only two who went the wrong way during the dance workshop. We both liked the absurdity of watching movies outside while wearing T-shirts and pajama pants. When you talked about feeling out of sync since you were one of the few Asian Americans at your school, I understood perfectly. You were always quiet. Is that why I never heard you before?

(2)

Friendship can begin with a meal. A plunked-down tray, a saved seat, then a text asking where you are for breakfast. The comfort of being expected, of having a place, was a relief. It made me tell you things, like how I had a fear of squirrels and an unreasonable love for stickers with googly eyes. You broke your arm while playing tetherball when you were six. Your brother, the golden child, constantly belittled you. Your mother still believes you lost a sweater your grandma gave you; it's hidden in a Monopoly box. We were in a magical bubble.

(3)

The day before we left, we decided we would watch the sunrise together. There are times when I catch you staring at me. You are the first boy I have ever stayed up the whole night with. We sneak out by the river, our feet swinging over the bank, and we are talking. We are always talking. Even when the sun begins to come over the horizon and the light hits us, the words don't cease. I don't want the last day to arrive and carry us back to the real world. But it does.

(4)

The day we leave, I see my mom and some aunties chatting. I see you behind them, then you stop. You hear everything; you can't help it. You hang your head. You pivot and walk in the other direction.

The next time I see you, you are a stranger. I ask what they said, but you won't tell me. You are what we were before these two weeks, but it's worse because you are edgy and standoffish and I remember when you weren't.

I remember everything. I don't know if you do.

6

LESSONS IN NEGOTIATION

IF I WANTED to find Garrett, I knew exactly where I should go: the Taiwanese cultural center in Old Taipei. It was relatively close to his parents' veterinary office, and was where he volunteered every weekend, sometimes leading art classes with the little kids or teaching Taiwanese. He probably hung out at that place more than his own home. If there was a spot I should check first, that was it.

I got into my car and gunned it to Old Taipei. It had been a while since I had been in this neighborhood; my mom and her friends stopped coming after the opening of the newer Dynasty Mall across town. The cultural center was inside an old warehouse, which at one point used to be a school, then an office building, and was now a multipurpose center. There was a big general/dining room when you first walked in and various classrooms down the hallways and upstairs. If there was any doubt as to the purpose of this place, one only had to see the one-story-tall Taiwanese flag hanging in the front of the main room.

After accidentally interrupting a tai chi class in one room and a cutthroat game of mah-jongg in another, I finally found Garrett in the back. He was lounging on an old couch as a bunch of kids watched a *Godzilla* movie.

He sat up when he saw me. "Juliana?" He stared at me like I was a kaiju that had materialized in the middle of the room. And in a way, I was. I hadn't been inside this place since Dad had been alive. It still looked the same, kind of, but way more run-down than I remembered.

I sat on the edge of the worn cushion next to him. Across the room, some of the little kids had snuck over and were trying to watch the movie from the side door.

"Are you sure Amy is old enough to see this?" I said as one of the monsters on screen had his head ripped off. I wasn't stalling, per se. I was just, you know, warming up.

Garrett frowned. "Ames."

She shushed him with a waved arm.

"Ames."

She sighed and came over to him.

"You know the rule," he said, but his tone was kind. "No grown-up movies. Do you want some of your workbooks instead? Or do you want to go back and watch the *Octonauts* next door?"

Amy was a major math prodigy. Even at her young age, it

was obvious; she was already two grades ahead and their mom had started to homeschool her. In Amy's spare time, she also competed in gymnastics, so she was often at tournaments.

Amy dug in his backpack and pulled out some books and a little knitted turtle. But she did it slowly, trying to sneak peeks at the screen.

"It's okay," I whispered. "Godzilla wins at the end."

Her eyes widened.

"You know the creature with the big wings?"

She nodded.

"He's totally a good guy."

"Hey!" one of the kids bellowed. It was David Chan, who I had also known since we were babies. "NO SPOILERS!"

I winked at Amy. "And," I said, "he brings a whole army with him and they all fight the bad guys and they win."

"JULIANA!" David shouted. "I CAN HEAR YOU."

Amy's jaw dropped, then she gave me a hug before she left. Garrett grabbed Amy's water bottle, then ran to give it to her.

His tablet was on the cushion, and I took a peek at what he was working on. He had told me at camp that he had started a webtoon, a revenge tale about a space pirate named Yen, whose crew had abandoned him for his former cocaptain/best friend. He hadn't let me read the whole thing, though the few panels I had seen were filled with an unusual melancholy. Was he still working on it?

Garrett jogged back, then flipped the tablet over. "Why are you here?"

I watched Godzilla stomping his way through the city. I would almost prefer getting crushed by one of his giant monster feet.

"I need your help," I said.

"What?" He was shocked. Believe me, if I had any other option, I would have taken it.

Think of Dad. The competition.

"Is everything okay?" he asked. For a second, he was almost like he had been once upon a time: concerned, caring. "Is something wrong?"

I wasn't fooled. I knew all too well how easily Garrett Tsai could turn into a stranger. How fast the walls could come up.

"It's the AABC." I might as well get it over with. "You know, the business competition? It's really important to my mom—and me, too—that I do well."

Garrett's face closed up again. Surprise.

"Of course it is," he said. "Of course that's what it's about."

"What's that supposed to mean?"

"What do you want."

Godzilla got bitten by one of the monsters, and he roared in pain. I feel you, Godzilla. "So, the challenge this year has something to do with a website."

"So?"

Godzilla ripped a head off another sea monster. "I was supposed to partner with Eric Lin, but it . . . didn't work out. He's doing it with someone else at our school."

Garrett was silent.

I thought of my dad again. About my mom, alone again on

a weekend night, quietly working in the kitchen, the dim light over her head. About that rat bastard Eric Lin.

"I don't know anything about coding or design," I said. "But you do. So I wanted to know if you would do the competition with me. As my partner."

Garrett looked like I had suggested that he enter an Olympic bobsled tournament. "Me?"

"Yes."

"Why would I possibly do that? I don't know anything about business."

"I'll take care of that part. You just need to do the art stuff. Like website design. Maybe a logo, some flyers. Not much."

"The AABC. The competition everyone talks about all the time." By everyone, I knew he meant the Linevine.

"Yes." I didn't see why it mattered to him. His parents worked in Old Taipei, so they weren't really in the center of the Linevine. Those uncles and aunties were mostly my mom's former friends: the doctors, engineers, and CEOs. The group here didn't socialize with them as much, except at the really big events, like the Mid-Autumn Moon Festival or the Lunar New Year celebration.

Garrett shook his head. "No way. I don't need to impress any of those people."

"It's not about impressing them," I said.

"Really."

Okay, it was about impressing them. But it was also about my dad and upholding his legacy, not that I would tell Mr. Garrett Tsai about that.

41

It was time to bring out the big guns. I had already anticipated his rejection and had come prepared. Dad always said if
you enter a negotiation, you must bring something to the table.
I knew Garrett had been working various jobs around Old Taipei, trying to collect enough savings for tuition to RISD.

"The AABC comes with a full scholarship for each person
on the winning team," I said. "To the school of your choice."

Now I had his attention.

I also knew the cultural center was in dire need of funds
since it—and all of Old Taipei, really—had not been doing well
financially. "A cash prize will also be donated to any organization that helps the Asian American community. Five thousand
dollars to the winner's choice. It can go here."

Garrett twirled his tablet stylus on his left thumb a few times.
I watched it turn in quick circles, his index finger neatly catch-
ing it after each rotation. I suddenly remembered a younger
him practicing this very thing, pen clattering on the table as
we listened to cultural lectures. Now it was smooth, reflexive.
Was there any part of him that thought of our time together at
camp? Or had he pushed it all aside? Forgotten it?

Was there even a small part of him that would want to help
me?

"I don't have anyone else to ask and it starts tomorrow," I
said. "I *have* to enter." I stared at the television screen, but I
could feel the prickle of Garrett's gaze on me. Seeing too much.
He had always been like that, even when we were kids. "I can't
do this competition without you. But if you partner with me, I
promise I will do my best to win. I *will* win."

I would give anything to know what he was thinking right now. But he had become impossible to decipher. He, who, once upon a time, I had been able to read better than anyone. Or so I thought.

He finally said, "The whole cash prize goes to the center. . . ."

Oh, thank goodness.

"*And* you have to volunteer here for the next four weeks."

"What! No way." I didn't have time to add anything to my schedule. I had to maintain my GPA in my regular classes in order to keep my valedictorian standing, plus continue my responsibilities as president of the Student Business Association. Now, more than ever, those things counted since I was in Yale's regular applicant pool. Plus, I needed to do all the work for the competition. I didn't have time to do activities and things with the little kids, even if they were cute.

"Plus," he said, "I know you're the president of your Student Business Association. We need more people to run an event in a few weeks. Maybe you can ask your friends if they want to pitch in? And help us to network so we can get more publicity."

What did he want, the entire kitchen sink? My wallet, too?

He said, "Take it or leave it."

"Come on."

"I'm sure you can find someone else, then." Garrett picked up his tablet and started sketching again.

"Why me? For the volunteering?"

"Grace Zhang left for college, so we're short on people." He swept thick, swooping lines across his screen. "Plus, it might do you good to spend some time around here."

"What?"

"Leave your ivory tower. You know, see how the rest of the world operates."

Was he trying to say I was sheltered? Or narrow-minded? Unbelievable. Leave it to Garrett to say he would help me and then insult me on the way out.

I wrapped Dad's key chain in my hand, the edges pressing into my skin. The other teams had more experiences with start-ups and competitions. Some might know a bit about websites. But I'd bet none of them had Garrett's experience with design or his eye for striking visuals. He could be my secret weapon. If that meant I had to suck it up and deal with his attitude, I would do it.

"Deal." I grabbed my laptop and got his information for the registration form. Sent him the packet of information I had gathered about the past competitions and winners.

"We can meet tomorrow at the library." I packed up my stuff. "The competition starts at noon."

He nodded once, then turned back to his tablet.

For better or worse, we were now in this together.

As I left, I noticed Garrett's parents in their car. They were frostily sitting next to each other, then his mom climbed out and slammed the door.

We all knew Garrett's parents were always fighting or giving each other the silent treatment. His mom didn't speak English well and spent all her time blaming Garrett's dad for dragging her to America and for not making enough money. He, in turn, blamed her for blaming him, and on it went. We all knew this, all the parents knew this, and we all tried to pretend it didn't exist. I think his uncle had been accused of embezzlement or something in Taiwan, but no one openly talked about that, either.

Garrett walked out of the cultural center, Amy's lunch box in one hand. He was smiling at her but stopped when he saw his mom, her arms folded. He looked toward the car, to his dad's stony face. He sighed, then grabbed Amy's hand. They drove off, and I saw a flash of his elegant profile through the car window—shadow then light then dark.

I hadn't told my mom yet about what Eric had done or how I had launched my contingency plan. I wanted to, as Dad always advised, come to her with both the problem and the solution. But this answer might not be one she would like, even though it was my only viable option.

I had a plan. I just needed to let my mother know. Later.

Ha-ha, just kidding. There is no *later* with Mom. There is only now and why-wasn't-this-done-five-minutes-ago. She pounced, like a plastic-hair-rollered tiger, as soon as I walked in the door.

"What's going on with the competition?" she asked. "Did you and Eric turn in your registration? Did you get any hints about what the challenge is? Did they post the total number of competitors?"

People say I have no chill. At least I come by it honestly.

But this was a total problem. There was no way I could tell Mom that Mrs. Lin was the one who made Eric drop me. She would be too hurt. But I didn't think I could keep the fact that Eric had ditched me a secret for long, either. That much, at least, I had to confess.

"He's partnering with someone else."

"Ai-yah!" she said. "What did you do? You know how important this is."

I felt the squeeze of anger, the hot pressure. Why did she assume it was my fault?

"I didn't do anything. He dumped me."

"Did you say anything? Did you argue with him?"

"Mom. He totally ditched *me*. It wasn't my fault." For one reckless moment, I wanted to defend myself, to let her know what Mrs. Lin had actually done. But I thought of my dad at the end, his eyes watery. His weak hands around all of ours—mine, Hattie's, Bella's, Mom's—bringing them together. His last wish couldn't have been clearer. He wanted our family to stay together. To protect each other.

Plus, it wasn't even about me. It was about the shame attached to our entire family. About Mrs. Lin's opinion of my mom and Mom's parenting skills. I didn't have the heart to tell her, no matter how mad I was.

Mom slumped in her chair. "You call Eric. You ask him for another chance."

I thought of my dad humming as he hung up some sheets over Hattie's bed, making a tent for us. Doing homework with me at the kitchen table. I pictured a sphere around the dangerous heat of my anger, containing it. The cleansing coolness of a breath inhaled, the warm and controlled exhale.

I said, "I found someone else. Someone better."

She stared at me. "Who."

I knew she thought Garrett was a slacker and that he was on the Short Road to Nowhere because of his interest in art. Even though I knew he was my best shot at winning this competition, I could never tell her about our partnership. She would make me end it before we could prove ourselves.

But who could I say instead? The person had to be Asian American but also someone Mom wouldn't have a chance to interact with or talk to their parents. So not Taiwanese. Someone academically strong. Someone she had heard of.

"Louis," I said.

"Louis?" she said. "Louis who?"

"Louis Park."

My mom was silent. "The salutatorian?"

Louis and I had been in the same classes since grade school, and he had always been in the top of our classes. Mom had met him and his family in passing at school events and was impressed by both of his parents being doctors.

Louis was also on the express path to becoming a zoologist, but Mom didn't need to know that. Details, schmetails.

The competition results would be posted under our team names, so she couldn't find out that way. Also, competitors were not allowed to use their real names while advertising their products or services so there would be no unfair advantages. This could work.

47

Mom appeared slightly mollified but then said, "Are you sure Eric is doing it with someone else? Why don't you ask him again?" If it had been before The Fall, Mom would already have been on the phone with Mrs. Lin, sealing this partnership. But she couldn't lose face by calling her directly now; it would seem too much like she was begging. Naturally, however, it was something that I could do.

Navigating the whole social thing with my mom and her so-called friends was super complicated. You almost needed a guidebook on the unsaid, the unspoken social rules keeping everything in place.

"Mom!" I said. "He already asked Albert Goda."

Her mouth tightened. "You sure Louis Park will do a good job?"

"You've met him," I said. "He always works really hard."

Mom leaned back, staring at the ceiling. A victory over Eric Lin in my father's competition might be even better than being his partner. I could see Gèi Wéi shifting, sharpening. She waved a hand.

But as I left the kitchen, she said, "Do your best."

I didn't need a translator to know what that meant: *You had better win*—i.e., Garrett and I had better win.

7

LOVE ADVICE FROM MR. GRUMPY
AND MS. SUNSHINE

GARRETT AND I arranged to meet at the library at noon. I got there at eleven thirty and logged into the competition website in case they released it early. Garrett wandered in about ten minutes before noon. He was wearing a manga tee/hoodie combination, which meant it was a day ending in *y*. I was faintly surprised he showed up, and early, no less.

"What have we got?" he asked. I was still getting used to seeing him with longer hair, how it curled around his ears, accentuated the lines of his face.

I had assumed that working with him would be like it was with Eric: pulling teeth. Especially given our past history. But Garrett quickly pulled out his laptop, which was plastered with stickers—*Dragon Ball*, *Naruto*, *One Piece*. He was all business, having preloaded some website templates and pages featuring different types of fonts. Fine, we could keep it professional. Civil.

He said, "We don't know what the challenge is, but we should probably scan a few of these and see what styles we like and which ones we don't?" He was in this to win, as well. I had seen him in Chinese class, exhausted, and I knew a scholarship could make his life infinitely easier. "Do we want modern or something more whimsical?"

Checking out different website samples had actually been on my list of things to do, but I hadn't had time to do it.

Garrett began scrolling through various options. He often doodled on his papers as Anna Lǎoshī droned on in class. But now he was almost animated, going through fonts and layouts, explaining how both could enhance or reflect the products or services offered.

I suddenly remembered walking through the woods together, him pointing out all the things I had never noticed: the shades of light through the trees spilling over the floor or the way the shadow would change the color and depth of a leaf. I didn't quite understand what he was talking about but had been fascinated with how he had looked: excited, his hands gracefully pointing out minute details.

"How about this one?" he asked. Unlike back then, he was matter-of-fact. Detached.

I focused on the website. It had sketches framing the site and a hand-drawn font. "I like it."

"I think the handwriting style is more appealing because

it might be more relatable and casual. Or we could go with a calligraphy-type one if we want to be more formal."

The light from the window was hitting Garrett's head, bright on his black hair. The curve above his lip was shaded, as was the side of his nose. These were all things I didn't want to notice. Not anymore.

Partnering with Garrett was bringing up things I had successfully buried. Things I didn't want to think about. Things I didn't have time to think about. I had to be careful, otherwise, they would float right to the surface, bringing all the dirt with them.

At exactly noon, both of our email accounts pinged with one message: a login and password to the official competition site.

Go time.

Welcome to the Asian Americans in Business Competition! We welcome all the competitors and wish you the best of luck.

Your objective this year is to create and promote a service that will directly benefit your target audience (teenagers from the ages of 14–18). For this first round, you must create a minimum viable service (aka a bare-bones, low-cost but still operational version of your service). Your goal is not revenue but audience engagement.

Garrett frowned. "Audience engagement?"

CHALLENGE #1:

DISTRIBUTION

Successful launches depend on positioning your product well. In order to learn this lesson, your first challenge will be to offer your service through a difficult distribution channel, namely a brochure-style website, which we will provide and you will design. (A brochure-style website is one that provides information only, much like its paper counterpart; there are no videos or GIFs or other advanced web features.) You will be evaluated on the amount of traffic you can create.

P.S. Paid advertisements are strictly prohibited at this time, but use of social media is permissible. As with all challenges going forward, you will have a week to complete this task. Good luck.

There was a link at the bottom of the page where we could sign up to get a free blank website. A biography of my father and a picture, taken before he had gotten sick. It was one I had seen before, where he was standing in front of the Sterling Memorial Library at Yale, smiling.

I scrolled, then scrolled some more. Checked for any more information. But that was it.

It was definitely not time to panic. But Garrett looked like I felt: panicked.

"We need to start a service benefitting *teenagers?*" he said.

"What's that supposed to mean?" He seemed vaguely horrified, like someone had jumped out of the bushes, wrestled him to the ground, and shoved a calculus test in his face.

"Okay," I said. "This will be okay. It's a broad topic, so it leaves a lot of room, right?"

I pulled out my journal, where I had taken notes on Dad's books. We would be evaluated based on the amount of traffic we could create. So we needed something broadly appealing. Garrett glanced at my color-coded tabs and almost smiled. But he quickly suppressed it.

"I think it would be best if we offered something we're good at." I uncapped a red pen. "Like an area of expertise. We need a wide audience to get traffic. Something everyone might be interested in."

What could that be? How about a link to medical services that could prevent panicking high schoolers from passing out? A place that could provide elaborate disguises so a person could walk through their community without having to bear the scarlet S of shame? An online ruler that could track changes in . . . height?

No, no, and *wow, no.*

Think. What could only we offer? What were we better at than everyone else?

I sat up. The answer was obvious: love advice. What could possibly interest high schoolers more than romance? And dating? Nothing! And who was the absolute master at romance? Why me, of course.

We were all super busy with school and everything, so we could give quick snippets of advice that people could scan on their phones. And maybe offer links to longer versions of the answers if they were interested.

"I've got it." If it was anyone else, I would have paused for dramatic effect. But I didn't. "A dating advice site."

Garrett laughed out loud. "Dating?" He looked like I had suggested giving advice on how to catch unicorns or lasso the moon. "Love advice."

"What?" I said.

"How are *you* an expert on dating?"

"I'm a natural. Did you not see Emily and Lewis?" I get a feeling—an intuition, if you will—when two people should get together. It might be how one person keeps glancing at the other. It might be how they silently check in before speaking, a tacit conversation. How they lean toward one another without seeming to notice it. When I saw that—voilà. Romanceville.

"Oh, please," Garrett said. "They totally would have gone out anyway."

"*And* I set up my friends Maria and Tammy. They are still together, thank you very much. You know what everyone wants to know about? Love. How to—"

"—hook up with other people?"

"*Date.* It's a perfect way to get tons of traffic since it interests almost everyone. Who doesn't love romance?"

"Who does love romance? It's like you're leading people to despair. It's better not to start it at all."

I was about to tell him he was *totally wrong* when a brilliant idea exploded like a firework shell in my brain. *How to Be Your Best Entrepreneur* said the best marketing comes from intrigue or tension. I totally believed in love and happiness. Garrett believed in some cold, dark prison of solitude. If we *both* did the advice column, we could draw an even broader audience: those who wanted to read about romance and those who didn't believe in it. Yet.

I said, "We need to do this together."

If Garrett had a drink at this moment, he would have done a spit take in my face. "Absolutely not."

"This is *perfect*."

"It is not." He scowled. "You said just art. Remember?"

"That was before the challenge came out. Audiences love intrigue and tension. I am a normal human being with actual human feelings, so I love romance. You are a curmudgeon with a heart the size of a raisin who thinks everyone should die alone. We can totally get more traffic if we both answer the same questions."

He didn't respond.

"We can be the only pair with an opposites vibe. It'll distinguish us. Make us intriguing," I said. "This can win, I know it."

He still didn't say no, which was a good sign.

I asked, "Do you have a better idea?"

Garrett paid a sudden, close attention to the bookshelves next to us, and I checked my watch. "Well?"

He sighed. "I do not."

"Great." I started setting up a joint email account before he could change his mind. "I'll even volunteer extra at the cultural center. Two more weeks."

He still didn't look convinced but seemed slightly less cranky and didn't say anything when I changed our social media profiles. He didn't know I would have agreed to five weeks anyway. Negotiation rule number one: never reveal your top offer. Always keep it in your pocket, just in case.

We worked side by side for the next few hours. I advertised our service on places where people who needed love advice might hang out, like Reddit. Sent texts to Hattie and people in the SBA, asking them to send in love questions so we could post something right away. Drafted some blogs on romance tropes.

Meanwhile, Garrett set up a simple but fun layout on the website, with casual fonts and cute drawings at the top of each page. "Voilà." He turned the computer toward me.

It was . . . really good. Mom had always been dismissive of art and the arts in general, but I saw now how design was the thing that could draw the eye in, make you want to stay on the website and find out what it was about. How much work it took to sketch something deceptively simple and elegant. After my own failed attempts to try and create my own website, I knew how hard it was.

Garrett had put a banner drawing at the top, of a guy and girl buried in envelopes with hearts on them, which I had to confess was pretty freaking cute. He had also created a logo of a cartoon guy and girl, with the guy wearing a hoodie and *Gintama* T-shirt, his dark hair falling over one eye. The girl was wearing a replica of my favorite skirt and was carrying a notebook with a little picture of this stuffed cactus I had won when we were kids.

It was honestly better than I had expected. Garrett had been utterly focused for the past few hours, adjusting details that I couldn't see. The end result was polished, professional.

He twirled his pen as I scanned his work. "Well?" he said finally.

"It's good," I said. He almost smiled. It was smile-adjacent.

But then I clicked on the "about" section; it had a cartoon of a girl in a field of heart-shaped flowers and a blurb: *"Sunny is a self-proclaimed expert on love. Even though it doesn't exist."*

"Are you kidding me?"

"We're not supposed to use our real names, right?" Garrett said.

I scrolled to his section. *"Cloudy is a digital graphic artist and romance cynic. All of his views will eventually be proven superior to Sunny's. He will save you from inevitable suffering."*

Unbelievable. "You can't say that." And was he kidding with *Sunny* and *Cloudy*? If I didn't know better, I could have sworn he was almost amused, like he was in on the joke.

"Intrigue and tension, remember?" he said innocently. "Shall we use different names? Delusional versus Realist?"

You know what would cause tension? Throttling one's partner.

Garrett tipped his chair back. "We're agreed, then. Let's get going with those love questions."

"Oh, are we finally getting some of your superior advice, *Cloudy*?"

"Bring it on."

I checked Reddit and the other sites where I had put out ads, but no one had responded to my request for questions yet. No problem. I checked my phone and luckily, my friends had come through. There were a few smart-alecky ones.

What should I do if my girlfriend always wants to get the bucket-sized popcorn when we go to the movies? We're only two people! **(Maria)**

What should I do if my girlfriend clearly can't appreciate the world's best snack? **(Tammy)**

Why can't life be like a K-drama? **(Hattie)**

People. Work with me here!

I finally found one we could use. I passed it to Garrett.

How can I tell if someone likes me?

Signed,

Not a Psychic

Garrett said, "You first."

"Easy. The person asks you out." I smugly typed my answer into the computer. I was a love goddess, truly.

"You're kidding."

"No."

Garrett leaned forward, his chair legs thudding to the ground. "What if the person is shy? Or is not sure the letter writer likes them?"

"Well—"

"Maybe that's been the case for you, but it's not true for everyone."

Garrett always said whatever thought was in his head, no matter the consequence. Food was too salty at the restaurant? He was the first to speak up. When Benny Yao was mean to the substitute teacher in Chinese class? Garrett called him out. It was one of the things that I had always found fascinating. One of the reasons I had wanted to be his friend, before. But he had given up any right to be that honest with me. Not now. Not after how he had left things.

"Okay, genius. What would you say?" I asked.

He typed: "The person will make it a priority to spend time with you."

"That's it? They'll make it a priority to spend time with you."

"Yup. That's it." He added a cloud emoji. "Next."

"What?" I said. "How about you and your friends? You spend time with other people all the time."

"Yeah, but that's different." He gazed at the ceiling, almost philosophically. "Priority is key."

"What are you talking about?"

"We're busy," he said. "Some of us have video games to play or have to hang out with our buds. Our schedules are crammed."

"Oh my God."

"And if *instead of all that* we choose to spend time with the person we like, then it's not small."

"You are making absolutely no sense," I said. "You need something more concrete, like 'the person gazes into your eyes.'"

"That only happens in the movies. Or if you have a stye."

"Give me the laptop." I amended my answer to: "Your crush will look at you longingly. And eventually, they'll tell you!"

Garrett snorted. He typed: "See if they want to spend all of their time with you. Also, find out if their friends know about you. If they're interested, they'll be talking about you *all the time*. Ignore Sunny—she thinks she's living in a K-drama."

"And what's wrong with that?" I asked.

"The same thing as rom-coms," he said. "It gives a false portrayal of the world."

"Why is it false? There are plenty of happy couples."

Garrett posted our answers to the most popular social media site, Chatty, as he said, "Maybe it starts out that way. Maybe people think they've found their person and nothing bad can possibly happen. But then time passes. They get stressed. Start to argue. They find out that love is not as strong as they thought. Like everything else, it can be broken." There was a sharp shard of bitterness poking through his words.

I thought of Bella, how Mom had taken a machete to the cord tying her to us. I remember Bella sobbing in her room before she went to medical school. She and Mom used to always cook together, in matching strawberry aprons. But then Bella had taken a spring break trip to San Francisco, had become infatuated with the city. *The food, Juju! The Bay is so beautiful.* She had met non-Asian Wesley, and they had moved in together. That's when the fighting started, when the line of

60

Mom's love had stretched thin. When Bella had started to say what she wanted. Bella had hugged me tight the week before she left, almost like she knew what was to come. Like she knew the rope would snap.

The memory of Garrett's parents' frosty silence hung over him; it almost always did, even when we were kids. When our families still had brunches together, he was always the silent one, watching his mom and dad. He didn't talk about them much. Ever. I wasn't sure what to say. I didn't entirely disagree that love could be broken, but it existed, and sometimes endured. I was sure of it. My grandparents had been married for fifty-six years. The only time they had been apart was after my grandma died. My mom never dated again after my dad passed. Love was serious business in our family.

"What do you mean?" I said. "When you find someone you love who loves you, that's it."

If it was possible to twirl a pen sarcastically, Garrett had just done it. "Hardly."

"It can last. People get married to their childhood sweethearts all the time."

"Or not."

"My parents did."

"Yeah? So did mine."

Oh. His parents must have been in love at some point, though, right? Could love turn to . . . that?

Well, we both knew it was possible. Well, not love but friendship. Maybe the line between caring and hurt was thinner than I thought.

"Well, you're wrong," I said. I had to believe in love. I had gone through too much grief and pain with my family. My father had always said love was the one truly magical thing in the world. It could invisibly connect people and last through time, distance. Death.

"We'll see," Garrett said.

We sure would. We would see exactly who was right, *Garrett*.

How long was this competition?

The answer: four more weeks. Four weeks too long.

8

SWITZERLAND

THINGS WITH GARRETT were not going well. And they were not much better at home.

"Hattie," my mom said at breakfast the next day. Even though she had a full work schedule ahead of her, Mom had gotten up super early to make our favorites: congee with preserved egg and Chinese fried donuts. "Go change. Why are you wearing the sweater with all the holes? Wear the blue one."

"I don't want to," Hattie said. "This is the same one Sonni wore in her music video! The one all over TikTok."

"Who? Who is this Sonni?" Mom said. "Go change."

I recognized Mom's tone. It was milder than the harsh one she had used on Bella, before Bella had left. But then, as now, it coiled through me, alarming.

"And you have to go with me to Auntie Liu's after school," Mom said. "She needs help with the Lunar New Year fashion show." The Lunar New Year celebration was one of the major Taiwanese events of the year. My mom had already booked her hair appointment and bought a new dress. It was also right before the end of the competition, which meant we were either going to have an entrance of triumph or we would have to fake an excuse and Mom would have to return her clothes.

Hattie said, "*Mom!* I'm busy. Why can't Juju go?"

"She has to work on the competition."

"Yeah? Well, I have things to do, too. I'm doing an article for the paper."

Mom waved her hand like Hattie was trying to excuse herself by saying she had to stay home and pick her nose.

Hattie dropped her spoon, the metal clanking against her bowl. "It's important."

Mom didn't say anything. Just one look.

When we were younger, we always had to go on these errands with Mom. Bella loved them and would push us around in shopping carts at the Chinese grocery store or would do crafts with us in Auntie Liu's living room as Auntie prepared for her annual fashion show. I remember right before she left for San Francisco, Bella gave me her canvas bag full of yarn and stickers and crochet hooks. I had always coveted it secretly but hadn't wanted it that way. Not like some sort of goodbye gift.

Hattie grabbed her spoon, then silently shoveled down the rest of her congee. What was she thinking about? Maybe about how she would have another year of getting dragged around, alone? First it was Bella, me, and Hattie; then just me and Hattie. And after next year, just Hattie. Or rather, Hattie and Mom, which meant it would be a year of war.

I kicked her foot under the table. Didn't she see how tired Mom was? Hattie would say Mom didn't have to work so hard; the sale of Dad's patent had given us enough of a cushion. It was true. We weren't private jet–level wealthy, of course, but were lucky enough to be able to pay off our house and have college trust funds for each of us. Plus a little extra. But Mom was always preparing for the worst. She had seen how everything could be taken away; it had happened to the people of Taiwan after World War II. When you live through witnessing massacres and bankruptcies and the loss of rights, there is no point where there is *enough*. Because Mom had seen what it was like when there was nothing.

Hattie dropped her bowl into the sink, grabbed her backpack, and marched outside.

"Sorry, Mom." I took a Chinese donut and wrapped it into a napkin for Hattie, then grabbed the other sweater off the couch. I packed another donut for Mom to take to work. "I'll talk to her."

My mom gave me a distracted kiss on the cheek. "Study hard today."

I sometimes visited Maria's house and saw how she and her mom would gossip at the kitchen table while prepping for dinner, how Maria could tell her all about her relationship with Tammy or her problems at school. We never had that. Our mom was always halfway gone, tangled in emails and profit-and-loss statements. Hattie had once tried to ask her what it was like growing up when Taiwan was in such turmoil.

She said one word: "difficult." It was a word with a different meaning than the American meaning. For my mom, "difficult" meant: "It didn't kill me, so . . ."

I tried to imagine what it would be like to ask Mom what she was feeling. Or to confess I was terrified I couldn't win this competition and I would let her—and Dad—down.

But I saw her tired face, her glance at the clock, and I couldn't. I remember right after Dad died, I once snuck downstairs after bedtime. I was surprised to find my mom in the living room; she was crying, but trying to do it quietly, swallowing jerking hiccups. Until that moment, my mom had been an immovable force, almost untouchable. It was the first time I had seen her wholly broken. It was terrifying.

My dad had been her best friend, the one she could always talk to about work or what was happening in the Linevine. They would chat in Mandarin on purpose, so we couldn't understand them, but we didn't need to know the meaning of the words. The way my dad would look at her, affectionately, or how she would lean on his shoulder made everything clear. After he passed, Mom's friends would stop by with platters of food and pull her to dinner parties and social events. Slowly, she started to laugh again. Smile. She wasn't happy, exactly, but at least she knew she had done this one thing: she had successfully raised their children. But then came The Fall. And Mom became quiet again. Would sit on the couch on Saturday evenings, staring at the television, her face bare. What she was thinking about those evenings, I had no idea. Her sisters in Taiwan? What had happened to us as a family after Dad died?

She never said. I sometimes sat next to her and tried to keep her company, but my Mandarin was not good enough and I was confused by the plots of her shows.

But since the competition had started, she had been dressing up more. Dropping hints of my prior accomplishments into the Linevine and talking to people on the phone instead of sitting by herself on the couch. She had even started shopping at Dynasty Mall on the weekends again instead of waiting for the off hours. How could I possibly add to her burdens with my doubts about the competition? The Lunar New Year celebration was only a few weeks away, and I knew everyone would be there. It could be a night of triumph. It could make Mrs. Lin eat her snobbery. I only needed to be at the top.

I said, "Thanks for breakfast, Mom." But she was already walking away and didn't hear me.

"What's wrong with helping Auntie Liu? She's, like, Mom's only friend," I said. Hattie was already in my car, scowling, and I pushed her feet off my dashboard. Then I handed her the Chinese donut and the sweater. "Why do you always have to argue with her? You wear this one all the time."

"Because it's ridiculous. And she always tries to control everything. Hey, can I drive?"

"Absolutely not." Hattie was sixteen and technically had her driver's license, but for the safety of everyone in Connecticut and the tri-state area, I drove.

Hattie slouched in her seat and turned up the radio, too loud as usual. "Why does it matter what we wear, anyway? What about not judging a book by its cover? Does she, what, want me to wear a ball gown to school?"

I turned the music down, then slowly pulled out of the driveway after checking both ways. "Come on, you know she didn't say 'ball gown.' She just doesn't want you to look like someone spilled paint on your clothes."

"It's the design, Juju. Aren't you on TikTok? These are *artful*. And why are you always taking her side?"

"I'm not." I was taking the side of our family. We had already been split into two. I couldn't bear to see us in any more parts. "Hattie. For me, please?"

She unwrapped her breakfast. "Only for you." I felt a little bad about pulling the Sister Card, but it was for her own good.

Done! One problem solved. I cheerfully made my way to school, only to be intercepted by Maria and Tammy.

"Juliana," Maria said. "Are you going to talk to Eric Lin?" I had given both her and Tammy a brief update on what had gone down, and they had been appropriately outraged on my behalf.

"Of course," I said as another one of our SBA members came up to me.

"Juliana," he said. "Mr. Veevers said there's a problem with the booking for the auditorium."

"I'll take care of it," I said.

"What a jerk," Tammy said. "I always said Eric was ruthless."

"You did!" Maria said.

Tammy beamed at her, and I felt something like envy. Maria and Tammy had always had a connection, even before they started dating. They would never leave each other, no matter what.

"We will give the stink eye on your behalf," Tammy said. "Tell us which direction to aim."

That was true friendship: those who will give dirty looks to those who have wronged you. I hugged them as the warning bell rang, then we ran into our homerooms.

No sooner had I sat down than a text from Garrett popped up on my phone.

Dear Sunny and Cloudy,
I am SO IN LOVE! I can barely function! I can't even remember my own name! Please help!
Signed,
Call Me Swoony

He was impossible. I typed:

Dear Swoony:
Check your ID card. Your chances of success will increase exponentially if you can introduce yourself.
Sincerely,
Sunny

By lunchtime, I was in my groove. I had fixed the issue with the SBA auditorium reservation, aced my calculus quiz, and sent messages to some vendors for the SBA fundraiser. But the competition was still a problem.

I had posted my blog on romance tropes last night. I had listed some of my favorite books as examples and pasted snapshots of their covers. I cross-posted to all of my regular social media accounts. Even though my followings were relatively modest, it had to help, right? I had gone to sleep happy, dreaming of all the likes and comments rolling in. Of it being the best love blog in the history of love blogs. But when I woke up, only two people had visited our new website.

Number of people not related to me who had clicked on our site last night: one. Number of people who wanted to sell me hiatal hernia medication: you guessed it.

What else could I do? We were getting some traffic from people visiting our social media accounts, but our numbers were still low. I was in a genuine— I wouldn't say panic. Let's say I had a genuine *concern*.

I was inhaling some meditative breaths when I walked into the cafeteria and saw Eric Lin. He was off to the side, talking with some of his friends. I marched over.

"I can't believe you," I hissed. "Two days before registration? Are you kidding me?"

Eric apologized to them and pulled me to the side. "Quiet. You're making a scene."

"Oh, you're worried about *a scene*? Not the fact that you're a total asshole?"

"This is a competition, Juliana." His face spasmed. "You knew we couldn't win if we stayed together."

"*You* knew the challenge had something to do with tech," I said. "But you didn't bother sharing that with me. We could have figured something out. Instead, you threw me under the bus." Dad had always said to honor your word, to stick by those you came with. It was the iron rule we had always lived by. "Besides, don't pretend this isn't all because of your mom."

He couldn't deny it, which made me even more furious.

"Good luck," I snapped. "I hope you can live with yourself."

Eric stopped looking sorry and began to get irritated. "You want to go into business? Like our parents want so badly?" He sounded bitter. "You want to be successful? Then you can't take things so personally."

"Stop justifying your shitty behavior."

"Your dad understood how the business world works," he said. "The priorities you need to have."

"My dad?"

Was that pity on his face? I wanted to claw it off.

"My parents were friends with Mr. Lee," he said. "They know all about what happened."

Was this about the fight between Dad and Mr. Lee? But they had made up. Whatever. He was trying to distract me.

He said, "I have to win."

"You think I don't?"

He looked away. "You wouldn't understand."

I was done with him. "Good luck in the competition. I hope you and Albert have a grand old time."

He didn't say anything as I left, just watched me go, frowning.

Now I was even more determined than before. I had to secure my victory.

Dear Sunny and Cloudy,

My crush walks his dog past my house every afternoon. Does he like me?

Signed,

Hopeful

Sunny: Of course he does!

Cloudy: Does he live on your street, by any chance?

10

BOBA WITH MR. McCRANKY PANTS

UNFORTUNATELY, WINNING THE competition meant I had to manage Garrett. I was supposed to meet him at the TeaTime dessert place after school so we could plan for the competition.

Garrett had been busy, much to my astonishment. He had posted more advice to our social media accounts. On Chatty, he replaced my plain blue banner with one featuring our new cute logo. Since then, our website traffic had steadily increased.

When I walked in, he already had a drink in front of him.

"Green tea?" I asked. Leave it to Garrett to get the most austere drink on the menu. "Where's the boba?"

"I like it plain."

Because why would Garrett Jun Tsai get boba at a *bubble tea shop*? Why order something that might actually, you know, make you happy? The whole Earth might go out of orbit. I got my usual: roasted oolong, full sugar, with crystal boba and red beans. I even asked for egg puffs on the side. Ha.

"Is that a meal or a drink?" he asked.

I stabbed my straw into the thin lid. "This is happiness in a cup."

"Or a stomachache," he muttered.

"No boba is straight-up evil." I took an enormous sip of my tea. Delicious.

He pulled out his phone and held the screen up. The traffic on our Chatty account had increased even more overnight. "You're welcome."

I grabbed it from him. Those were even better than an hour ago. Garrett had posted little sketches with each question: cute, cranky ones. He looked quietly pleased when I laughed. "You've been working hard," I said.

Garrett snatched his phone back. "Surprised?"

"No." I mean, kind of. My mom and the others had always talked about him the same way: *the youngest Tsai boy, always drawing.* I knew he wasn't in math competitions like Amy or cramming for prep classes like Patrick always did. Art didn't have a straight path to a high income and stable job, so it wasn't something the parents could understand or value. I never paid much attention when my mom said stuff like that. It was like she was talking about the weather or gossiping about the latest car someone bought.

But for the first time, I really considered what she and the Linevine were saying. I had seen how Garrett had carefully designed our website at the library, adjusting the size and colors until they were perfect. He worked on his webtoon at every spare moment in Chinese class and at the big potlucks. He was always drawing. People thought of it as only doodling, but maybe they were wrong. Perhaps he was practicing. Perfecting it. Working just as hard as me but on something different.

Garrett seemed testy again, so something compelled me to say, "You did a good job."

"You mean, a good job for *an artist?*"

I knew why he was still defensive. I had seen how Garrett's family dismissed what he did. When he was a kid, he always tried to give his mom his drawings. And she would always tuck them into her purse, ignored. His brother was worse, either rubbing in Garrett's face that he wasn't as academically accomplished or saying that he was wasting his time with art. I imagined what it would be like if the Linevine belittled my love of business, my goals of following in Dad's footsteps. That tacit approval was one I always had. It was something that I, admittedly, had taken for granted.

"No," I said. "I mean it's great."

Garrett had to check to see if I meant it, which was a little heartbreaking. He said, quietly, "Thank you."

I wondered what would have happened if we had somehow stayed friends. We could be having so much fun with this competition right now: him probably grabbing my drink and taking a sarcastic sip, me teasing him mercilessly.

I grabbed my phone. Pulled up our analytics. There was no use in dwelling on the past.

I said, "We're getting a lot more engagement on our Chatty

account, but it doesn't count for the competition. Only website hits do."

Garrett was also businesslike. "I noticed a spike in visits every time we posted new advice. Some people are clicking over."

"But not enough." Think, Juliana. The goal was to direct eyes to our website. How could we transfer followers from one platform to the other . . . ?

I was sprinkling a little extra sugar into my drink but dropped the packet on the table. "Wait. The competition doesn't care about social media hits, only website views. What if we post the questions on Chatty and people then have to go to our website to get the answers? We'll use it more like a portal to attract and redirect followers."

"*Yes.*" Garrett smiled then, one of the few I had seen directed at me in a long while. It rearranged time, yanked me back to when a younger him tried to make a Chinese donut fort at breakfast or sketched goofy animals on my Chinese calligraphy practice. When he uncurled my fingers once and placed a perfect white stone in my palm.

I pulled up our shared email mailbox and tried to read the questions. But the memories were still there, tangling through everything.

"All right, then," I said. Focus, Juliana. "Let's try to answer some of these."

Dear Sunny and Cloudy,
I had my first kiss with my boyfriend. Unfortunately, our braces

76

got stuck together and it was horrible. Should we just break up?

Signed,

Straight Teeth, Broken Heart

We both winced.

"Ouch," I said.

"Relatable," he muttered.

"Wait." I started to snicker. "Did that happen to you?"

Garrett suddenly became very preoccupied with the menu above the cash register.

"No! Seriously?"

He appeared to be reading every single boba option, line by line. But his ears were red, a reaction of his that I vividly remembered. It made him seem more . . . vulnerable. Like the boy I used to know.

"I have no idea what you're talking about," he said.

I did the math: he had braces when we were in middle school, around seventh or eighth grade. I pictured a young Garrett Tsai temporarily tangled in a lip-lock. I couldn't help it: I laughed. A lot.

His mouth twitched.

"And how did you . . . disengage?" I asked.

"We're not talking about this, Juliana."

"Did it involve wire cutters? Just tell me if you had to use tools."

"Juliana." He shook his head but not before I heard a small laugh, smothered in a fake cough.

My answer:

If he really likes you, it won't matter! Try again!

Garrett's:

Orthodontic wax. Wait a week to heal.

The server came up to us with my egg puffs.

"Nice." Garrett pulled off a puffy circle, then passed me the plate. He used to do that all the time, jogging to the dessert counter in the camp cafeteria and coming back with one serving that we could share. Cake or cookies (but never pie since we both didn't like it).

Our eyes caught, then he looked away.

I concentrated on the sprinkle of powdered sugar on the puffs. "No, thanks," I said. Ever since I had accidentally inhaled some sugar straight into my lungs when I was a little kid, it gave me the heebie-jeebies.

"What's wrong?"

"Nothing."

But of course he wouldn't let it go, puzzling through the options.

"Oh, right," he said. "Didn't you order a plain one?" When I didn't answer, Garrett raised his hand. I waved it down.

"You can have it," I said. "Take some home to Amy."

He frowned. "You can tell them they got the wrong order."

I could already feel the discomfort spiking through me. Having to tell this person, this stranger, that she made a mistake.

78

Enduring the veiled anger or disappointment.

"It's not a problem," I said. "Really." It was only an egg puff.

The server came over, and Garrett said, "Excuse me—"

"—we'd like another plain egg puff, please," I said. "To go."

He said, "Seriously?"

I shushed him.

After she left, he said, "All you have to say is, 'I would like a plain egg puff, please.'"

"That's what I said!"

"*I ordered a plain egg puff. Would you mind bringing me that instead, please?*"

"You're ridiculous," I said. There was no reason to make a fuss. I had seen what happened when people, like my mom or the people in our community, got mad at you. You either had to live with the buzzing gossip following you, forever, or you got cut off entirely. There was no reason to go through that.

Garrett crossed his arms. "Do you never say what you think?"

What? "I do."

"Really." His voice was hard.

"What's that supposed to mean?" Why was he suddenly so peeved? I didn't think it was about egg puffs.

He said nothing, and now I was the one getting annoyed.

I said, "What are you talking about?"

He stared at me. "Do you ever disagree with people?"

"Yes." I did! Sometimes. Mostly.

"Go against what everyone tells you?" He was focused on

me, like the answer really mattered.

Where was this coming from? Did he mean the uncles and aunties? Garrett had such scorn for the system, the narrowness of it. After what all of them had always said about him and his family—the gossip about his fighting parents, his uncle's legal troubles, his own choice to pursue the arts—I could see why. But why was he was lumping me with everyone else?

"I do." I had, hadn't I? I had been so fixated on keeping everything afloat that I had never really thought about it. And even if I hadn't, it's not like I had much of a choice. Other people—people with less complicated families, those not tangled in the mess of the Linevine—might be able to. The rest of us had to stay and hold everything together.

Garrett shook his head once, and I almost heard it: *Sure.* Why did he even care? It's not like what I did or did not do was any of his concern. Not anymore.

The server eventually came by with the plain egg puff, and I snatched it off the table. "I'll email you the rest of my answers," I said, then chucked my cup into the trash.

Garrett was back to his usual self: prickly, standoffish. "Great."

That was perfectly fine with me.

Two days later I waited for the results of the first challenge. At five minutes to four p.m., I stepped out of a conference room at the local library. I was supposed to be finishing my meeting with the SBA fundraising subcommittee, but I had to check.

At exactly four p.m., I refreshed the website. Again. Then it finally changed.

I looked at the top ten.

Checked again.

We were not on the board.

11

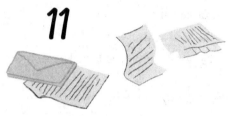

THE SECOND CHALLENGE

BUT ERIC AND Albert *were*. Right there in stinking seventh place. We were Team SunCloud, so they must be Team Esher since there weren't any other competitors from our school.

This was impossible. I was valedictorian of my class. President of the Student Business Association. National Merit Scholar. I did *not* ever get second place, even.

This . . . this was a mistake. This was unacceptable.

I refreshed again. And again.

And even though I would rather have jammed a handful of Q-tips up my nostrils, I sucked it up and called Garrett.

"Did you see it? It's wrong, right?"

There was the sound of kids shouting in the background, laughter.

"Hello? It's Juliana."

Maria poked her head out of the conference room and said,

"We're almost done. Do you have anything else to add?"

"One minute!" I said, and she ducked back in. I got back on the phone. "The results? Did you see them?"

"I saw them." There were more kids shrieking in the background. Where *was* he? A three-ring circus?

This was bad. Maria and Tammy knew I had entered this competition. And so did the rest of the SBA, who I had asked for help earlier. Would they now think I sucked? Ask me to step down as president? How could I lead the group if I couldn't even win a simple challenge?

Even though I knew I shouldn't, I opened Line and took a peek. Sure enough, there in the Linevine was a message from Mrs. Lin: So grateful for the opportunities provided by the AABC! Eric and Team Esher are learning so much! Honestly. She should be in the humble bragging Olympics. "Accidentally" revealing Eric's team name? Masterful. It was practically a banner advertisement to check the competition results every week.

A text came in from my mom: Juliana. She always used periods in texting, which made all of her messages seem super severe. Or maybe that was the intent. She didn't have to say more; the Lunar New Year potluck was around the corner. I pictured my mom and me walking into the room with the stink of failure wrapped around us as all the uncles and aunties gossiped about Dad's competition. About Dad.

"Hello?" Garrett asked. "Are you still there?"

If we couldn't figure out how to fix this, we would continue to fail. This competition depended on traffic, and I wasn't sure how to get more. Then we would be out, and I would lose everything. I knew as well as anyone that everything—class standing, leadership positions, accomplishments—was all sky-scrapers balanced on landfill, and it would take only one quake to bring them down.

I could almost feel it, the cold slice of getting cut off. The free fall.

Maria leaned out of the meeting room again. "Juliana, I think we're done. Do you want to end the meeting? Or I can do it for you if you'd like?"

"Sorry! I'll be right there." I quickly apologized to Garrett and hung up.

Maria stepped out and closed the door behind her. "Hey. Are you okay?"

No. I'm in huge trouble and I don't know how to fix this. I had to do one thing—win my father's competition—and I am failing. My mother—and the rest of the community—is watching, and I am choking.

"I'm fine," I said.

Maria and I had first met when we were ten and were friends when Bella was disowned. I had come to school after crying all night, and Maria had asked what was wrong. And like today, I couldn't quite tell her. There was a logical part of me that knew she would try to understand. But there was a more powerful part of me that was afraid that sharing what had happened would change what she thought of me. If she knew not only what Bella had done but what my mother had. Because her parents never would have done the same.

How could I explain that not winning would be unforgivable?

That the only thing I wanted to do—honor my father and his legacy—was going up in flames? This wasn't the world Maria lived in. It wasn't something she could even comprehend.

So I said nothing.

Maria's concern sharpened to disappointment. But she would never push it. She gently squeezed my arm, then disappeared back into the room. I refreshed my email; to my surprise, a new message was already waiting.

CHALLENGE #2:

PARTNERSHIPS AND COLLABORATIONS

You have hopefully selected your idea and established a minimum viable service. But you may have also discovered the difficulty of creating audience engagement without a proper launch.

One way successful businesses solve this problem is by partnering with different corporations and piggybacking on their already established audience bases.

Your next challenge is to approach a company and to convince them to advertise your service. Points will be granted for those who can increase the traffic to their websites the most. Best of luck.

Were they kidding? I knew I had just ended our call kind of abruptly, but I still grabbed my phone and texted Garrett. This was an emergency.

We have to meet, stat! They released the next challenge.

I'm in the middle of something. Let's meet in half an hour.

Where are you? I'll be there in fifteen.

I hurriedly ended the meeting, and exactly fifteen minutes later, ran toward the cultural center. When I dashed in, Garrett and a bunch of little kids were painting a huge banner with gold paint. He had gold and black streaks on his jeans and what appeared to be a tiny handprint on the edge of his shirt. The kids were chasing each other with brightly colored hands, giggling.

"Good job," Garrett said to one of the little boys, in Taiwanese, and handed him a Sharpie. "You can go sign yours."

How could this possibly be more important than our competition? "What are you doing?" I asked.

"Donfield, Inc., wants to construct an arena on the edge of Old Taipei," he said.

"Okay?" Esher was an up-and-coming city, and it seemed like there was a construction project on every corner. But how was this more important than the latest challenge?

Garrett said brusquely, "If it goes up, it'll destroy the businesses and communities here. We have to stop the city council from approving its permit."

My mom said this neighborhood had been in a steady decline since the building of the Dynasty Mall. All of her friends had switched as soon as it opened, now going there for their grocery shopping and dim sum. I hadn't thought too deeply about what happened to the places left behind or pushed aside. I had just assumed it would be fine.

Garrett apparently knew exactly what I was thinking and was not impressed. I remembered what he had said before: *Do you ever go against what everyone tells you?* I felt a bloom of indignation. Did he think he was so much better than me?

"And what's the banner thing supposed to do?" I said.

"It's a sign for CultureFest next week. We're trying to bring attention to what's going on. That's why I need help with publicity and volunteers."

I didn't see how it was going to help. CultureFest was an annual community event in Old Taipei, one that used to be really popular. When we were little, Bella, Hattie, and I loved getting the street food from the booths and watching the lion dances. But attendance had become more and more scarce these past years. I didn't think a few booths could stop a major construction project.

Plus, if they really wanted to get attention, wouldn't a professional banner be better, like the ones they had used to advertise the Dynasty Mall's grand opening? I still remembered the event, which was more like a party. They had hired a band and set up a beverage service, and there had been people walking around serving small samples from all the new restaurants. That was how to get some real publicity.

Here, someone had painted a gold slogan in large Chinese characters, but they were kind of crooked. The cloth was wrinkled, and it was frayed on one end.

I was about to say something to Garrett when an older woman came over. I kind of recognized her; she sometimes came to the big Taiwanese events, like Lunar New Year and the Mid-Autumn Moon Festival, though she wasn't close friends with my mom. I think she ran some sort of tutoring thing? She had a son, Kevin, who was going to community college next year. The little kids all called her Ms. Vivian; it was a cute, informal nickname, which she seemed to prefer.

"Juliana," she said. "So nice to see you again!" I waited for her to ask the usual questions about where I was going to apply for college or how we were doing in the competition, but she instead handed me a squeeze bottle of paint. She always seemed more relaxed than the other parents. Was this because she grew up in America? "Add your print! We've all done it."

Her palm was light purple and Garrett's left hand was vaguely stained blue.

The little kids gathered around me. "Can I paint your hand?" a boy asked.

"No, me!" another one said.

How could I say no to those adorable faces? I held out my palm and let them both do half. When they were done, I pretended to give them a high five and they squealed and ran away. Garrett's expression softened, and he seemed almost entertained. What? I could be spontaneous. When it fit into my schedule.

"Where should I put my handprint?" I asked.

The kids shouted and pointed at different spots. I put mine on the corner and signed my name with a flourish. *Juliana Zhao.* What I didn't add: *Winner.*

* * *

After I had washed and rewashed my hand, it still looked faintly red, like I had spent my afternoon playing a particularly vicious game of slapjack. I shoved it in Garrett's face. "This is your fault."

"How?"

"If we had just met at the library, I wouldn't have been sucked into—"

"—having fun?"

"Staining my hand."

"Oh. No. Not staining your hand." But there was a small upturn of the corner of his mouth, something others might call a smile.

I pulled out my phone and laptop. I needed to get to work. I could feel it, what I had briefly forgotten while I had been painting: the stress. We needed to research companies. See if we had connections. Find out which types of ads might be the most effective. There was so much to do, and the minutes were leaking out and being wasted, endlessly.

Garrett was studying me. Unlike the other people I usually hung out with, he never seemed like he had a million things running through his head at the same time. He was just quietly watching. Listening. It had been one of the things I had always liked about him, before. What made me want to open up to him. But now it made me feel like he was seeing too much. Deciphering things that I didn't want him to.

"Time to get back on track," I said. "We only have a week to finish this challenge."

"We do. But we have plenty of time." He looked like I was a photograph whose composition was slightly off and he couldn't figure out why. I knew I was tense. Maybe too tense. But how could I not be?

He said, finally, "So what's the challenge? We have to partner with a company? Like a sponsorship?"

Another round. Another chance. Focus on that. We were offering dating advice, so which corporations might have the same target market, aka teenagers with love problems? Maybe the question and answer–type social media sites, like Reddit? But its audience was too broad, and almost everyone our age used other social media sites. I needed something like YouTube or TikTok but for love problems. A place where everyone our age hung out all the time.

Of course. The answer was, of course, on their phones.

The top app for people in high school was, obviously, coffeematch.com. It had been started by a sixteen-year-old high schooler who couldn't find anyone in his school that he wanted to date. His idea was to get kids from around his geographical area to enter their information and interests into a magical algorithm that suggested matches. They could then all meet in person for coffee on preset CoffeeMatch Days. It was in public, so it was safe, and was also a fun way for people to mingle with people outside of their school. It was a little retro to do all of this in person, instead of online, but it had caught on quickly, much to everyone's surprise. CoffeeMatch had recently partnered with national coffee companies, who started sponsoring monthly CoffeeMatch functions. It was brilliant. I wish I had thought of it.

I pulled up their website. "This is it."

"Coffeematch.com? The dating app?"

"They're national now," I said. "Everyone's heard of them and uses their app all the time. One ad from them could skyrocket our brand awareness and traffic."

Garrett scrolled through the site. "Why would coffeematch.com want to advertise a high school love advice column? Wouldn't it be a better idea to do something in person? Like pair with someone local and get to know them? How about the *Esher Times*? They might want to sponsor us. Support local teens in their effort to win a prestigious competition?"

"Sincerity does not sell," I said. "Advertising on a nationally recognized app does." It was one of the first lessons I had learned from my mom: the power of name brands. I had gone with her to meetings, had seen people who had been rude to her on the phone reconsider when they saw her pristine BMW, Louis Vuitton bag, Louboutin heels, and discreet Cartier watch. Mom never collected things just for the sake of collection. Rather, every item was strategically purchased and worn to telegraph success. It was necessary when she had to face racism and sexism every day; these items were her armor and they were powerful. Even for the rare Taiwanese functions that we attended, Mom always made sure she was impeccable, since she knew wealth, at least, could offset some of the gossip.

Advertising was the same: it was taking the feelings generated from one item or brand and transferring it to yours. The most effective thing would be a well-known national company. I scrolled to the bottom of the coffeematch.com website and then searched around a little more. But there was no information on how to buy an ad or how to contact the head office.

"It's the top matchmaking company in our demographic," I said. "You can't find anything better."

Garrett looked faintly bitter. "Of course. It has to be the best, right?"

Obviously. What did he know about business? Had he been studying it for years like I had? Gone through old textbooks and case studies? "We only have a week. We don't have time to meet some random newspaper people and become all buddy-buddy with them. The Lee Corporation always has ads on prime-time TV. And they partner with huge software companies. They're always trying to get their name out there. Like James Lee did with the AABC—and now all the colleges know about it."

"Yes, those huge corporations love to splash their names around. But does it really make a difference in the end? Are people really going to pay attention to a little pop-up ad while they are trying to swipe right? Even if it's from a large company? It's too impersonal."

"Of course they will," I said. "Who are people going to listen to—some little Podunk paper they've never heard of or coffeematch.com?"

"A trustworthy local source?"

"No way," I said. "Which car do you think is better? A BMW or some car made in someone's garage?"

"That's not even a thing."

"Companies are famous for a reason. People like brands," I said.

"People are brainwashed by brands. They just look at status symbols without bothering to find out if the thing is actually good or not." Garrett's mouth twisted. "Besides, coffeematch. com only offers ads for big companies. See? These are all huge corporations." He tilted his phone screen toward me.

"I'll get one."

"Then I'll be working on our backup plan," he said. "With the *Esher Times*."

"Is that a challenge?" I was beyond irritated with him, but the idea of a competition was slightly thrilling. The old us had done this so many times, jokingly—racing to the entrance of the camp dorms or seeing who could swim the most laps in the shortest amount of time. "Winner is whoever secures an ad first?"

"Done," he said. He held out his blue-stained hand, and I smacked it with my red-stained one.

"Game on, Tsai."

12

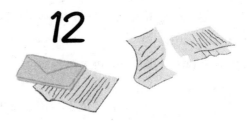

Dear Sunny and Cloudy,

My partner and I fundamentally disagree on the direction of our business venture. She is terribly misguided and is convinced it is her way or the highway. How can I prove I'm in the right? Because I am.

Signed,

It's Me

J: Ha-ha. Stop cluttering our inbox, *Garrett*.

G: You know what's the best flavor in the world, Juliana? The sweet taste of victory.

J: The only thing you'll be eating is my dust, sucker.

13

STEP ASIDE, DON DRAPER!

IT'S NOT THAT I'm competitive, per se. I was just absolutely certain I was 100 percent correct. And Garrett was wrong. It probably wasn't the most efficient for us to be focusing our efforts on two different things, but I didn't really need him in order to finish this part of our challenge. I had one secret weapon he couldn't beat: I was a master on the telephone.

I started with the corporate hotline. Most people would bypass this step, thinking it wouldn't lead to anything helpful. Au contraire. I knew from my days at Mom's office that even if they couldn't make corporate decisions themselves, all people who answered the phones had access to someone who could.

I also knew, from hours of fielding the customer service hotline myself, that these poor people were often treated the worst by those on the other end of the phone.

"CoffeeMatch.com. How are you doing today?" The girl on

the other end of the line already sounded defeated.

I worked my magic. I asked her how she was doing (it was surprising how many people failed to do this). She sounded like she was about my age, so I joked with her about time differences when I found out she was stationed in Nevada. I told her how much I loved coffeematch.com since I was an advice columnist myself. We chatted about relationships.

(Being good on the phone really isn't so hard: just remember every person is another human being, and don't be an ass. Those two things will get you 90 percent of the way in almost any situation.)

"So, what's up?" she said, almost cheery now. "How can I help you?"

"Well, I love CoffeeMatch so much. I was wondering what their advertising policies are. I can't seem to find anything on their website."

"You want to advertise CoffeeMatch? Yourself?"

"Actually, Brenda, I was wondering how to advertise my advice column *on* coffeematch.com."

"I think they only work with big companies. But let me ask my manager."

"Thank you," I said. "And, listen, if Jake doesn't ever call you back, you should ask yourself: Is this really what I want out of a relationship?"

She thanked me, and I felt almost as good about helping her as I did making progress on our ad. Maybe even better. I eventually talked to her manager, who then talked to his boss and so on. I eventually discovered Brenda was right: they normally only did advertising contracts with larger companies. But I explained to Michaela Simmons, head of Advertising and Sales, that I was a participant in the AABC, and if I won, I would be very happy to publicly express my gratitude to the companies that had helped me along the way. She finally agreed to a small pop-up ad, which would run three times over the next week.

Bingo.

I sent Garrett a short and sweet text.

I got it.

The response came in a few minutes later.

You did?

It's done.

The world was sunny. The future was bright. And, once again, I was on the straight path to victory.

14

THE CENTER MUST HOLD

I WAS FINALLY feeling better about the competition. But my happiness didn't last long. I got home after school the next day, and my mom was in her super-cleaning mode. She usually worked from home in the afternoons and wore athleisure wear in her office. Today, her hair was freshly done, the curls tight. And even though it was freezing outside, she had opened the windows to let the air in.

"What's going on?" I asked. This couldn't be good.

"Dinner tonight," Mom said. "Mrs. Lin and her family are coming over."

"*Here?*" I said. "Why?" They wouldn't talk about the competition, would they? Would Eric somehow spill the beans about my nonexistent partnership with Louis Park? And Mrs. Lin was the one who had told Eric to dump me. Did she think Mom knew and had invited her anyway? Oh, this was very not good.

Mom pulled out our fancy plates—the delicate ceramic ones we never used—and started to set the table. "We have to fix things with them, because of the competition. We can't have bad blood." She had no idea. If anyone had to fix things, it wasn't us.

"Eric dumped *me*, Mom!" Was she kidding? I tried all of my usual tricks to calm down: visualizing, deep breaths. But I couldn't contain it, the anger. The sense of injustice.

Mom found a set of cloth napkins and pushed them at me. "I talked to Mrs. Lin before the competition about you being partners. We can't have her thinking it's your fault it didn't work out."

"But it's *not*." Even if Mom didn't know that Mrs. Lin was the reason Eric broke up our partnership, she still knew it was *him*, not me, behind the split. And yet she was still ready to lay all the blame at my feet. Wanted to apologize for *me* during this dinner.

Unbidden, a memory came of Bella in this very room, belly round, shouting. *You are always worried about what everyone else thinks. Why does it matter so much?*

My mom, equally as loud: *You don't understand.*

Then explain it.

My mom, her voice cracking: *You have brought shame to this family.*

And that one word—shame—was like a bullet. Bella sagged, her hand on her stomach. *You'll never put us first, will you?* It would have been worse had she shouted. But she said it like it was an undeniable, terrible fact. Like she had pulled a ribbon off the neck of a doll and the head had rolled off.

I had run up to Mom, had hugged her out of her stiff anger as Bella strode to her room and slammed the door. But today, watching Mom furiously scrub the table to a shine, I thought about my sister. I had made Bella a small pouch filled with my favorite candies and had left it outside her closed door. The next day, it was gone. And so was she.

When had Bella gotten to the point where she couldn't hold her feelings down anymore? Had she tried, but they kept bursting through her fingers?

Even worse: once it started coming out, was she able to stop it? Not the anger. The doubt.

I dropped the napkins on the table, unfolded. Mom didn't notice when I left.

Hattie was missing. I poked my head into her room, then under the tent Dad had made for us when we were kids, which hung over her bed. Empty. She also wasn't in Dad's office. I finally found her in the backyard, angrily cleaning out our old shed.

My dad had also made this himself, so the walls weren't quite straight and the paint was uneven. But we had never loved a place more. We used to pretend that it was a clubhouse; Bella had set up a reading station with tons of pillows and stuffies, and we had sleepovers there on warm summer nights. After she left, neither Hattie nor I could bear to go back. It gradually filled up with our old lawn mower and snowblower, shovels, and cobwebs.

"What are you doing?" I asked.

"I needed to get out of there," Hattie said. "You know how she is. She even laid out an outfit for me."

I thought about Mom and there it was again: the fist of rage, pulsing. But I couldn't release it. Not in the house saturated with the ghost of my father. Not when my last memory of him, his weak hands over mine, was pulling us together. I was the center and I had to hold. I had to wrap the memory of Dad around me, and let it keep everything in.

Hattie said, "I'm going to study out here from now on. Like Bella did." Bella had set up a desk in the shed when she had started fighting more and more with Mom. But she still kept coming home from Yale on the weekends, mostly to see us. Hattie and I would snuggle into the beanbags and read while she memorized her notes.

"What happened?" I asked.

Hattie stopped sweeping and glared at me. "She doesn't want me to talk about Wisconsin in front of Mrs. Lin. Like it's something to be embarrassed about. So what if I want to go there? Not everyone wants to go to Yale."

Hattie said it so easily. Like she could pick what she wanted and just do it, go anywhere. Maybe that was the privilege of being the youngest. When she was in college and out of Mom's house, would my time come? When could I think about these things? The betraying thought wormed its way through me, tearing things up. I quashed it.

"It's one dinner," I said. "We just have to get through this." *I just had to get through this.* Somehow keep it a secret that Mrs. Lin wanted Eric to dump me and that I was now partners with

Garrett. I knew Hattie had no idea this was all going on, either. I wanted to keep it that way. There was no reason to burden her with my problems.

Hattie was sweeping again, the broom scraping against concrete. "It's like I'm lying. So I want to go to Wisconsin! So I want to be a journalist! It's not a big deal."

Hattie had always wanted to be a reporter, even from a young age. She used to pretend to interview our nanny and would take notes in orange crayon on a little notepad. ("Who is your favorite child?" was one question she had asked her. She wrote down Cynthia's answer—"I don't have one"—then crossed it out and replaced it with "ME." Hattie had never lacked confidence.) Later on, she wrote articles for the middle school paper, focusing on issues impacting the Asian American community, like the arena going up by Old Taipei.

But it was true that journalism pay wasn't tops. And there would be a lot of potentially dangerous travel if Hattie did the kind of investigative reporting she wanted to do. Plus, going to Wisconsin? She would be in the Midwest, Bella on the West Coast, and us on the East? How would that even work? How could we be a family if we couldn't even be in the same part of the country?

I said, "I mean, it *is* a hard field."

Hattie started sweeping again, forcefully, the dust puffing around her broom. "You always take her side."

"I do not." I was seeing the bombs planted in the ground and trying to navigate a safe path for us all. Hattie and Mom were like oil and fire; they fed off each other and combusted.

And I was the only force keeping them peacefully apart. After I left, what would happen? Would Hattie spend all of her days out here while Mom was home alone? That was another reason I absolutely needed to get into Yale: on the weekends, I needed to come home and pull our family back together.

She said, "Don't you think we should do something with *meaning*? Find out the truth of things? Help others?"

I didn't have the luxury to think about any of that. My first and only priority was to keep us going. It always had been. Getting preoccupied with significance and meaning? Those were the distracting rabbits on the side of the road; you followed them and suddenly you were off your path, lost in the woods. And who knows what could happen then?

"It's not bright enough in here to study," I said. "You'll strain your eyes."

Hattie said, "Okay, *Mom*, I'm going to use an extension cord to hook up some lights."

"Isn't it going to be too cold later?"

"Space heater." Hattie was getting her stubborn look, the same one she had since she was three years old and, legend had it, refused to use the potty for a year until the one day when she decided she was ready. She always did things on her own time.

A part of me wondered what it would have been like if Bella was still at home. Would some of the load be off me? Would she have done a better job of keeping us all together, like Dad would have wanted?

Before he died, Mom and Dad had once taken a rare day off work, and we had all gone to a water park together. I remember

Dad and Bella going down a huge slide, screaming. Mom laughing as the water splashed over her. She used to laugh a lot. Dad was wistfully happy, almost as if he had known that there wouldn't be many days like that left.

But then Hattie and I got into a fight, which escalated into a lot of crying and the totally unjustified yanking of someone's pigtails. My dad finally pulled me aside.

"Juliana," he said. "You have to take care of each other."

"But she pulled my hair!"

"Juju," he said. "You're the jiě jie. And you are the middle. Like Bàba is in his family, okay? That means we're special. It is our job to keep everything together. We're the center."

I had reluctantly listened and tried to keep Dad's lesson in mind from then on. But I seemed to be the only one who did.

Hattie tried to untangle a huge pile of Christmas lights but kept yanking them tighter, which made it worse. I took them from her and started working out the knots.

Hattie tried to take them back but then gave up and started pushing all the tools to one corner. "Hey," she said. "Did you do a Rube Goldberg project for your physics class last year? I was trying to make this ramp thingy, but the sides keep falling over."

I looped the plug through the rest of the line. "I can help you with it at the end of the week. Is it due soon?"

"No. But I just want to figure out why it's not working. Do you have any notes?"

"I'll meet you after school at the lab."

"Juju, I only want to borrow your notebook."

I put a reminder on my calendar to meet her after my last class on Friday.

I finally got all the lights loosened and stretched them out. "You going to use these now?"

"No—in the winter. You'll see." She stopped. "Oh, I guess you won't be here." She stared at the ground. "I'll send you a picture."

Even when we were little, even if we were fighting, I was always sad when Hattie was sad. Whenever she got her toys put in time-out, I always snuck her one of mine so she wouldn't cry. I also slipped her my extra desserts and let her borrow all of my stuffed animals. But college—and leaving—was not something I could fix. Another fissure in our family.

I almost wanted to talk to her about the pressures I was feeling. To tell her about how I had lied about partnering with Garrett and about what Mrs. Lin had done. To admit I was terrified I couldn't win Dad's competition. That I would lose and the Linevine would stop talking about how prestigious the AABC was and would start tacking it with an asterisk about how *His daughter couldn't even win, though.* That I would sully Dad's legacy with my failure.

But I couldn't. I was supposed to be the jiě jie. The big sister. After Dad died, it had been only us sisters and Mom. Then, Hattie, me, and Mom. Our family couldn't get any smaller.

So I said nothing. Instead, I helped my baby sister clear out a space of her own, one she could use after I was gone. When she was the last one left.

15

BRIEF ASIDE TO EXPLAIN MOM
AND THE DUCK CLEAVER

WE ALL MIGHT be familiar with the concepts of rage posting or rage cleaning. My mom rage cooked. She had a variety of items she liked to chop when she was especially peeved: carrots, lotus root, daikon.

But when she was mad—really furious—she took out the duck cleaver and went to town on some raw poultry.

To a lot of families, chicken soup was comforting and healing. In our family, it was a sign that something had gone terribly, terribly wrong.

When Bella played hooky from math tutoring and snuck to dance classes instead? Duck cleaver. When Hattie decided to play kickball in the living room and broke Mom's favorite vase from Taiwan? Cleaver. And when Bella told Mom that she was pregnant and dropping out of medical school, Mom didn't say a word. She just drove to the store, came back with three whole chickens, and started chopping.

The next day, all of the pictures of Bella were gone.

"She is no longer a part of this family," Mom said.

"What?" I glanced at Hattie, but she was as clueless as I was. I didn't know that was even an option. How can you un*family* someone? It was like saying you were taking away someone's lungs, or heart.

I was twelve years old, and there were certain things I knew to be immutable: gravity pulled down and not up; jumping off the top branch of the tree in our front yard was a really, really bad idea; and your family was your family no matter what.

After that day, only two of those things were still true.

16

HUMBLE BRAGGING, A DISH BEST SERVED WITH A SIDE OF RICE

THE DINNER WITH the Lins went about as well as expected. That is, it was a disaster.

It all started out as per usual. Their family arrived and my mom made the loud noises reserved for Other Taiwanese People, topped off with *Ai-yo! I Haven't Seen You for So Long! You Look So Wonderful!* Mrs. Lin gave her a fancy paper bag filled with oranges and a tin of cookies, which resulted in a round of *Ai-yo! You Shouldn't Have!* And yet another round of *Ai-yo! It Was Nothing!* Eric stood off to the side, silent.

Mom had put out brand-new slippers in the front. They were not the usual white flimsy kind. No. Mom went all out with the extra fuzzy, memory foam Isotoners. She was playing to win. She had also dusted off two old pictures of Bella and put them back on the shelves, behind the other ones. Mrs. Lin glanced at them as she and Mr. Lin took off their shoes.

I had been stressing about this dinner all day, running through the scenarios in my head. The first problem, of course, was that Mom didn't know Mrs. Lin was behind Eric dropping me. I still couldn't bear to tell her. However—and this might be the first time I have ever, ever said this—this was the one situation where the Linevine's inability to speak about things directly could actually be an advantage. Mrs. Lin herself certainly would never bring up what she had done. Nor would it be unusual for Mom to avoid confronting her openly. In fact, this dinner might even be perceived as a passive-aggressive *In your face.* Like, *I will shame you with my politeness, biach!* Which, frankly, might be deserved.

No, the bigger problem was that I had said Louis Park was my partner. So long as Eric didn't say anything with his big mouth, things would be okay. Mom never talked to Louis's family, and there were no school functions where they could accidentally run into each other. If I won, it wouldn't matter anymore. I just had to keep up the charade for a few more weeks.

But, of course, all the competition stuff remaining a secret was dependent on Eric. Which meant I was screwed.

Hattie gave Eric the stink eye, but the grown-ups didn't notice. Eric did. Mrs. Lin said, loudly, "Eric, why don't you and the other kids go to the basement?"

He sighed and followed Hattie. We sat awkwardly on the couch until Hattie turned on the television and clicked it over to a super violent movie. She crossed her arms and turned up the volume. She clearly knew what Eric had done but still didn't know Mrs. Lin was behind it.

"How is the competition going?" Eric asked. He had the nerve to sound slightly remorseful.

"We don't have to be polite," I said. "Just watch the movie."

Hattie and I were used to forced socialization. Before The Fall, we used to take trips during the summer to visit my parents' friends. (We, of course, stayed at their houses. For my mom and her friends, staying at a hotel in a city where a friend lived was roughly equivalent to sleeping on the ground in an unmarked jail cell.)

We spent a good number of school vacations on lumpy fold-out couches in strangers' basements, next to unused Ping-Pong tables and stacks of dusty cardboard boxes. We had been forced to have awkward conversations or deal with outright hostility. There was Tom, who woke all of us up every morning at 5:30 by shouting, "ZĂO ĀN!!!" After three days, even my mother stopped being polite and hid in the guest room to nap. There was Willy, who literally said four words to us over a three-day period. (Those words were: "This is your room.") There was Kenneth, who put signs all over the house that said, "STAY OUT—KENNETH."

All this to say that I could deal with an evening with Eric Lin. But I didn't have to be nice about it.

We all stared at the screen for a long while. It was not awkward at all.

Eric pulled out his phone and started texting someone. I was surprised to see his expression soften, his normal edge temporarily dulled. I had seen Eric around school and hadn't talked to him much since the beginning of the competition. I didn't see the need to. But I couldn't help but notice him hanging around Siobhan Collins, who was in the SBA with us. They would have lunch together, him sweetly picking up her leftover napkins and paper food trays and dumping them in the trash for her. She was super smart, driven, and 100 percent Not Taiwanese. Did his mom know? I somehow doubted it. Allowing her only son to date someone not of the mother country? Mrs. Lin would rather impale herself on a chopstick and roast herself over a hot hibachi grill.

Eric eventually put away his phone and faced the movie again, but I could tell he wasn't watching it.

I have to win this competition.

Was it possible he might have his reasons for doing what he was doing? Maybe.

But so did I.

Dinner was even worse. Since there was only one other family over tonight, we were allowed to eat at the main table instead of the kids' tables set up in the basement. It was definitely worse to be upstairs.

Eric was an only child, and I have to confess this was the first time I noticed the pressure of *undiluted attention*. Eric was all his parents could talk about. Eric loved to play tennis. Eric won a math competition when he was in middle school. Eric once made a bridge out of toothpicks when he was eight. Eric seemed like he was one steamed bok choy away from chucking his dinner across the table.

Honestly, his parents should hold a master class. Humble

bragging is a delicate craft and difficult to explain to my friends. In the Taiwanese culture, it was considered poor form to directly boast about your children; it's considered conceited, since children are a reflection of their parents. However, your social standing was totally dependent upon having successful offspring. This tension led to the world's most subtle martial art: the humble brag.

Other non-Taiwanese people might be offended by this whole dance. My mom was once invited out to dinner by Maria and her parents. It was an hour of total confusion and chaos.

Them: "Maria loves singing! She's the lead in the musical!"

Look from Mom to us, translated: *Hah, who do these people think they are? So boastful!*

Mom: "Juju hates studying. *Ai-yo*, so lazy. It's a miracle her grades are so high."

Maria's mom and dad looked shocked at her use of the word "lazy." I could totally tell what they were thinking: *Did Juliana's own mother call her lazy? Isn't that too severe?*

Nope, that's just dinner, Maria's parents.

All of this drove Hattie up a wall, especially when it escalated into forced musical recitals by the kids. It's all fun and games until the violin comes out.

"So, Eric, you want to go to Princeton?" my mom asked him, in Chinese.

Eric opened his mouth, but his mom said, "Yes. Like his father."

Eric's dad let out a loud "Hah," which roughly translated to: "Yup."

But Eric told me he wanted to go to Dartmouth. *I want to go as far away as possible.* I glanced at him, but he was eating, silent. When I didn't say anything, he looked vaguely surprised.

During the rest of the dinner, his parents kept speaking as if Eric wasn't *right there.*

"We have to make sure Eric gets into the best school."

"Business is definitely the best for Eric. Like James Lee and their family. So successful!"

And: "Now that Eric is ready to go to college, it's time to think about his future. I hope he meets a nice girl at Princeton."

What about Siobhan? It was 100 percent obvious they didn't know about her.

Eric's face spasmed. He was staring at the center of the table, like he wanted to rage teleport straight out of this meal. His parents had said they were only going to let him leave the tri-state area if he got into an Ivy. Was he going to—what? Hope he got into Dartmouth so he could be free? Or win AABC, use the tuition to go to a non-Ivy school of choice, and cut his parents off?

His parents had pushed him hard his whole life. Mom always told us that when she was growing up, there was fierce competition to get into the right feeder high school, which could get you to the right college. There was an even worse battle for employment back then; in a place with limited options, only the top people could get jobs. And how did you figure out who was top? There was only one way. The difference between being employed and not employed at certain places might be the name of the college on your résumé.

This was the world Mom and Mr. and Mrs. Lin came from. They had moved here, and they had—relationship by relationship, child by child, school by school—rebuilt the system they had known. An island in a strange and occasionally hostile desert of English.

Eric looked like he was waiting for me to say something about Siobhan, and was then shocked when I didn't. He knew I had seen them together at school, and I could bust him twenty ways to Sunday right now. But I felt a little sliver of pity for him. And for Siobhan, who had always been nice. So I didn't bring it up.

Mrs. Lin tapped Eric's back, trying to get him to straighten up. He glared at her.

Mr. and Mrs. Lin kept pushing Eric. But were they shoving him right out of their lives? I don't think they had ever considered the possibility.

Mrs. Lin was talking, and then I heard something mixed in Taiwanese and Mandarin: the AABC. "They were so excited to do a piece on your husband."

My mom beamed.

What? Who was?

"And James Lee and his father, of course. There is even someone from Harvard who is going to talk about how so many of the past winners do well. The paper is going to follow up with the AABC alumni and see what they're doing now."

"The *Taiwan Times*," my mom said, and didn't even try to appear modest.

The *Taiwan Times*! Everyone would read it! It was the Bible of the Taiwanese community, landing in driveways and mail-boxes around the country. Nothing was news until it was printed there first.

Mrs. Lin clasped her hands together. "It would run in a few weeks, so they'll have time, of course, to interview this year's winner."

Oh my God. The *Taiwan Times*. Everyone would read it.

My mom gave me a Significant Look. "Well, the winner*s*." The slight emphasis on the plural was subtle. "They needed partners this year, right?"

Oh no. Red alert! Red alert! Must change the subject!

"Mom, do you want me to cut some oranges?" I said.

She would not be deterred. "Such a shame that Eric and Juliana were not able to partner this year." Mom politely left it in the passive voice. No blame assigned, just a general mis-fortunate event. I knew she was trying to segue into clearing things up.

But Mrs. Lin didn't comment. Did she think Mom had just low-key insulted her by bringing up our broken partnership? She didn't know Mom didn't know that she had asked Eric to drop me, and OH MY GOD, WHY WAS THIS SO COM-PLICATED?

Mom passed Mrs. Lin the fruit tray as Mrs. Lin stiffly agreed it was unfortunate, then quickly changed the topic to the *Tai-wan Times* again. As she kept talking about how wonderful the article was going to be, Mom placed an orange on my plate. It was a citrus-infused message that said, *You had better get this victory for our family and our ancestors' ancestors.*

Next to her, Eric was texting someone under the table. Probably Siobhan. I didn't have enough energy to figure out what was going on with him anymore. I had bigger problems to worry about.

17

EVERYTHING IS COMING UP HEARTS

OVER THE NEXT few days, I kept having nightmares about the *Taiwan Times*. One where I answered the door and a giant newspaper swatted me like a fly. One where I became King Midas but everything I touched turned to newsprint.

I kept refreshing the coffeematch.com website, frantically. Finally, I saw it: an ad with a flash of Garrett's logo and a link to our website. It was beautiful, a tiny fierce engine that would drive visitors to our site. It had better or else my shame wouldn't be only local. It would be throughout the whole freaking Taiwanese American community, from sea to shining sea.

I sent Garrett a screenshot. He responded with a picture of the cultural center.

Tomorrow. Don't forget.

Leave it to Garrett Tsai to spoil my moment of triumph.

Volunteering was a great way to test out fresh outfits, since I didn't know many people at the cultural center. In honor of today's art project, I wore a dark blue skirt, white sweater with a whimsical design, and a powder-blue coat. The vibe I was going for was winter but in a fun way!

Garrett was wearing jeans and a *Steins;Gate* T-shirt. And *Totoro* socks. I was going to make a crack about them, but he wasn't his usual self today. He was coiled, quiet. Next to him was Amy, clutching his hand and a knitted turtle.

"I thought she had a gymnastics competition today?" He didn't answer. I crouched down to her eye level. "Didn't you have a meet?"

She hugged her turtle tighter. What was going on? I glanced at Garrett. For once, there was no snark between us.

"What happened?" I asked. It wasn't like her to skip a meet—ever. And Garrett looked askew; his shoelaces were untied, and he wasn't wearing a jacket even though it was freezing.

Garrett's phone buzzed. He ignored it. "My parents were fighting. So I brought her here." I saw him like this, occasionally, sometimes in Chinese class when his dad dropped him off, his mom silent in the passenger seat. Their arguments would worm their way into him, consuming. Our weeks in New Hampshire, when he was away from them, were the only time I had ever seen him free of it.

His phone kept buzzing. He rummaged around his backpack, then pressed a water bottle into Amy's hands. "Go ask Chef Auntie for a snack and then come back, okay?" She hugged him, then ran off. Garrett watched her, unsmiling.

His phone buzzed again. He finally picked up.

"Yes, we're here." He dropped his bag on the ground. "No, it's too late to bring her back. Well, you should have thought about that before. We'll be back at dinner."

He hung up and stared at the wall. Then grabbed his backpack and strode to a table. I followed him but didn't know what to say.

"It's like they're children," he said. "Honest to God." He opened his backpack and pulled out some of Amy's workbooks and a small iPad. He dug around some more, then zipped up the pocket with a quick yank. He pressed his hands to his head and stayed like that for a moment, his fingers tangled in his hair. "Do you have a charger?"

Of course I did. Because Hattie never brought hers and you never know. I put a regular charger, a fast charger, and a battery pack on the table. "Which one do you want?"

Garrett huffed out a short laugh and picked the fast charger. "Hattie's?"

"Of course."

Garrett was the center of his family, too. Both of us carrying supplies for the younger ones, running interference, shielding our mèi meis. Keeping everything afloat so they wouldn't have to. But seeing Garrett exhausted, fed up, I wondered how we had gotten the short straws.

I grabbed a bottle of water from the communal fridge and brought it back to him.

"Are you all right?" I asked.

"Not really."

I didn't know what to say, how to pry open the firm lid covering what he was thinking. I didn't say, *It'll be okay,* because sometimes things aren't.

"It was a bad one?" I asked finally. I thought to the fights Mom and Bella used to have, the shouting. The tight, spiraling feeling of dread I would feel as Hattie and I would hide in her room, staring at the tent over her bed.

"They're all bad ones." Garrett glanced toward the kitchen, checking on Amy. "They should just get divorced. But they couldn't deal with the gossip." The last word was coated with bitterness.

"No one can deal with the gossip." It wasn't only us kids at the mercy of the Linevine or my mom. It was everyone.

"It's ridiculous." Garrett was different from everyone else; he always said what he thought, did what he wanted. Was so scornful of people who followed what everyone else did without question. Was this why? Because he had seen his parents doing the opposite? Letting everyone else's opinions control their lives?

He bent his head and there was something unbearable about the sad line of it, the weight. When we were kids, I remember we had been at his house for a dinner once. This was before my father had gotten diagnosed, before his passing, before The Fall. His mom and dad were in their silent-mode phase, carefully socializing with everyone else but not each other. That evening, his brother and the others were playing video games loudly in the basement, but he had disappeared. I had found him alone in his room, reading an old volume of *Dragon Ball*.

"You all right?" I had asked.

He said a quiet yes. I turned to leave, but he asked, "Have you read these?"

I hadn't and had never really wanted to before. But then, as now, there was something haunting about the sorrow he wore, how it seemed to wrap around and seep into him. I had taken the book he had offered and sat next to him. We read until the end of the party, and as I was putting on my shoes to leave, he flashed me a small smile. I remembered it vividly because it was the first time I had felt a glow that had not come from grades or being the best at something. Later, Garrett would be back to his usual self, especially in Chinese class. But for that small moment, I had made him feel better. He hadn't needed me to accomplish something or do anything or be anyone. He only needed me to sit next to him.

I had always wondered if he remembered. But years later, during that summer, we had a free period after dinner one day. Garrett had come up to me and wordlessly passed me a battered issue of *Dragon Ball*, which he had found somewhere. We had read it, side by side.

So I sat next to him now. I didn't get up as he became lost to thoughts I could only guess. I didn't check my phone or ask him too many questions or give him any advice. I just stayed there. And when he finally glanced over at me, the prickliness he usually wore was gone. Like he was too raw to keep it up.

"Are you all right?" I asked.

He didn't answer.

Finally, I said, "Hey. You know what I once read about?"

He shook his head.

"This is totally fictional, mind you, so take it with a grain of salt. But I once saw a story about high schoolers who kind of did whatever the hell they wanted."

He laughed, a surprised exhale. I felt unreasonably pleased.

"You mean they didn't spend their time being a mediator for their parents?" he said. "Or double-checking elementary school homework and packing lunches for their sisters?"

"Nope," I said. "And they just let those school projects *fail*."

His eyes widened. "My God," he said. "I can't even imagine." We smiled and understood each other perfectly. Because neither could I.

Amy came running back to us, a plate full of Chinese sponge cakes in her hand. In the kitchen doorway was a middle-aged woman, apron tied around her waist. She looked concerned and waved at Garrett. *Eat.*

He put a hand on Amy's head, then offered me the plate. As I took some, we started to eat together. Something shared.

Later on, Garrett helped me to bring the supplies for our project into the classroom: boxes of egg cartons and scissors. I gave Amy the bag of googly eyes and the sparkly pipe cleaners, and she quickly cheered up.

I had planned the perfect project: making tiny animals out

of egg cartons. The only problem was that a lot of the little kids didn't speak English, and not all of them spoke Taiwanese, so I was supposed to do the whole thing in Mandarin.

"Now let's take the . . . er"—I pointed at the egg carton—"egg . . . box and . . ." I made a slicing motion. "Cut! Cut!"

Garrett stifled a smile. He started to look better after we ate our sponge cakes, almost back to his usual self. Actually, almost like his old self, the summer one.

"Then small child string!" I held up a pipe cleaner. "Red okay!"

Garrett laughed. And I was reminded of all the projects we had been forced to do together: paper lanterns, origami animals, Chinese seals we had to carve out of Styrofoam. Garrett's was like calligraphy. Mine looked like a headless stick figure with three legs.

"Hole, so tiny," I said in Mandarin to the kids, holding up my sample egg carton. "Small child string horns."

"Oh my God," Garrett said as several of the children waved their small safety scissors, confused.

I mimed putting the pipe cleaners into the egg carton. I glued on the eyes. I drew a happy face. Each I accompanied with a helpful "hmmm?" noise. Who needed Mandarin? This was totally working.

The kids broke out into chatter, most of which were variations of "I don't get it!" One girl looked like she was going to cry. I glanced at Garrett, panicked, and he joined me in the front of the room. He recited the instructions in Mandarin, and the kids became much happier. But he was soon overwhelmed as three kids asked for his help all at once. He threw up his hands and made a goofy face, which made them giggle.

"Slow down," he said. "There is only one of me."

My mom would have told the kids to do it on their own and figure it out, but Garrett sat next to them and walked through each step, helping some of them to poke holes in their cartons or to glue eyes on the front. He drew a fancy unicorn face on one and cute dog ears on another. He took care with every creation, cradling each carton in his graceful fingers, his left hand sketching.

One of the little girls wrapped her hand around mine and pulled me to her project, an egg carton cat.

"What is the name for this?" she said in Mandarin.

"Cat?" I said in English.

"Cat," she repeated in English.

I pointed to the scissors. "Scissors." That one was tougher, but she got it. We went through other words: crayons and pencils and paper.

Garrett came up to us. "Giving English lessons?"

I said, "She's teaching me Mandarin, too." The girl giggled. "Right?"

I helped her and some others gather some paint and brushes. And when they were finally done and I saw the row of carton animals lined up on the counter to dry, I felt as happy as if I had made them myself. It was a pure feeling, not laced with anxiety, like when I got my class ranking or ticked something off my to-do list. Just . . . satisfaction. Joy.

Garrett stood next to me. "They're cute."

"Right?" I said.

We both gazed at the projects together. My dad had taught me how to make these cartons one afternoon when he was off work. Now, looking at all the crooked pipe cleaner arms and googly eyes, I thought he might be happy that I was sharing his knowledge. Keeping it alive.

Here is the thing about grief: it is always there. You think it has receded. You think you can carefully scoop up the sand of your life and pat it together into a little castle and pretend things are fine. But the feeling of loss will still come, when you least expect it. It will crash and swallow everything.

Now, here in the middle of Old Taipei, I felt a crush of sadness that I had to guess what my dad might like. That I wouldn't know him well enough to be certain he would be proud of me. Instead, I had these fleeting reflections of who he was. Guesses.

It was that, more than anything, which made me say, "I think my dad would have liked me helping out here."

Garrett looked surprised. "Your dad?"

"It's why he started the competition in the first place," I said. "To support the community."

"He did? I thought it was only for college applications."

I had forgotten that Garrett had not grown up with this competition like I had. Had not seen its evolution. "No, in the beginning, it was more about encouraging Asian Americans to go into business. When it was under Mr. Lee, it was about giving opportunities to people who didn't have them. It's what my dad wanted the most. It wasn't until James took over that things changed."

Garrett was gazing at me like he was processing what I was saying, recalibrating.

He said, "What was your dad like?"

Some people might hate this question, but it was my favorite one. It meant I could share him, keep his memory alive.

"He loved everything," I said. "Never halfway. He made the world seem like it was made of infinite possibilities."

Garrett seemed wistful. "Sounds nice."

I was used to moments of silence with Garrett, but each time was subtly different: companionable at camp, detached in class, sometimes inexplicably scornful. But this quiet was almost alive with the unsaid, pulsing.

Garrett said, "Do you . . . want to meet some of the other people? See what we do around here?"

I nodded.

"Really?" he said.

"Yes." To my surprise, I meant it.

The center was pretty crowded by late afternoon. I recognized a few folks from the big Taiwanese functions but not that many. None of them appeared to be in my mom's close circle of friends. On the wall, someone had taped up copies of a petition with a lot of signatures. It looked like it was for their efforts to stop the city council from approving the arena. They were in for a battle. I had read in the Linevine that some of the wealthier uncles and aunties had decided to invest in it, so there were a lot of people who wanted to make sure it went forward.

"Do you know anyone here?" Garrett asked.

"Not really." One uncle I recognized from the grocery store around the corner. He used to give us free candies when we were little kids, when my mom still shopped there. I think one auntie owned the local bookstore, maybe?

"They're from around the neighborhood," Garrett said. "Some people rent apartments a few blocks away; some are store owners."

I followed the smell of delicious food to the kitchen next to the main room. In the middle was the woman who had given us the sponge cakes. She was expertly flipping a pile of rice and veggies in a huge wok.

"This is Auntie Qi. She runs the Asian fusion restaurant next door. She's friends with Auntie Liu, your mom's friend? I think they knew each other in Taiwan." Garrett said in a stage whisper, "We all call her Chef Auntie, and she'll say she hates it, but she secretly loves it."

The woman shook her spatula. "No Chef Auntie!"

"That's a lot of food," I said. It all smelled delicious. I wondered why she was cooking here if her business was next door. "Are you preparing for your dinner rush?"

She laughed. "No, volunteering. A lot of the uncles and aunties recently arrived here or are having a hard time to find jobs. We give food to everyone."

Most of my mom's friends at the big Taiwanese functions were like my mother, financially well-off and comfortably successful in their careers. My mom would say the people here were *different from us*. I had never thought about what that meant before. Did "different" mean less wealthy? Not in white-collar jobs? More recently immigrated?

I thought about my struggles with Mandarin just now, how difficult it must be to come to another country and try to get a job when you couldn't even communicate the basics. The contentment that could come from teaching a little girl the word for cat.

"Do you need . . . help?" I asked.

Garrett looked at me curiously. "Aren't you busy this afternoon?"

I was. I was supposed to set up the venue for the SBA fundraiser, contact local businesses about sponsorships, cram for my AP Calc test, and pick up Hattie from tennis. My mom definitely would have said to go straight home. But the thought of being squirreled away in my empty room with a pile of books was suddenly . . . unappealing. I quickly checked the competition website: no updates.

A few of the dishes had been plated and were sitting on the counter. "Can I take these out?" I asked.

Garrett strolled behind me. I expected him to make some sort of sarcastic comment, but he didn't. In fact, he almost seemed impressed.

I first went up to a gentleman sitting at a side table, who was about a decade younger than the age my father would have been. He didn't smile as I put down the plate or say thank you. I liked him instantly. My grandpa had also been charmingly grumpy. I noticed the man shared his nicest dumpling with his elderly neighbor and made sure everyone else had water before getting it himself.

"Uncle Jing has been living in this neighborhood since he arrived in Connecticut," Garrett said. "He and his wife ran the fortune cookie company down the street, but she died about ten years ago. Now he runs it with his brother."

I brought out some more plates and gave Uncle Jing an extra dumpling to make up for the one he gave away. He promptly handed it over to another lady at the table, a quiet auntie with a knitted flower headband in her hair. Then he gave me the stink eye.

Garrett laughed at my expression. "Not used to people being immune to your charm?"

"You just wait," I said cheerfully. "Uncle Jing and I are going to be BFFs."

It turned out that Chef Auntie liked to test out her new dishes here, so I handed out food and took back feedback.

"Uncle Jing says there should be no truffle in the dumplings."

Chef Auntie strode into the main room, spatula in hand. "You ate five!"

Uncle Jing said, "What about plain dumplings, huh? Why are those so bad?"

She stomped back into the kitchen. Then threw some oil on her pan, cackling. She fried up a ginormous dumpling and plated it with extra truffle sauce on the rim of the plate. "This is for Uncle Jing."

I brought it out to him, and he grumbled. But I noticed he

ate the whole thing himself, and when I picked up the plate, all the truffle sauce on the sides was gone.

Over the next hour, I got roped into a surprisingly lively game of mah-jongg and a fun game of tag with the little kids. I met more of the uncles and aunties. The auntie with the flower headband seemed to be very quiet, always sitting by herself and not talking to others unless they came up to her first.

I found out her name was Auntie Cindy. "She doesn't seem to talk to the others much," I said to Garrett.

"She's a little shy. She doesn't have family here, so she comes here for company."

"What happened to her family?"

One of the little girls came up to her, and Auntie Cindy opened her purse. She pulled out a little knitted animal and pressed it into her hands. The girl squealed and gave her a huge hug. Auntie Cindy hugged her back, and she looked wistful? Heartbroken?

"I think she has a son, but they got into a fight, and they both won't make up with each other," Garrett said. "That type of thing."

I knew all about that type of thing, unfortunately.

A boy ran up to Garrett and wrapped himself around his leg. "More tag!"

"More tag?" Garrett said to me.

"No, I'm too tired . . . ," I said, then smacked him on the arm. "NOT!" I tore across the room. Garrett raced after me, and the kids followed him. I led them all into an empty room where they wouldn't accidentally run into things and then spent the next hour sprinting and laughing instead of worrying about the competition.

At the end of the hour, I staggered back to the dining room and sagged into a chair. I was tired but not the weary-to-the-bones kind. The gratifying kind.

But the first thing I saw on the table was a crumpled copy of the *Taiwan Times*. The worry, the pressure, which had been dormant, wrapped around me like a spiked vine. I flipped the newspaper over and pulled out my phone. Surely the competition results must be out by now, right? I could check before going to pick up Hattie.

Garrett came up to me.

I said, "Time out." I didn't look up from my phone. "I'm in a safe zone."

He slid a beef roll in front of me. It was perfectly crispy, with sprigs of cilantro sticking out of the sides.

"Eat," he said. "I'll check."

I had been smelling its delish crispiness all afternoon. "You sure? Did you already have one?"

Garrett tucked a pair of chopsticks into my hand, his fingers brushing against mine. I startled, then held the chopsticks tightly. He pulled up his phone, and I tried to process the rare sensation of someone else taking care of things. I took a huge bite of the beef roll, which was heavenly.

"Did you try this?" I asked.

Garrett's attention was on the screen.

"What? What is it?" We definitely got to the top with this challenge. It was CoffeeMatch! Do you know how many people go on the CoffeeMatch website each day?

Garrett tilted the phone toward me.

Fail.

18

THE BITTER TASTE OF FAILURE

EVEN GARRETT SENSED how bad this was. We were two rounds in and hadn't made any progress. But Eric and Albert had; they had moved up one spot, to sixth place.

How was that possible? I frantically did some research: the top five teams all had totally different projects. Team Dresscycle had developed a service that could help coordinate homecoming and prom dress exchanges. I bet that was Kelly and Linda's project; it sounded like something they would both be interested in. Eric and Albert had created a central information hub for college scholarships, complete with deadlines, stats, interviews with past winners, and resources for assistance in applying. But how did they get traffic?

Linda and Kelly had paired with a TikTok influencer and offered a free trial for her and her friends. They were thrilled with the results and had posted about it on social media. Albert and Eric's service was promoted through a network of schools, through flyers, the PTA, and the school newspapers.

Garrett said, "We still have a few more rounds. It'll be okay." But I heard it, the curiosity: *Why are you freaking out so much?*

I refreshed the page without answering. But the results were the same again and again. Worst yet, the next challenge had already been released.

CHALLENGE #3:
MARKET FEEDBACK

Your service is now up and running. You have marketed with corporate sponsors. This week, we want you to try and engage your target audience in a different way.

Accordingly, we will be hosting a two-hour event where you will promote your service in person. The venue will be at the Esher Convention Center, and we will provide each team with one table and a budget of $50. We will also provide computers so participants can enter in their reviews of your service. We will provide an "audience" of fifty members of your target demographic. Points will be awarded for each person that you can convince to leave feedback.

A live event. Could this be our opportunity to get ahead? It could play to our best strengths: in-person charm, direct interaction with our target audience, and a subject area that could draw others in.

I said, "A live love advice booth."

Garrett looked horrified.

I could see it now. Blast on social media with promotions for the event. Use of our color scheme for décor and online advertising. A replica of our website banner for the station. "We should spend our budget on great decorations. Ones that will really draw you in."

Garrett, as usual, seemed like he wanted to say something.

"What?"

"We're not getting measured by how many people will check out our table," he said. "We're getting points based on how many will actually leave feedback. That's much harder."

"But every team is going to be there. How are we going to get people to come over if we don't have something splashy?"

I was the one who had been studying the AABC for years. I had taken notes on every textbook in my dad's office, had read case studies for fun. I should know the best way to go forward.

But the sting of the ad challenge was still fresh. I had ignored Garrett last time and . . . it hadn't turned out well.

He was right. But so was I. How could we get people to leave feedback if we didn't stand out visually?

I was at a loss. But then I remembered something I had read in one of my dad's old negotiation books: sometimes you had to figure out what the other person wanted and see if there was a way you could both win. On the margin of my dad's copy, he had written a huge star by this section, in blue ink.

"You're right," I said. "*But* I think we need to bring attention to our booth; otherwise we aren't going to get any traffic at all. How can we do both?"

Garrett leaned back in his chair. "We do need to draw them

in. And somehow also motivate them so they will take the time to fill out a review. Like some kind of hook or incentive."

That was a good idea. Why would a stranger take the time to give feedback? And how would we get a whole bunch of them to do it? Of course. "A giveaway!"

Garrett started to smile. "A giveaway."

Ads on social media. All of our décor could focus not on our website but on the giveaway itself. What else had my dad said? Always bring something to the table. We could do it here, literally.

"In exchange for filling out the form, the person's name could get entered into a raffle to get—"

"—a lifetime supply of tissues for use after their breakup?"

I elbowed him. "A twenty-five-dollar gift certificate to a romantic restaurant," I said. "Is there any way to add to our prize pack without spending more money? Maybe an extra live love advice session with the winner?"

"What about donated items?" he said. "Maybe Chef Auntie or Auntie Cindy could give some stuff?"

We smiled at each other. And, treacherously, I was reminded of the closing ceremonies at camp when we had finished our last skit and it felt like everything clicked together perfectly.

But then my phone pinged. Mom.

Juliana. Your team name is not in the top ten. Why

And just like that, all the stress came flooding back. I flipped my phone over without reading the whole message. If we lost this next round, we would really be in the hole. And then how would we recover?

Garrett said, "Your mom?"

"Yes."

He looked bitter. "Let me guess: She really wants you to win?"

"You could say that."

I could almost see it, the war between him wanting to say something snarky and him wanting to know more. He chose the latter, to my surprise. "What if you don't?"

I could have said, *You don't understand*, but he had taken the high road. I suppose I could do the same. "The aunties, the uncles, the comparison game. You know. Public failure." I picked at the remainder of the beef roll with my chopsticks. "Since my sister . . . My mom's been keeping herself away from everyone. Because of the shame."

Garrett didn't respond, and I thought of the weight that comes when someone listens, really listens to you. At camp, we had hours of talking, deliriously long stretches of time when we had slowly opened up to each other, one story at a time. There were a lot of people around us now, but it seemed like we were in a pocket, alone.

The pressure was the thing I never talked about. Not with Hattie, not with Maria and Tammy, not anyone. I had the sudden, overwhelming memory of the sunrise Garrett and I had watched together, our arms brushing against each other. We had spoken about so many other things that July. But never about past relationships, never about our parents, and never about academics. New Hampshire was a magical oasis where we could just exist without grades or college or social standing, so we never talked about any of it. We hadn't wanted to.

I wasn't sure why I was telling him this now. But being able to say it out loud, finally, was an overwhelming relief.

But the last piece he didn't quite understand, and what I still couldn't bring myself to say, was that both Mom and I were holding up the weight of Dad's legacy. But for a ridiculous, impossible second, I wanted to tell him that, too. I wanted to tell the memory of the boy I remembered Garrett to be, his face lit by the orange rising sun, his hair blown by the wind as we sat by the river. To pass him all of it and let him hold it for a second, like he had with my phone. Just one second, so I could breathe.

But then I remembered the happiness I felt when I thought that we had become friends. That I had found someone who understood me. Then the desolation of the last day, when he had morphed into a stranger.

"Never mind," I said. "It's okay."

"It doesn't sound okay." His attention was focused on me, prickling.

"It's not your problem." Maybe that was a little sharp, but I didn't care. I needed to stop remembering how we used to converse like this, how he used to ask me questions. *What was it like for you at school? When you visited your relatives overseas, did they treat you like an American? Tell me about your first concert.*

And he would tell me things, too. *I'm sorry I never got a chance to know my grandparents. I'd love to study abroad in Taiwan.* Then there was the afternoon he stepped close and said, *No, it's not like this with everyone. Not for me.*

I still held all of his answers inside me, like letters in a box. I had his, as he had mine.

"You can still talk to me." His voice was soft.

"Really."

He looked away. He knew exactly what I was talking about. And yet he still dared to act like he cared.

I said, "We're not—whatever we were—anymore. You've been very clear."

His words were so quiet that I almost missed them. "I didn't think it mattered to you."

And now I was pissed. I picked the words that would inflict the maximum damage: "It did."

He looked like someone had shoved him in the chest and he couldn't quite keep his balance.

"But clearly," I snapped, "it didn't mean anything to you."

He was still dazed. But then he leaned toward me. And for once, he let me see all of what he usually kept hidden: sorrow, regret, fear. Something rawer, which was starting to flare. "You're wrong."

I felt each word like a hand running down my spine. He couldn't be saying what I thought he was. He had written off those weeks in New Hampshire. I had been the only one reminiscing, like a fool.

Because if he cared, at all, then why had he done it in the first place? Broken us? I was about to say something when Amy barreled across the room with a knitted octopus. "Look look look what Auntie Cindy made!"

We both tried to pay attention to her, but we were only focused on each other. His mouth twisted. "Juliana?" he said. "I—"

But I couldn't bear to face the past again.

"I gotta go." I grabbed my stuff, and before he could say more, I ran.

19

Dear Sunny and Cloudy,

Every time I try to talk to the girl I like, I get hiccups.

Signed,

Hiccupping Alone, Forever

Sunny: Take ten sips of water in one breath. Then go for it!

Cloudy: Pretend you're in love. It'll be so terrifying, the hiccups will disappear.

20

CULTUREFEST

WE WORKED TOGETHER over the next few days. Garrett designed some posts, and I blasted our socials with the news of our giveaway. He didn't mention what we had talked about, and neither did I. But it was there.

He came with me to the cultural center to ask Auntie Cindy for some cute knitted hearts and to a super cheap printing place across town to make an economical banner. We secured the promise of a pastry plate from Chef Auntie and convinced Auntie Beth from the bookstore to give us some romance books for our prize pack. But Garrett never said a word about camp. He was back to keeping things distant. Professional.

If he wanted to pretend that we never had that conversation, then that was fine with me. It didn't matter that those two words would sometimes melt through me at random times: *You're wrong.*

No, I couldn't allow myself to become distracted. Couldn't let messy feelings derail me.

I sent Garrett a short message telling him that I could help set up for the CultureFest in Old Taipei, which was being held tomorrow night. True to my word, as I had promised in the beginning of the competition, I put out a request for volunteers to the SBA. I also made some flyers and advertised on my socials about the event. He responded with a thumbs-up emoji. I refused to let myself text him back. Because then I would ask him what he had meant, and I would have to finally find out why he had cut me off after our summer together. Why he had sliced everything between us, like Mom had with Bella. And I didn't think I wanted to know.

Hattie somehow found out that I was going to CultureFest and immediately offered to come along.

"Why?" I was taping the circular ramp for her physics project and trying not to think about Garrett. I forced myself to focus on her structure. As I suspected, there wasn't enough support at the base. Hattie pushed me aside.

"I can do it," she said. "I just needed to know what's wrong."

I handed her the tape but sneakily put an extra piece on the side where it was really needed.

"Stop, Juju." She ripped it off. "I can do it myself."

I waited until she turned around, then put it back on. It had been just the two of us after Dad died, because Bella had been at college and Mom had always been at work, trying to keep the company afloat. I had been the one who had walked her home from school, who had prepared her snacks, who had comforted her at night when she got scared. When she was crying about Dad. Helping with a physics project was the one thing I could do. That I could make better.

"I'm only helping Garrett set up some of the booths," I said. I just had to win this competition and then Garrett and I could go back to our former separate ways. That's what he had wanted, right? Right? "And don't you have tennis? It's Friday."

"There might be people there that we know," Hattie said innocently. "*Plus,* helping others is good for the soul. And I did a whole article about Old Taipei. Don't you remember? The arena is going to destroy the area. It's going to be like all those other minority communities who've had development projects take over their neighborhoods. How's this for my follow-up: 'Local Community Fights Back against Huge Corporation'?'"

"Is Donfield, Inc., a huge corporation?" I had seen some of their logos on projects around town but hadn't known they were into big projects like stadiums and arenas.

Hattie pulled out her phone and typed a note. "Oooh, that might be an interesting thing to investigate. Who's funding this whole thing?"

"Probably the city? Or some corporate sponsor?"

Hattie made a face. "They probably want to plaster their names all over it or something. Like the Chase Arena."

"What about your homework?" I asked. "Shouldn't you be focused on that first?"

"It's done," she said. "And I'm going. It's for my future career, Juju."

Huh. That sounded kind of legit, but considering that Hattie was wearing her favorite sweater and jeans and had done her hair more carefully than usual, I found this highly fishy. Still, I let her tag along.

We finally found a parking spot and made our way over to where the festival was going to take place. I checked my phone: no messages from Garrett. Not that I had texted him either. That was fine. The way it was supposed to be.

As we passed the stores and restaurants on the way to the park, I realized I did have vague memories of some of them, back from when we were kids. The dim sum place with the huge aquarium in the back. The grocery store with the sticky floors where the owner and his wife used to slip us free boxes of Botan Rice Candy. We passed Uncle Jing's place, with its cute ginormous fortune cookie in the front. I waved at him. He scowled.

"That's Uncle Jing," I said. "He totally loves me."

"Sure."

I saw a box of decorations, with CultureFest flyers on the top, through the window. I walked in.

Uncle Jing was stirring some batter, and another man was seated at a table, folding the discs of cookies into their distinctive shapes. There were photos in the back, some of a young Uncle Jing and a young woman, smiling. I almost didn't recognize him. Then a few of an older Uncle Jing, alone.

"Is that for CultureFest?" I asked in Taiwanese. "We're on the way to help set up. Do you want me to take it over?"

He grunted. "Don't need fancy decorations. Everyone knows my cookies."

Uncle Jing, unsurprisingly, was a purist. There were no fancy flavors or toppings, no industrial assembly lines. The only concession was offering a slightly larger-sized cookie for fifty cents extra.

I walked around the store, and the other uncle gave me a toothy grin. He waved me over and stealthily passed me a free cookie. It was delicious—crisp and buttery, completely different than the ones we got in restaurants.

"This is amazing!" Oops. I probably got the other uncle in huge trouble.

But Uncle Jing looked almost cordial. "All handmade," he said. "All fresh."

Delicious. I gave the other half to Hattie, who immediately went over to grab a large bag to take home.

I asked Uncle Jing some questions about his business and found out he had this store for over thirty years and had fielded several huge offers to franchise.

"You turned them down?" I didn't even know that was an option. Why would he say no to so much money?

"Of course!" Uncle Jing said in Taiwanese. "Who is making your cookies, then? Who knows if they are good or not? Some strangers?"

The other uncle sighed, deeply. "He should have taken the money."

My mother probably would have agreed, seeing as how his store was almost empty. But I saw the care he put into each cookie, meticulously pouring the batter and smoothing out each one. Wasn't there something noble about that?

Uncle Jing finally agreed to let me take his decorations and almost smiled when I promised to make his booth the cutest one.

"Just make it better than Chef Auntie's," he said, then paused. "But make sure hers is nice, too." He fussed with some cookies in the front, arranging them. But if I wasn't mistaken, he was blushing.

By the time we got there, the park was already filled with volunteers—some of them, I was happy to see, from the SBA. There were piles of signs next to the gazebo, with slogans like "SAVE OLD TAIPEI!" and "CITY COUNCIL—SAY NO!" They had hung the banner we made, handprints and all, in front of a large table at the entrance. On the top of the table were several fresh petitions to the city council, urging them to withhold their approval for the arena construction.

There were definitely fewer booths than I remembered from years past. Part of the park was also blocked off with construction netting, some of which featured Donfield, Inc. signs. I saw Hattie examining them to see who else might be funding the project, but there didn't seem to be any clues.

I carried Uncle Jing's stuff to an unoccupied booth, one in a spot sure to maximize foot traffic. There was a reason that real estate was all about location, location, location.

A group of people had started stringing up some hanging lanterns. Down the path, a couple was setting up the sound system. Vendors were preparing their food trucks, and there were different signs going up for bubble tea and mochi donuts.

Ms. Vivian, Kevin's mom, was with the little kids, who were practicing a lion dance. Kevin saw us and waved, which was surprisingly friendly, considering we hadn't talked much. Then Hattie beamed and called loudly, "Keeeevin! You owe me!"

I didn't know they knew each other so well. I was familiar with most of Hattie's friends. They used to come over after school and hang out in the kitchen or in her room. In the last few years, though, we had been so busy, me with SBA and her with tennis and journalism. She now hung out with her friends on her own and was always on her phone, texting. Seeing her now, dressed up, made me wonder what was going to happen next year when I wouldn't see her every day. When we would be living totally different lives.

I was about to ask Hattie how she knew Kevin when I spotted a tall guy next to one of the booths. His back was to me, but there was something about the confident line of him that caught my attention. Then he turned. For a second, my brain struggled to put two separate sets of thoughts together, like two magnets pushing each other apart. The guy. Was Garrett?

He had a bottle of water in his hand and tipped it in my direction. He was wearing a slim dark shirt, tucked into black pants. His hair was casually styled, a thick chunk hanging over his eye.

I was walking toward him when he was intercepted by a pretty girl in a bright pink dress. She touched Garrett's arm, and they easily started chatting together. What was this? He had other friends? I was so used to seeing him in isolated misery in Chinese class or attached to his tablet at one of the big

Taiwanese functions. It had never occurred to me that he might have an outside social life. With girls.

It was clear from the way he was laughing that he and this girl knew each other well. She reached over and touched his arm again, and he let it stay there for, really, a moment longer than was appropriate. Not that it was any of my business.

Hattie came up behind me, holding a pile of red streamers. "Hey, where do you want these?"

She said something else, but I wasn't really listening. The girl was now all into Garrett's personal space, and he didn't seem to mind. I was just about to walk over to them when Chef Auntie came up to me.

"Are those Uncle Jing's?" she said.

"Yup."

"Which booth is his?"

I pointed at the one I had picked. I explained my theory about traffic to Chef Auntie.

"Auntie Liu always said you were so smart," she said, and patted my shoulder. "Which direction will the people usually come from?"

I scanned the area. "From the left? They'll probably start at the petition table and then come over."

Chef Auntie walked over to the stall to the left of Uncle Jing's. "So people will see this one first?"

"I think so?"

She chortled, then called in a loud voice, "Bring my things! This one is mine!"

She examined Uncle Jing's space carefully, and then took a

stool from her booth and placed it in his.

"He has a bad back, so he can't stand the whole time," she said. "Don't tell him I told you."

Hmm. Chef Auntie (single, also exacting about food, suspiciously cranky about Uncle Jing) ignored my Significant Glance and strode off toward the sound system, with dignity. Veddy. Veddy. Interesting.

I felt a light touch to my waist, and I turned. It was Garrett, freed from his pink-dress-wearing fan club.

"No, Juliana."

"What?" I said.

"I see that look," he said. *"No."*

"I'm not going to do anything! But they have a certain chemistry, don't they?" I said. "Didn't Uncle Jing's wife pass away a long time ago? He might be lonely. And Chef Auntie is also single."

Chef Auntie flipped on the speaker system and started blasting Chinese music at a volume that was way too high. Garrett leaned toward me and said, "Unbelievable. It's like you can't help yourself."

"I'm only noting it for the record. You wait and see."

He couldn't quite hear what I had said, so I placed a hand on his shoulder and pulled him closer. He jumped a little, then bent down as I repeated what I said in his ear.

He turned and spoke in mine, his fingertips light on the small of my back. "Put the love on hold, Juliana. I have a project for you."

He stepped away quickly, then grabbed a fortune cookie

from Uncle Jing's box, not looking at me. We made our way to a table littered with vegetables, fruit, and small carving knives. Kevin and Hattie were already seated. Garrett took the chair next to Kevin and cracked his cookie open.

He pulled out the fortune. "'Happiness is an illusion.'"

"It does not say that," I said.

"Seeking happiness will only cause you unhappiness," Garrett said in Taiwanese. "Everything is temporary, including happiness."

"If everything is temporary, then that includes unhappiness." I also spoke in Taiwanese. "So it is possible to be happy."

Garrett flipped back to English. "Only temporarily."

"You're such an Eeyore," I said. "'The sky has finally fallen. Always knew it would.'"

"Exactly."

"He does have a certain undercurrent of darkness," Kevin said. He had a small watermelon in front of him and was in the middle of a nearly surgical crafting of the fruit. In a moment, an intricate flower spouted from the rind. Hattie clapped.

"How did you . . . ?" I asked.

Garrett laughed at my expression and palmed a pink radish and a small knife. In a few seconds, he presented me with the most adorable little creature, complete with little Sharpie-drawn eyes.

"It's so cute!" I said.

"It'll wither in a few days," he said, "like all human joy."

Another person might recognize he was kidding and find it amusing. Not me. Absolutely not me. "What are these for?"

"Chef Auntie's restaurant has been losing business recently, so Kevin came up with the idea of decorating her dishes with these fancy garnishes. The customers love them. We're making a few for her booth."

Next to him, Kevin was creating a very impressive duck from a potato. Garrett started slicing another radish. He handed me a carrot and a knife.

"Try not to slice off a finger," he said.

"Me?" I was not remotely artsy. The last time I tried to carve anything was in the empty parking spot next to never.

"It's not a piranha, Juliana," Garrett said. "It's a carrot." But he carefully walked me through the steps. I was reminded of the way he had patiently explained my art project to the little kids.

"The world won't collapse if your garnish is not the best garnish in all of the universe," he said. "Try having a little fun with it."

"I am having fun," I gritted out. I put the tip of the knife into the carrot and pressed. It slipped and nicked my finger. I inhaled sharply, and Garrett immediately glanced over.

He dropped his knife and ran toward the front table. He returned a second later with a Band-Aid and a small tube.

"You okay, Juju?" Hattie peered at my hand.

"I'm fine." It was only a tiny nick, but a surprisingly large amount of blood was oozing out.

Garrett took my hand, his fingers quick and sure. "This may sting," he said. He pressed a small paper towel to my finger, then wiped a dab of cream on my finger. He ripped open the

Band-Aid and wrapped it around the cut.

He held my hand in his, his face unreadable. I was conscious of the air in my lungs thickening, barely pushing in and out of my throat. Garrett looked at me, his hand warmly around mine. A flush appeared on his neck.

"Thank you," I said. How could two words sound so awkward?

"The little kids at the center get a lot of scrapes." He dropped my hand and began carving again. But the moment was still there. Between us.

After he finished his garnish, he placed it in my palm. It was a beautiful radish flower, the petals gently unfurling. It wasn't a part of the dish, and it obviously didn't add any flavor. It had no purpose other than to make you happy. And yet, that was enough.

Ms. Vivian came up and put a hand on Kevin's shoulder. "Kevin's dad loves the tomato fish. He taught him all of these."

Kevin ducked his head, smiling.

She continued. "Since he started helping Chef Auntie, all the customers now put their food on the . . ." She waved her hand. "You know, Instagram thingy."

"OMG, Ma."

She said, "In our day, we wrote letters, you know. We didn't even have email. None of this TikToky business."

"That's horrifying," Kevin said, and they both laughed. I wondered what it would be like to have shared jokes with your mom. Mine didn't get sarcasm or irony, and I had seen her laugh only at these Chinese television shows we didn't understand.

Ms. Vivian was always relaxed and open and talked about the movies or books we had all seen. It made me realize there was so much separating me from my mom—not just language, but what we read and watched. How we thought about things.

We carved for a bit, and I felt an almost unfamiliar sense of peace. A quiet happiness. Like when I had taught the little girl English or set up Uncle Jing's booth. We were doing something to help Chef Auntie's restaurant, so she could continue to make food for those who needed it. Was this why Dad had gone into business? It must have been.

Right?

At the end of the evening, I was about to go home when Ms. Vivian came up and asked me to set up a craft booth where kids could make paper lanterns. I was exhausted, but I didn't want to disappoint her. But right when I stood up, I yawned. Not the small dainty kind. The huge jaw-stretching, weary-to-the-bones kind.

"Oh, you poor thing," she said. "Get some rest. I'll ask Kevin."

"I got it." I pulled the box from her hands before she could say anything. Before I could see her disappointment.

She put a hand on my arm. "I'll find someone else."

"I'll do it."

She scanned my face, long enough to make me uncomfortable.

I said, "Really, it's not a problem."

Ms. Vivian's voice was gentle. "It's okay to take a break."

I didn't know why she was making this into such a big deal. I thanked her politely, took the box, and quickly set up the supplies. Then—at long last—I went home to get some sleep. Tomorrow was round three—and we had to win.

21

DEAR SUNNY AND CLOUDY

THE NEXT MORNING, Garrett and I both skipped Chinese class to set up our table at the Convention Center. When I got there, the room was packed. I waved at Linda and Kelly. Both of them had dressed up in prom outfits, complete with corsages and fancy hairstyles. They were playing dance music and had set up their display with a mirror ball and two mannequins with sparkly dresses. It was a brilliant way to advertise their dress exchange service.

The competition had randomly assigned tables, and ours was thankfully close to the center of the room. Garrett was already there when I arrived, in a white T-shirt and a dark pair of jeans. He was grace in motion, and I couldn't help but notice the shift of his back muscles, the shadowed dip of his T-shirt between his shoulder blades.

I walked up to him, but he didn't notice me. I put a hand on his arm.

"Juliana." Garrett yanked out his earbud and it fell to the table.

I had dressed up for today in my cutest dress, one that said, *I am a professional at love advice*, but also, *I am super fun, come visit our table!* Garrett stared at me, then fumbled with his headphone, jamming it back in his case.

I nudged the cardboard box next to him. "What's all this stuff?"

He pulled his attention to the table, which was covered in a red sparkly cloth. The box was full, paper streamers and other decorations spilling out.

"They're from the bookstore. Auntie Beth said we could borrow them."

"Those are great. But don't we need something with a little more pizzazz?" I whipped out a set of sparkly heart wands, which I had found for two dollars. "Like *these*?"

"My God," he said. "What is going on right now."

I reached into my purse, gleefully. "I got something for you, too." I brought out a special hat I had found on sale. It had two floppy ears, which were connected by a hidden air tube to long dangly paws hanging on the sides. One squeeze of a furry paw, and the ear would shoot up. It was exactly the sort of thing he would hate. I bought it on the spot and had the ears outfitted with gray knitted covers, à la our favorite cranky donkey, Eeyore. "Auntie Cindy is so talented."

I pulled the hat over his head, then stepped back, cackling. Garrett's hair was smushed down, the longer strands in the back curling at the ends. His face did not change expression when I reached over and squeezed one of the paws. When the ear shot up, I doubled over, laughing.

"So glad you find this amusing, Juliana."

"This whole event is worth it for *just that*."

But he didn't take it off. He merely grabbed a box, hat paws swinging, and set up our stand. With dignity.

The wands and the hat were a success. Our table started off pretty empty, and we had to answer some previously emailed questions so we wouldn't just be sitting around. But then I started squeezing one of Garrett's Eeyore ears before he spoke or he would wave one of my wands. We were having so much fun that the people started gathering and our traffic started to soar.

Toward the end of the session, a small group came to the front of the line. As promised, the competition had provided fifty random, unbiased volunteers from around the city. Instead of name tags, they were all given numbers, which they would use when they entered their feedback on the computers that were stationed throughout the room.

"You give free love advice?" one of the boys asked.

I waved my sparkly wand. "Sure do! You can also enter our romance giveaway if you leave a review. Give us your number, and we'll randomly draw one at the end."

He nudged one of the girls, a brunette. "Ask her!"

The girl stared at her shoes. I leaned forward. "Is there something you'd like to know?"

She shook her head. I glanced at her friend, who pulled her arm. She didn't budge. The friend sighed, then stepped forward.

"So," he said. "*Someone* I know has this problem."

"Okay." I smiled encouragingly.

"This someone—let's call her Nora—has a boyfriend who wants to be exclusive. Only Nora doesn't know if what she is feeling is serious. How can she tell?"

The girl glanced up hopefully.

"Well," I said. "If you like him and he likes you, it must be love. Go for it." I waved the next group over. I was on a roll.

"Wait," the boy said. "That's it?"

"What do you mean?" I said. "It's great advice."

"Just because they're dating doesn't mean it's love."

"Why not? They like each other. Voilà!"

"Have you been in love before?" the boy asked. "It's not that easy."

Garrett had gone quite still next to me.

"Well," I said, "no. I haven't. But you just know. You can tell."

The boy said, "Well, that explains a lot. What about compatibility? Emotional connection? Vulnerability?"

Sure, I hadn't wanted to get close to a lot of people, to tell them everything about me. But that didn't mean I couldn't recognize love. It wasn't why I had never been in love myself.

Was it?

Before I could answer, they stomped off.

More people came and went. We got a steady stream of traf-fic. But what the boy said kept coming back to me like a snag, one I couldn't quite sew together.

At the end of the event, even my sparkly hearts were sagging. But we had seen a lot of people, and I hoped the giveaway would translate into feedback.

Eric and Albert passed our table, and they were arguing. I couldn't hear what they were saying, but it didn't look good.

I carefully peeled off Auntie Beth's paper decorations and removed the tape so she could reuse them again for Valentine's Day. I should have been thrilled at the number of people who had stopped by. Our website analytics were also spiking up. But our test audience didn't seem as happy as I thought they would have been.

I tried to stretch out the tablecloth so I could fold it in half, but it was too long. I lined up the corners and tried snapping it in the air, but the ends slid into tangles. I tried to fold it from the middle, which was even worse. I threw the whole thing on the table, and the words spilled out before I could stop them: "Do you think that boy was right? About the love advice?"

Garrett picked up one end of the tablecloth and handed me the other. He walked out until it was straight, then walked back and neatly lined up his end with mine. "Now you're asking me about love? You must be desperate."

"How am I supposed to be an expert if I don't know what it is?" I clutched the ends of the cloth.

Garrett had an odd expression. "Have you never been in love before?"

"No! Have you?" I thought of his ex-girlfriend. I had heard that he had dated her in the beginning of his sophomore year. "Did you . . . love . . . your ex?"

"I did." The way he said it—quiet, certain—threw me into a sudden weightlessness. What would it be like to be loved by Garrett Tsai? I knew what his parents' messed-up relationship had done to him; love was not something he would ever give lightly. As I knew all too well, any parts of his personality that he chose to show to others had to be earned.

Was that what the boy was talking about? Love wasn't as easy as two people wanting to be together? There was something deeper and more complex to it. Something involving vulnerability and risk. Two things that were, frankly, terrifying to me.

I had always gone with my instincts, watched how people interacted with each other. I believed people in love would always find each other and have their happily-ever-after.

Had I been wrong this whole time?

The rest of the day was impossibly busy. I picked up Hattie, ran to the grocery store for my mom, called some of the vendors for the SBA fundraiser, then gathered all of my things to study. I had to skip CultureFest since I had to cram for my Spanish exam. But before I tackled my vocab, I had to check on the competition.

I logged in and there, at the bottom, in the last slot, was the following:

10. Team SunCloud

We were on the board.

22

WINNING

I RAN DOWNSTAIRS to tell my mom, but she was at the office. Hattie was gone, too. I knew Garrett was at CultureFest, so he might not have seen the results. I called him.

He picked up, and there was a lot of shrieking and laughter. "Juliana?"

"We got in the top ten!"

There was loud Chinese music. "What?"

"TOP TEN."

"I'm so sorry, it's really loud here—"

"I'LL TEXT YOU!" I shouted, then sent him a message.

Top Ten!

No way.

There was a pause, then a video popped up on my phone. It was of Garrett, Kevin, and Chef Auntie, and they were all cheering. Behind them were lion dancers and the flares from sparklers.

I sent a smiley-face emoji, then played the video again. After it was done, my house was quiet. I pulled out my Spanish textbook but kept my phone out, screen up. I wondered if Uncle Jing liked his booth. If the food from the vendors was delicious. If the little kids liked the crafts we had set up.

I memorized exactly one verb conjugation, then decided I should check to see if the competition had forwarded our feedback. The reviews could be waiting, like little presents, in my inbox *right now*. A bag full of gold coins. Or rusty nails. I mean, I wasn't *worried* about what they would say. It would be great. The boy this morning was just being rude. A total outlier.

But when I opened our messages, there they were.

Must be nice for Sunny to think love is so easy. But how about some answers for real people?

Sunny seems like she really cares about people, and I like Cloudy's tell-it-like-it-is attitude.

Does Sunny really think people are going to fall at your feet if you are interested in them? That's not the real world, honey.

Sunny's optimism is nice.

Love is more than what you see in the movies. Advice seems a little naïve.

For a tiny frozen moment, I thought some of these must be fake. Maybe the boy had submitted a bunch of entries himself. But these were all from different volunteers, and I knew the software would only allow each person to enter their feedback once. There were quite a few different entries, and a lot of them said the same thing. A LOT.

Which meant . . . people thought I gave terrible advice? I had thought the boy was simply being rude. But could he have been correct?

I checked the clock. Ten o'clock. Too early for Garrett to be home. He definitely hadn't seen these yet. I thought about texting him again, but I didn't want to ruin his night. I read and reread each entry, skin prickling, and counted how many people had hated what I said.

My mom knocked on the door; she must have gotten home earlier. She popped her head into my room, then put a plate of apples on my desk. Each piece was carefully cored and had the skin peeled off. She had put my favorite two-pronged fruit toothpick on the side, along with a few slices of candied mango.

"How is the competition?" she asked.

"Top ten." I showed her the screen with our team name, but not the feedback I had just received. I should have been thrilled we had placed so well, but I was miserable. Everything felt twisted and askew. If there was one thing I had always been certain of, it was that I was a great matchmaker. But I wasn't. Another earthquake shaking the landfill my life was resting on.

I suddenly, violently, wanted to see my father. I wanted to be six again, when I could run up to him and tell him all about the ugly secret parts of me, like the time I was in a store and accidentally ripped a page of a magazine and got so scared that I ran out without telling anyone. Or the time I wished Hattie and Bella would stay at Grandma's forever so I could have him all to myself. I would confess these terrible things, and he would always wrap himself around me and hug extra tight. We would talk about why it was wrong, how we could make it better. Then he would hug me again. He never forgot the last hug.

But this was my mom. Her world was very focused and clear. There was no acknowledgment that I could be in a complicated place. Or that I might need space to work things out. There was only the end result, which was okay . . . or not enough.

Mom shook her head. "I don't think the Park boy was a good choice. You could have done better in the earlier rounds. You sure he is a hard worker?"

"He is." I thought of Garrett quietly designing our website, hair brushing his cheekbone, the quiet joy of creation. Gamely wearing my Eeyore hat, one ear up.

"Auntie Liu heard you were at the Taiwanese cultural center. Why are you spending time over there? You need to focus on the competition."

Focus. I had heard it my whole life. For my mom there was

only one path to the top, and it was narrow and full of potential traps. Any misstep—any stop to look at the flowers—could lead to catastrophe. And might have been true in her day; the competition may have been so fierce that if you stopped to rest, there were twenty other people who would climb over you.

But was that the world we lived in now, in America? Wasn't the reason they came here so we could have more choice? So we could take our foot off the pedal?

But maybe there was no room for failure for her. There was no backup. Dad was gone, and he had left Mom as the shepherd of his last wishes. If we failed, she had failed him. He was the ghost haunting us all. I saw her in Dad's office once, removing pictures of Bella. In the old days, people used to fall to their knees, bowing, when they made a mistake. They would press their foreheads to the cold ground and beg for forgiveness. Mom didn't do that, but she sat in his chair, cradling Bella's pictures to her chest. Shame weighed every part of her, heavy. She carried our mistakes, too.

Given that, there was no room for emotion or risk or deviation.

Mom kept talking, but I wasn't listening. I was carefully wrapping the small part of me that, like Pandora's box, contained a force too dangerous to let loose: hope. Hope she would, for once, notice and ask why I was upset. Hope she would help me untangle my feelings, my doubts. Hope that this competition would be the thing bringing us together. I closed the box, locked it, and sank it at sea.

23

SPICY ADVICEY

I MET GARRETT at Super T Hot Pot for brunch the next day. He was waiting when I arrived, with a paper menu and a tiny golf pencil already in front of him. "Half and half, right?" he said.

I didn't mind getting right down to hot pot first, especially when the last thing I wanted to do was talk about my sucky reviews. Garrett seemed to want to do the same, as well, since he passed me the menu as soon as I sat down. He had already checked off half and half for the broth, but the rest of the food items were blank.

Garrett knew as well as I did that choosing the right broth was the key to a successful hot pot experience. You had to get the classic broth, of course, but the serious connoisseurs always got a split pot with half classic, half spicy. I knew Garrett wouldn't wimp out on me. We used to get into these contests with the other kids to see who could put a Chinese Szechwan pepper in their mouth for the longest amount of time. He always won. Unless I did.

"Of course," I said. "And Kobe beef." I pulled the menu toward me. Each check helped me to distract myself from the competition. Shiitake mushrooms, fish balls, sliced pork, tofu. I could do this all day.

Garrett grabbed another pencil. "We have to have pumpkin. And you forgot the noodles."

Oooh, good catch. "Of course."

I checked the menu, and then Garrett double-checked it. He raised his hand, and our server nodded at him. He unleashed his most winning, adorable smile.

"Ugh, you're shameless," I said. "That's not going to get us our food any faster."

He turned the full force toward me. "Really?"

"You're terrible."

The server came over with two pitchers and filled our pot with soup—original and spicy, as ordered. She turned on the burner and both sides started boiling.

"Okay, now we can get serious," he said. "Don't you think we need a catchier name for our website? How about Spicy Advicey?"

"Oh my God." He looked pleased when I laughed.

"Nooky for Rookies?"

"Garrett." Was he trying to cheer me up? I remember I once

had gotten upset at camp when I slipped and our small group lost in tug-of-war. Garrett had dragged me to dinner that night and soon had me cracking up with ridiculous suggestions for our final skit.

It was a rare event when Garrett Tsai would outright grin, but one of my favorite things—one I would never acknowledge was my favorite—was when I would catch a quick flash of dry amusement, a lift then a drop of the corner of his mouth. It seemed like he was letting me in on a secret. The other campers were sometimes surprised to see me snickering at something he said, but to me he had always been hilarious.

Garrett split his disposable chopsticks into two, then quickly folded the paper wrapper into a little stand. He dug into his bag and passed me a sack of fortune cookies, a crooked paper lantern, and a knitted bao with cute eyes. "These are from Uncle Jing, Ames, and Auntie Cindy. They all say hi."

I took them. "Uncle Jing did not say hi."

"No, he did not. And I got you those cookies myself. But he was thinking it, I'm sure."

I sniffed and swept them into my purse. Garrett hesitated, then pulled out his phone and slid it toward me. I swiped through his photos from last night: one of Uncle Jing walking up to his booth, smiling. One of Auntie Cindy and the little kids making lanterns. One of a pigtailed girl holding a knitted fortune cookie. They were all like Garrett's drawings, capturing a feeling in time.

After Mom left last night, I had forced myself to memorize

the rest of my verb conjugations, sitting in my room alone. There were bright colors in these pictures, the mist of smoke from the food carts. Uncle Jing and Chef Auntie shouting and laughing at their neighboring booths—were they comparing how many customers they had? Chef Auntie wearing the string of paper fortune cookies around her neck. Even through the small phone screen, I could feel their joy.

"It looks like it was fun. These are great photos." A wisp of wistfulness curled, grew. I had been driven for so long, wrapping my fingers around each rung of the ladder of success, always focused above. What would it be like to stop and see the view? Did I even know how? And now that I was failing so badly, was missing everything even worth it?

I passed him his phone back. I had been stalling but knew I couldn't do it forever. "Did you see the feedback?"

"I did." I braced myself for the *I told you so*.

"It's not the end of the world." Garrett stirred the broth slowly. "We got in the top ten. That's got to count for something."

"I guess." I opened a cookie, broke it into small pieces.

"The actual reviews didn't count. Only the number of people who filled out forms. And we got a lot of people."

That was technically correct. Which was a little odd. Why would they have us collect the feedback but not have it count for the final score? Ugh, it didn't matter. Nothing did. "What about—?" The fact that I sucked? I put my arms on the table, my head banging down.

Garrett said, "It's only one round. Let's try again. Answer some questions."

But for the first time, I didn't want to. I could now feel the eyes of everyone on me, judging. Even if my advice had been wrong, I still didn't know how to fix it.

But I thought of my dad. I had to continue.

"Okay," I said. "Okay." I grabbed my phone, pulled up the emails, and randomly picked one.

Dear Sunny and Cloudy,
My boyfriend wants to see other people. What do I do?
Signed,
Devastated

Garrett stopped smiling. He picked up a small pencil and flipped over a blank menu, sketching a heart balloon made of strings, the strands unraveling and dangling.

"You can't do anything about it. That's the answer." Garrett darkened the lines, his left hand drawing quickly. A little figure stood below the heart, staring mournfully at it.

"What?" I wanted to say you can fight for the relationship, make them change their mind. But the reviews I had read were in my head now, the scorn.

Garrett was still drawing. "Maybe you thought they loved you back, but you were wrong. It happens."

That was oddly specific. I looked at the little person on the paper, the sad curve of his spine.

"How?" I asked.

Garrett drew the ground tumbling underneath the figure, a deep hole only one step ahead. The heart balloon—the thing that could have lifted him to safety—remained beyond his grasp. "Maybe it's not necessarily black-and-white. Maybe the other person is just better. More handsome, the better hunter-gatherer. Or more beautiful and intelligent. The person is simply picking the superior option. It's evolution, right?"

It didn't seem that coldly scientific to me. It sounded tragic. Was that what happened to him? With his ex?

I wrote:

The person who will cherish only you is around the corner. Don't settle for anything less.

Garrett wrote:

You just have to move on.

Here was another thing I remembered about Garrett Tsai: the way he would hold heartbreak in the lines of his mouth, his eyes. He kept sketching, his dark hair shielding his face.

"Do you really believe that?" he said.

"What?"

His hand and pencil moved as if in a dance, the lines trailing behind it. "Every person will have someone who cherishes them?"

I was reminded of the girl staring at her shoes at our event. I wanted to give my usual cheery answer, but I saw the fragility of his question, the gift he was passing to me.

I said, "I want to believe it," and he looked up. He had a dark freckle on the corner of his right eye, lashes that seemed to want to hide everything. But he kept holding my gaze.

"Why?" he asked.

"Because I've seen it." He waited, and I said, "My grandparents were married their whole lives. My grandma lost her sight early, but my grandpa would always read to her in the afternoons. And she would massage his hands because he had bad arthritis. Even my parents . . ." Love was the thing that could tie you to the people you chose. It could cut through the acid of loneliness. Bind people together.

His voice was quiet. "What were they like together?"

"He . . . made her laugh." Mom had always been focused, worrying, even then. But Dad was the one who could tickle her out of it, who could do something silly and make her relax. "I would catch them sometimes, you know, when we were supposed to be sleeping? They would be on the couch, watching TV, and my mom would always be snuggled next to him, her head on his shoulder. They couldn't stand to be apart."

Garrett looked wistful. What had it been like for him, growing up in a house full of turbulence?

I remember learning about colors in grade school, how shades like orange are actually a mix of two primary colors. Garrett's expressions had become like that to me, mixes of fear and hope, affection and longing. And my own feelings were also swirled, streaked with trepidation, the shadow of what had happened between us.

Garrett was thoughtful as our plates of food arrived: a beautiful array of thinly sliced meat and veggies. I dropped some beef into the broth and added some veggies. Scooped them into a bowl after they were cooked, then passed it to him. He switched his empty bowl with mine, then scooped some hot pot sauce into both bowls.

"Hot pot is seriously the best," I said.

He finally smiled. "The best."

"Check for the new challenge?" I pulled up my inbox. After I refreshed it a few times, it finally changed.

The message was shocking.

CHALLENGE #4:
PIVOT

You have gotten your feedback, so it is time to review it and adjust your methodology if necessary. Many start-ups crash because companies fail to take this step or are unwilling to make the difficult choices required to succeed. Hopefully you will not be one of those. Sometimes the corrections are minor; sometimes they are more radical.

Accordingly, partners are no longer required. If you separate and both individuals decide to stay in the competition, you must both offer the same service, with the understanding that you may be splitting the pool of potential customers. Further, all contestants are no longer limited to a brochure-style website.

After you make your adjustments, we want you to market your service using only one hashtag. Points will be awarded based on the amount of new traffic you can generate this week.

Garrett and I looked at each other, our phones in our hands.

24

CHOICES

THE HOT POT bubbled between us, the liquid pushing up, then breaking into small waves.

Partners were no longer required? I had assumed we would both be in this to the end. But now there was an off-ramp. A seismic shift.

Garrett said, finally, "That's an interesting challenge." I couldn't tell what he was thinking. If he wanted to quit. After all, I had ignored his opinions and had been giving terrible advice the whole time. Would he really want to stay?

I forced myself to imagine this competition without him; I could get it done, could finish it. He had already designed the basics of the website, and I knew enough now to maintain it. It would make my mom happier, and she would never find out I had partnered with him at all. It would be everything I was supposed to do.

The choice should have been simple. But now, it . . . wasn't.

"Do you—?" I said.

"Juliana—"

To anyone else, Garrett might look as he used to in Chinese class so long ago: nonchalant, indifferent. I wasn't fooled. I knew him well enough to see the uncertainty threaded through the angles of his face, the vulnerability in the corners of his mouth.

We both needed to win this competition. Him for his scholarship, me for my dad. I knew we were better together rather than apart. But I wanted to know—I needed to know—did he *want* to continue? With me?

I said, "I know you've got a lot going on with volunteering and helping out with the arena thing. . . ." I would give him an easy out. Then I would know.

Garrett was pale, like he was bracing himself. But he didn't take the exit I was offering.

I should have just said it: *But do you want to stay in it? With me?*

But it was a question I was terrified to ask. I didn't want the answer.

Instead, the silence got awkward until Garrett said quietly, "I think we're a pretty good team."

I dared to look at him then. But he didn't try to hide behind indifference or sarcasm. And neither did I. "I think so, too," I said.

Garrett smiled, and I felt the force of it. It was like a match lighting fires through the whole of me, one flame after the other.

He said, "So . . . we should keep working together?"

I nodded.

There was a pause, then we grinned at each other. Giddily. Ridiculously. I lifted my glass. "Sunny versus Cloudy?"

He clinked his glass with mine. "Sunny versus Cloudy."

Nothing had changed. Everything had changed.

We brainstormed some hashtags. Worked out a schedule for some posts and researched what had recently gone viral.

When we eventually took a break to eat, Garrett had me laughing with the little sketches he made of the vegetables on a plank, ready to jump into the hot pot pool. One of a little me and a little him in a tug-of-war, a ribboned heart tied to the center of the rope.

"You know that little me is totally going to win, right?" I was feeling downright cheerful. The feedback was still looming over me, but it suddenly felt manageable. Workable.

Garrett sketched extra muscles on himself, and I snorted. He picked up a chunk of glass noodles and held it over the spicy broth.

"Ready?" he said.

The glass noodles were always last—the sublime end. We watched them cook, then Garrett spooned them into our bowls with extra sauce.

"Hey!" A great idea occurred to me. "If customers really like those carved veggies, we should start an Instagram account for Chef Auntie's restaurant! It might get her some more publicity."

Garrett shook his head. "You can never take a break, can you?" He sounded almost affectionate.

"No, this is a great idea! We can feature Veggie Art of the Week. And Hattie can write some captions. Like 'world peas.'"

"Lettuce pray for world peas?" Garrett said.

I snickered. "Exactly! And we can post how-to videos on carving the garnishes! I can set up a YouTube channel."

Garrett sighed. "Send me your list. I'll help."

"This! Is! Great!"

"Okay." But he was smiling.

As we were leaving, I stealthily swiped the menu with Garrett's drawing and stashed it in my purse. Later that night, I tacked it to my bulletin board, staring at the little figure and the dangling heart strings, which were just out of his reach. But there was a little detail I hadn't previously noticed on the side: a ladder.

25

Dear Sunny and Cloudy,

Every time I like someone, they never like me in return. What is wrong with me?

Signed,

Sad

~~Don't worry, they'll like you eventually!~~

There is nothing wrong with you. Sometimes we can spend our energy on those who could be the wrong fit. What matters is the trying. And trying again.—Sunny

There is nothing wrong with you. You will find the right person, maybe when you least expect it.—Cloudy

26

QUESTIONS

I STARED AT our draft advice and then texted him.

Are we actually agreeing?

Garrett immediately amended his answer on our shared document.

There is nothing wrong with you and everything wrong with love.

Whew, that's more like it.

He texted back a picture of Eeyore. But the world must truly be askew, because it sounded an awful lot like Garrett Tsai was becoming optimistic. And if he could do that, then it was time for me to do something equally as inconceivable.

I was going to learn how to give better love advice.

Oddly enough, the pivot challenge made it far easier for me to face things. It was like when Hattie was trying to untangle those Christmas lights. She only made it worse by yanking them harder. That's what sometimes happened to me: the torturous thoughts of not being the best wrapped and pulled, tighter and tighter. But with Garrett by my side, I could finally take a moment to loosen the strings. To find a solution.

He had put his trust in me for this competition. I owed it to him to really study the feedback we had gotten. To do the hard work and figure out how to get better.

I remember when we were younger, before Dad had sold his patent, he and Mom were struggling. They worked all the time, but their tech business wasn't quite getting traction. Then Dad had an idea, one that would eventually become a multimillion-dollar patent. Only he didn't know it at the time.

I was crying one day because Mom had promised we would all draw together in the evening. Bella had repeatedly reminded me not to leave the crayon box outside, but I had done it anyway because I didn't believe her. As she had predicted, they had all melted together.

"What's wrong, Juju?" my dad had said.

I told him and then held out the big plastic box, which was now filled with smears and swirls of wax and collapsed wrappers. I was sad for me, of course, but I felt worse for Hattie, who had been looking forward to this day for ages, since Mom was often at work or busy at home. It was our one chance to spend time with her. And now I had ruined it.

"We can fix this!" he said, but I started crying harder. Even I, at age eight, knew we couldn't. You couldn't fix melted crayons; everyone knew that.

But Dad had other ideas. Humming, he pulled out an old, unused chocolate mold tray, which we still had from Bella's baking phase. Hattie and I both stopped wailing. He carefully shaved the melted wax into the tray. We were now excited to help and spent a few happy minutes filling the molds. Then he put the tray into the oven.

By this time, Bella and Mom had both come back from her violin lesson and were sniffing the air, confused.

"Set up the paper, Juju," Dad said.

Hattie and I both cleared off the table and got the construction paper. He pulled out the tray with a grand flourish and we clapped. When he popped out the new crayons—now in the shape of hearts, with swirls—he said, "These are your new magic crayons to use with Mommy. They will keep changing colors, so draw something pretty!"

I remember I held the little heart in my hand, the wax still warm. Dad told me, "It's not a bad thing to make mistakes. But you have to figure out what went wrong and why. Have the courage to face the truth so you can try a different direction."

I mean, I was eight. I had no idea what he was talking about. But his words stayed with me, years later, like a treasure box buried through time, waiting for the moment when I could open and understand it. Was today the day?

Figure out what went wrong. Or where I went wrong. I didn't want to. It was a thorny sinkhole that I 100 percent did not want to jump into. I had seen what happened with Bella once she started asking questions like *Why can't I go to San Francisco?* It led to the duck cleaver, disownment.

But there was no way to go forward, to get better, unless I could be brave enough to face the bright glare of the truth.

I forced myself to read the feedback again. Then I pulled up our email box and started scanning the questions. Yes, there were a few messages asking about what to do when two people were on the cusp of a relationship and the feelings were clearly reciprocated. But the other ones, the ones I had assumed were about how to get together with someone else—those were actually more complicated.

As I flipped through question after question after question, I finally noticed how many of them had been about how to navigate fear and risk, how to walk the sharp edge between vulnerability and recklessness. These were the people who had the bravery to open the crate of their feelings, to look inside and ask the difficult, terrifying questions. The ones that could lead to joy, or heartbreak.

I had thought I could give great advice, but how could I, when I didn't have the courage to ask what mattered?

That night, I went downstairs as Mom was prepping dinner. I checked the colander: all hard veggies, like potatoes and carrots. Not auspicious.

"How is the competition?" Mom asked. "Do you think it is still a good idea for you to be partners with Louis? You're not doing well."

"We did better than last time. Top ten, remember?"

"But not top five."

"We just need more time."

Mom chopped, her knife tapping the wooden board in a steady rhythm.

Garrett had been in my thoughts, as had my alleged partner in the competition, Louis Park. When we had first started this competition, I didn't think my lie to Mom about Louis was a big deal. I thought I was protecting our chances, giving Garrett and me space to win without her interference.

But as this competition had continued, I had the uncomfortable realization that I hadn't considered Garrett's feelings at all when I made the decision. Hadn't thought about how it would likely crush him if he found out. How he might think I was trying to hide him or was embarrassed by him. I needed to come clean.

"You know who's really good at web stuff?" I said. You know, as casual as pie. "Garrett Tsai."

"Tsai Mei-Ling's boy? The one going to art school?" She said it like Garrett was going to double-major in Nose Picking and Poverty. "And his uncle. Stealing." Mom tsked, like it was Garrett who had been accused of a crime.

This was not going well. "That was his uncle, not him."

Mom looked at me suspiciously. "Why are you bringing him up? He never takes things seriously."

186

I thought of those questions coming in to our email account, the person at the other end, typing, pouring tears or uncertainty or rage into the ether. The fearlessness it takes to seek the answer no matter how ugly it is.

I asked, "Why would you say that?"

"He's studying art." Things were binary for Mom, and Garrett was not in the Good Taiwanese Boy box like Eric. He was in the other one. But her metrics had nothing to do with his personality or values. Like our competition, it was only about raw data, credentials.

A part of me shrank before I could stop it. I should drop it. I needed to, but this time I couldn't. I dared to say, "That's valuable, too."

Mom tossed some of the veggies into the hot pan, and it crackled. Popped. "It's a hobby. Not a job." She tilted the board over the pot, scooped in the cut veggies. "You tell Louis to start working harder. Focus on the competition, Juliana."

Mom hurried to the garage to get some daikon radish from the second fridge. Our talk was clearly over.

But I hadn't been able to say anything that I needed to.

I snuck into Hattie's room and flopped under the peak of the makeshift tent above her bed. I remembered Dad taking some sheets we had each picked out and sewing late into the night, humming. We sisters had been so giddy when he hung it on the ceiling, laughing. This was before Dad had died and Bella had left, when we lived in a world where a homemade tent could make all of us happy.

But I couldn't let it go, this terrible, twisting feeling. Couldn't stop thinking about what my mom had said.

The binary world my mom lived in, one I was always taught, was this: Ivy League or failure. It was an immutable truth, like the sun rising in the morning or stinky tofu smelling foul. I had heard it since I was a baby in my Yale onesie, had listened to the gossip since I was old enough to understand language. *Oh, did you hear? John Tai couldn't even get into medical school. Ai-yo, Winnie Chao is only going to a state school.* Non-Ivy was horrifying, terrifying, and definitely a Failure.

And below *that* was pursuing any kind of career in the arts. Those jobs, thought my mom and her friends, were for people who couldn't hack it in medicine or engineering. Or those who wanted to throw away their parents' sacrifices. Maybe both.

Had I subconsciously absorbed all these judgments, like I had absorbed Taiwanese? Had they all seeped into my brain like a language?

I had to be honest: I had underestimated Garrett when we first had started this competition, and thought the people in Old Taipei were *not like us.* That Ms. Vivian might be *less than* because she only ran tutoring classes. I had assumed things were true because my mom and her friends had told me they were so.

But I had seen Garrett these past weeks. Saw how hard he worked, how he pulled his family together, took care of Amy. I learned the people of Old Taipei looked out for each other, like a true community. And Ms. Vivian had more empathy and understanding than anyone else in the Linevine.

If what I had thought about them had been so wrong, what

else could be? Everything? The ghost of Dad was pointing the way: *Have the courage to face the truth.* To ask the hard questions.

I started with the biggest pillar: the Ivy League. Was it actually the be-all and end-all? I checked the background of some Fortune 500 CEOs. The majority of those must be Ivy League grads, right? But as I scrolled through article after article, I discovered that not only was it not true—it wasn't even close to true. Some were—famously—even undergraduate dropouts. But they were all more than successful.

But the more I thought about it, even the premise might be wrong. What's to say the Fortune 500 was the right metric? Or even financial success? I had assumed our ads for CoffeeMatch would be the best because it was the biggest and most famous company of its kind. But I had been wrong. Maybe there was some other, unquantifiable metric for success, both for ads . . . and for everything else. Like having a life in the arts, doing what you loved. I thought of Garrett quietly drawing, free of the clawing uncertainty that gripped me and many of my classmates.

That was the problem with questions—they only led to more questions. It was like those old pick-up stick games that my grandparents used to give us: you pull out one stick, and the whole structure collapses.

I was terrified of everything falling. I had spent my whole life climbing to the top of the pile. I had no idea what to do if it all came down.

27

#CANDYBARCHALLENGE

THE NEXT MORNING, my phone buzzed. Garrett. I had been sending him suggestions for the hashtag, but he clearly refused to take them seriously.

#LoveSchmove

#SufferingThyNameIsRomance

#Eeyore, I typed. How about something more upbeat?

#Why

What kind of hashtag could go viral? #Love was too generic, as was #LoveAdvice. I thought about what the boy had told me during our live love advice booth. I had been looking at the surface of love, to the signs that people were attracted to each other. But I needed to dig deeper. Be more honest.

Dad's words were still running through my head. *Have the courage to face the truth.* I flipped through the inbox again. So many questions, so much openness.

Vulnerability.

Maybe that was the element I had missed. The thing necessary to achieve a truthful, authentic type of love. A lot of these questions were about having the nerve to face a crush or significant other, to find out the person's true feelings. Even if the answer was one you didn't want.

What if our hashtag could help to do that? Help people to discover the truth, like I was trying to do? Instead of being trapped in the unspoken or a one-sided, imagined connection, they could get real, so they could move forward or move on.

I grabbed my phone and texted Garrett.

You remember that one TikTok challenge where people kissed their best friends? What if we set up something similar, but for people who are too scared to confess their feelings to each other? We can have people give their crushes a specific gift—something small. . . . It would be meaningful if you know about the challenge but totally innocent if it turns out the person doesn't like you.

#SmellyGymSock?

#CandybarChallenge.

We're going to go on TikTok?

We are gonna rule TikTok.

Garrett texted me a video a few days later.

It was a guy and a girl exiting Piccolo's Chocolate Company. The guy slowly handed the girl a chocolate bar, and she, oblivious, took it. But then she looked at him, her fingers curling over the candy. She stared at the camera.

The cameraperson cheered.

"Is this . . . ?" she said.

The boy didn't need to answer; it was right there, in the way he cupped the back of his neck, in the hopeful slant of his body toward hers.

The cameraperson whispered, "He's been in love with her for four years! Four years!" Giggles off to the side.

The girl clutched the chocolate bar as the boy hung his head. She caught his hand. As he turned toward her, she launched herself at him and planted a kiss.

Wild cheering.

The boy and the girl slowly melted into each other, his arms sliding around her waist, hers encircling his neck. The camera shook with a wobbly close-up of a chocolate bar.

More and more videos began to appear, the hashtag #Candybar Challenge trending on TikTok and Chatty.

Two guys who pulled out candy bars at the same time, beaming.

One girl who gave a bar to a guy, and when he said no, she snatched it back and gave it to the hot guy standing next to him. He kissed her.

One older gentleman who put his bar on the table and waited to see if anyone would pick it up. Five minutes later, an elderly woman did. The video cut to the two of them in front of a store, dancing.

28

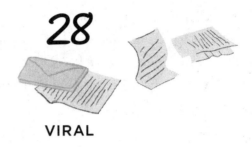

VIRAL

IN A FEW days, the #CandybarChallenge was officially viral.

Someone had set the #CandybarChallenge to music, so the presentation of the gift would happen at the proper, chorus-swelling moment. I managed to secure a partnership with Piccolo's Chocolate Company, and they made flyers for their store and mentioned us on their social media sites. It turned out the owner was part of a small business association, so they all started advertising our challenge as well. Auntie Beth helped us by hanging a big sign in her front window and in the romance section of her bookstore. The uncle and auntie who owned the grocery store put up posters by their candy section.

More important, it turned out that the son of the chocolate shop owner had a longtime crush on a girl named Mia Susanti, who was a huge social media influencer. After she got her bar—and her happy ending—she posted to all of her accounts, and we were off to the races.

I texted heart eyes at Garrett.

Who says I'm not Cupid?

Even I have to confess that these videos are not . . . terrible.

Wait, who is this? Did you steal Garrett's phone?

He texted back a GIF of Eeyore.

That's more like it.

But I wondered if he really meant it. If Eeyore was still all that he believed in.

29

LOVE-DEUCE

MOM SAID NOTHING more about the competition, probably because her mind was otherwise occupied. She came downstairs on Saturday morning dressed up in a tennis outfit instead of her usual robe.

"Girls. Mrs. Lin has invited us to the athletic club," she said. "We're going this afternoon."

I glanced at Hattie, but she didn't know what was going on, either.

"Why?" I blurted out. Mom was invited every week. She always said no, after The Fall.

Mom pulled her tennis equipment out of the closet. "Mrs. Lin is getting very serious about Eric's college applications and his grades. I think it's a good idea to talk to her about what you've been doing. After tennis."

Everything happened before or after tennis. Before The

Fall, we used to spend every weekend at the athletic club and some holidays, too. I remembered one Thanksgiving when Garrett and I and our siblings had a sad little meal by the racquetball courts. We had been mad, thinking of all our friends eating their turkey in their warm homes. Our parents didn't understand the holiday, of course, so it became an odd combination of tennis as usual plus piles of Taiwanese food. Like everything else, it wasn't quite one culture or the other.

But this was a disaster. Mom still didn't know about what Mrs. Lin had done. If she went to the athletic club today, wouldn't it seem like she was trying too hard?

"I . . . can't go," I said. "I really need to do work on the competition."

"This is important," Mom said. I knew why: if I won, she couldn't abruptly show up to all the social events afterward. That would be like boasting. She needed to make her comeback gradually, then heroically fake modesty when the accolades rolled in.

Like I said, all the unspoken social rules were super complicated.

"I have a lot of homework," I said. "I need to pass my Spanish exam or I'll get a B. It'll go on my transcript."

"Juliana." That meant: *You've never gotten a B in Spanish in your life.* And: *Stop making excuses right now.*

I looked to Hattie for help, but since I hadn't told her what Mrs. Lin had done, either, she was confused.

I tried my best argument. "The competition isn't over yet.

What if we don't do well later on? Won't that be bad?"

My mom was dead serious. "You had better do well, then."

When we got there, Eric Lin was wandering out of the men's locker room with another one of the kids, Dylan Lo. Eric had been looking miserable at school lately, and Siobhan Collins hadn't seemed much better. She had gone to our last SBA meetings with puffy eyes, and she and Eric now sat apart from each other. But they still kept glancing at each other, like they couldn't help it. Had Mrs. Lin somehow found out about their relationship? Made them split?

Garrett came out of the locker room next, looking slightly more cranky than usual. He stopped when he saw me. Smiled.

"Juliana?" He was carrying a tennis racket, his hand loose around the grip. "What are you doing here?"

I checked: my mom had already disappeared, probably to change her clothes. Guilt, clinging and clammy, wrapped around me. I needed to tell her that Garrett was my partner. But even the thought of it and her reaction were enough to make my stomach roll. I had spent my whole life avoiding the Duck Cleaver Glare. This would be willingly sticking my neck under the blade. Much to my acidic shame, I couldn't do it. Not yet.

I said, "My mom decided to come. You?"

"Mr. Peng pulled his back, so my dad is making me fill in for him in doubles."

Garrett was wearing a pair of tennis shorts, dark blue, with white stripes down the side. His calves were surprisingly muscular, and I wondered when he had time to exercise when he spent all of his time indoors with a tablet or art supplies. I knew he took wushu classes—could those make him this fit?

A silence fell between us as I concentrated on not looking like I was ogling Garrett Tsai's legs.

My mom strode over to us and gave Garrett the barest greeting. He stared down at his racket.

"Juliana," she said. "You and Hattie play with Dylan and Eric today."

Mrs. Lin was next to her, and she looked uncomfortable. Had Mom steamrollered her into agreeing to a game? And did she seriously mean play . . . tennis? Had she met me? And with *Eric Lin*? Who, as far as she knew, had ditched me? But I knew it didn't matter. Nothing could outweigh *Taiwanese, son of a National Taiwan University grad, heading toward Princeton engineering.* For Mom, this was an ideal opportunity.

Eric was equally as horrified. For a second, we were in total agreement: we wanted nothing to do with this. Besides— tennis? That was bad enough. But doubles? Even worse. Singles meant I only had to concentrate on swinging at the ball. Doubles meant I had to both return the ball and avoid hitting my partner. Disaster. Even Garrett looked alarmed. He was probably remembering all the times he had to play on the courts next to me when we were kids and he got beaned in the head.

But my mom was chatting with the other aunties in the lobby. Actually being social. I picked up one of Hattie's extra rackets.

I guess it was only one game.

Garrett leaned toward me. "Juliana. Don't you hate tennis?"

It was the one sport I had always tried to get out of playing. Even in the early days, before The Fall, I had tried to make excuses every time people wanted to pair up for matches.

I knew there was a lot he was holding back from saying, mainly *You never tell people what you want.* But there was a distinct possibility that I was about to bring eternal shame upon our family by losing the AABC. All of my mom's hopes for social redemption, her careful climb, could shortly be torched. I owed her. If I had to string myself up from the gallows of tennis, so be it.

We played indoors today, which was marginally better since I didn't have to worry about my tennis ball going over a fence. Garrett was on the court next to us, and I was well aware that most of his attention was on our game and not his. This was probably because I hit the ball toward the ceiling, into the net, toward the game on the other side of us. Where I did not hit it was within the bounds of our own court.

I knew I could get it if I just tried harder. But it seemed like the more force I used, the less I made contact. I pictured smashing the ball like a neon-yellow rocket, but I missed and it flew past me. I tried again, but now I was fixated on how I was obviously not doing well and that only made things worse.

It soon became my turn to serve. Hattie flicked me a thumbs-up from across the net. "You got this, Juju!" she said.

I had actually liked tennis a lot when I was a little kid. I loved the sound of the racket hitting the ball, watching the arc of yellow soar across the court. But I had seen the other kids, how they had been able to play at the net and serve aces, seemingly effortlessly. I knew it wasn't an efficient use of my time to work at something I was already behind on. Why invest in something I couldn't excel at?

But Hattie had never worried about being the best. The only reason she played was because she liked it. And now she was clearly having fun, running after every ball and joking around with the boys.

Bounce the ball. Toss. It flew up, then down, and I swung my racket. Yay! Contact!

The ball sailed in a perfect path . . . into the center of the net. Next to me, Dylan said nothing; he just grabbed the ball off the ground and shoved it into his pocket. We started playing again, and eventually Dylan started yelling, "Got it!" for all of them. I stood by the net and tried not to get hit. We still lost.

Hattie said, "Another round?"

Both Dylan and Eric winced, though they both tried to hide it. But I saw it.

I politely passed, then ducked out and headed toward the water fountain. To my shock, Eric followed me out.

"Juliana," he called.

I didn't know what he wanted to say. Clearly we both just had to finish this tennis charade, make our moms happy, then continue on with our lives.

He said nothing at first, standing with his hands in his pockets.

"Okay, then." I started to leave.

"Have you talked to Siobhan?"

"Siobhan?" She was friends with Maria, but we weren't super close. "No. Why?"

I saw a crack in his normal expression, and at the bottom was heartbreak. Whatever had happened between him and Siobhan had clearly not been his idea. I couldn't help it; I felt a small sliver of pity.

Eric looked like he was trying to say five things at once and they were all jammed in his mouth. "I was wondering if she was doing okay."

If Mrs. Lin had found out that Eric was dating Siobhan, I could only imagine what his last few weeks had been like. The thought of Mom and her duck cleaver, more than anything, made me choose a kinder answer than I normally would have picked. "I can check in on her."

He gave me a tight smile. "Thanks, Juliana."

I still hadn't forgiven him, but I began to see that we were both trying to navigate the same suffocating system. Trying to find a way to survive.

It was after the game, when the parents were hanging out in little chatty clumps around the lobby, that I heard it. I was sitting on a couch, waiting for Mom and Hattie to come out of the locker room, when some of the aunties started talking behind me in Taiwanese.

"I see Sùyīn came today," one said. She was talking about Mom?

The other tsked. "It's been a while."

"She's looking a little—" The auntie used a word in

202

Mandarin, which I was 90 percent sure translated to "rundown."

The other auntie agreed. "Doing too much. You think she sees the baby?"

"Oh no. Not at all."

More tsking. "Such a shame, the daughter leaving Harvard Medical School."

The other auntie let out the Taiwanese equivalent of "I know, right?"

"And the middle one. She's not doing so well in the AABC."

"Well, probably not. Sùyīn hasn't been preparing her enough. She's too loose with those kids. Look at the other two."

There was the faint squeak of a door opening. Their voices fading. But not before I heard: "Mèng Yáo's son, though. Eric. He's very focused. . . ."

I poked my head out from behind the couch, wanting to catch a glimpse of who was trash-talking. To see their faces. But the aunties had already vanished into the locker room. My mom, pale, was a little distance behind them. They must not have noticed her. But I knew from the way she wouldn't make eye contact with me that she had heard them, and knew I had, too.

I didn't know what to say. *Those old bats aren't your real friends? Forget them?* These were not things that were said in my mom's group. It was all about preserving the illusion of civility, even as they stabbed at each other on the way out. I couldn't do anything about it, but I could at least give my mom the dignity of pretending it had not happened. I slipped off the couch and quickly headed toward the lobby. As I got close to the front door, I heard my name. Garrett.

From his expression, I knew he had also overheard. Of course he had—the one thing the aunties did not have was volume control. They were so used to talking about people in Taiwanese while on the streets of America that I honestly thought they forgot other people could understand them.

"You okay?" he asked.

"Just another day in the Linevine." I tried to sound flip, but I had never been flip about anything, ever. This was too much like after The Fall, when the stares were one second too long, too smoothed over with politeness. What had Mom been thinking, coming today? How had I let it happen?

Garrett glanced around the lobby, then led me outside to some benches by the parking lot.

"Do you need a moment?" he said. "Away from everything?"

This was my worst nightmare, the eye of gossip turned toward me. And Mom. It was my fault. I had tried so hard to do the right thing. But because I couldn't bear to tell Mom about Mrs. Lin's snobbery, I had let her walk right into the viper pit.

What had I done?

I hadn't meant to hurt Mom. And yet, here we were.

"They don't beat around the bush, those aunties," Garrett said.

"No, they do not."

He was struggling, I could tell, with wanting to say something. "Is it always like that?"

"It's been worse. Since Bella." I pressed my hands to my eyes as if I could block out everything. "We shouldn't have come today."

It was all my fault.

I felt a hand on my shoulder, so light I could have imagined it.

He said, "I didn't know it was that bad for you."

Garrett's parents weren't close with my mom and her friends, so I guess he hadn't really seen the extent of the gossip or why Mom had shut herself off. How isolated we had been. How the same conversation happened every time we went out. I hadn't talked about it, or The Fall, when we were in New Hampshire together. The same way he hadn't talked about his parents. We had both wanted to be in a place where we could be free of all that, for once.

"It's so screwed up," he said. "All of it." He was sitting close to me, his arm almost pressed against mine, but neither of us moved.

"It is." It was a labyrinth full of mines. There was no way to escape without injury.

Garrett was starting to look irritated. "If you know, then why do you care so much about what they think?"

"How can you not?" They seemed inescapable, the suffocating tendrils of the Linevine. But maybe Garrett had seen how things could be different. And hadn't I, too, in Old Taipei? I thought of Chef Auntie fussing over everyone, Uncle Jing quietly making sure the others had food and drinks. Auntie Beth saving books and giving them to Garrett.

I thought he would return to his scornful self, but he was studying me again. Like he had just figured out something unexpected. "Have you been trying to do all of this for your mom? The Ivies and the grades and everything? To give her something to brag about since she's been getting such shit from everyone?"

I didn't need to answer.

Unhappiness shaded Garrett's face, tightened the line of his shoulders.

"I . . . ," he said. "I assumed you were like my brother. That you wanted the Ivies for the sake of the Ivies."

That stung. I knew that's how I might appear on the outside to nearly everyone. How people in the SBA and at school and maybe even the Linevine saw me. But I had always hoped—had once upon a time believed—that Garrett would be different.

He clasped his hands together, his knuckles turning pale. "I'm really sorry."

"For what?" But a part of me already knew the answer; it was in the way the silence now was weighed down with the memories of our past together. That summer was always there between us, undeniable.

Was he finally going to tell me what happened?

Garrett always demanded the truth from everyone, and that included himself. "For what I did," he said, "on the last day, at camp. . . ."

I didn't want to hear it. I didn't want to know. I needed to know.

He sighed. "Your mom came early. And I heard her talking to some of the others. One of the aunties said she heard that you and I were hanging out a lot. And then your mom said—"

Oh no. I could only imagine. *The Tsai family? They have a vet office, for the animals. I know, it doesn't make much money for so much work. You heard about the uncle. . . . Yes, they have to send money back for the lawyer, too. Embezzlement, how terrible.*

Garrett's hands were still clasped, his fingers gripping each other tightly. "She said, 'I hope not.' That you would never hang out with someone *like me*. From *that family*. You would know better."

What? "But you didn't believe—" I said. "I would never—"

Garrett looked miserable. "I don't know. I heard it and . . . it made me think. I mean, we never talked much growing up. We weren't friends. Why would I believe that we would go back to Chinese class and potlucks and the Linevine and things would continue like they were in New Hampshire? Especially when your mom had those feelings about me and my family? I had never seen you go against her wishes. You could have thought the same thing, for all I knew."

It was a stab. "You would think that, even after . . . ?" All the time we spent together? But the truth was there, undeniable: I had been surprised he was so committed to the competition. That he worked so hard. I had not seen the value of what he had loved. And if I couldn't do that, how strong a friendship could we have had?

I had been so busy being hurt that he had cut me off, like Mom had disowned Bella, that I hadn't thought about what could have caused it. And the ugly truth was this: he was right. I still hadn't told my mom we were partners. I was exactly who he thought I was. I was worse.

He said, "I convinced myself that our time together was this little . . . detour for you, and you would go back to your usual life once we returned to the real world. That you didn't care. And it would be easier if we just ended it." He stared at the ground.

His guilt was unbearable. "Garrett." *You weren't wrong about me.* "I—"

I wanted to say it. *I didn't tell my mom we are partners.* I should have just told him. But I couldn't. Because it would open up more questions, like *Why* and *How could you?* And *I knew it.* An endless well of hurt for him, an arrow right into the one hole in his armor. And scorn, again, for me. Him looking at me like he could see my small cowardly self. I didn't know if I could face it again. Because this time I would know that he was right.

My mom strode through the front door of the racquet club. Hattie was behind her, clutching my bag from the locker room.

"Where were you?" Mom hissed. "We were waiting." She must have wanted to leave as soon as she overheard the aunties gossiping about her.

I sprang to my feet, Garrett behind me.

Mom smiled politely at some people across the parking lot, then hustled us off to the car. She didn't notice Garrett; she was only focused on leaving.

Garrett stayed in the doorway, watching our car as we drove off. I didn't want him to suffer. Not for me. Not when I should have been the one apologizing.

* * *

Mom didn't say anything on the drive home, and Hattie was confused. Would this set Mom back? Would we find her on the couch again?

Apparently not.

As soon as we got home, she slammed her purse on the table, then strode to the kitchen and dragged out a large pot from under the cabinet. Hattie's eyes widened, then she totally peaced out. Chicken. She shot me finger hearts as she dashed up the stairs.

Mom filled the pot with water and then began yanking veggies out of the fridge. And one packet of raw meat. Oh boy.

I knew better than to say anything.

"Mrs. Peng thinks I'm too loose with you?" The end of the carrot was *thwunk*ed. "I put all of you in every prep class. Bella got into Harvard, early. You're valedictorian."

She chopped. I hoped the recipe called for extremely minced carrots.

"And AABC, hah. You can still win." She stared at me. "Right?"

"Um," I said. This was the worst time to drop the *Hi! I've been totally lying!* Bomb on Mom. But maybe I could lay some groundwork. Try to show Mom that Garrett wasn't a slacker.

"If we really want to win," I said. "I should know more about design."

Mom was fixated on her chopping. I see we were escalating to a ground meat situation. "*Hi-yah*, are you talking about that Tsai boy again?"

I felt terrible having to say it, but there was only one

209

currency that my mom would understand. "He got into RISD early admission, Mom," I said. "It's one of the top art schools in the country. He's won lots of awards, too, including best in state. Maybe I can ask him for some general pointers."

Here's what I actually wanted to tell her: *He listens, Mom. He watches out for me. He takes care of everyone, just because it's the right thing to do.* But I knew those were things that she wouldn't value as much as prestige.

She said, "He will not help you win."

I wanted to push more, but if I told my mom about Garrett, wouldn't it be subjecting him to her scorn for the rest of the competition? Wouldn't she blame him for all of our bad results?

Was that what I was really worried about? Or was I just afraid?

I wanted to reach for Dad's jade key chain. He had died when we were young, so we had never been old enough to ask the complicated questions. For us, it had been easy: *Can we stay up later? Can I eat this cookie? Can I buy this dress?*

How was I supposed to decide what to do when both choices were so fraught?

I pictured Garrett smiling at me. There were times recently when he looked so much like he used to—it was like we had gone back in time. Like we could start again.

But could we? Without ending up in the same place?

30

HAPPY BIRTHDAY TO US

THE NEXT DAY, I received a text.

Cultural center, after school?

For the past day, I hadn't been able to think about anything but what Garrett had overheard at camp. What my mom had said about him. The lie. I needed to confess. Confessing would devastate him.

But if I told both of them the truth now, what would happen? Mom would force me to cut him out of the competition. He would never forgive me. Mom wouldn't either, for lying in the first place. She would become fixated on why Eric had dumped me and would probably find out what Mrs. Lin had said, which would lead to even more embarrassment, and then suddenly we would be in a raw poultry farm with a duck cleaver and no exit.

Every path, terrible. If I kept everything a secret and we won the competition, would Mom let everything go? And if she was happy, then there was no reason to tell Garrett and he would never have to find out. Right? If I could keep the lie going long enough to win, could I get myself out of this mess?

Even I didn't believe that.

The truth, insistent, would not be denied: *You are a coward. And the facts will always come out.*

I had stayed up late last night reading all of our advice emails. All the questions. These people weren't writing in because they wanted to take the safe path. You don't pour your heart out to a stranger if you think the answer is *Don't do anything. Stay exactly the same.* These people didn't want to know if they should take action. They wanted to know *how.* What action to take. How to tell your crush, confront the problem, end the broken relationship.

The old me would have said to go for it and things would all work out. But that wasn't helpful. For each situation, there was a thorny, terrifying point where a hard choice had to be made. Like now. How did people know what to do? How did they make their decisions? That's what I wanted to know.

It's what everyone wanted to know.

But I had no more answers than anyone else.

I arrived at the cultural center early, but there was no sign of Garrett. Chef Auntie waved at me and so did Auntie Cindy. I said hi, then made a beeline for the vending machine. I didn't think chocolate could solve my dilemma, but it might be a good start.

Much to my surprise, Garrett had gotten there before me and was carefully studying the selections. He always gave things his full attention, even with something like picking out a snack.

"Chocolate craving?" I asked.

"Juliana." His hand dropped from the keypad.

"Found some change in your bag?"

"I have exactly enough quarters," he said. "I can't pick anything. It has to be special." He gave me a wry look.

We were silent as he scanned the selections. I thought that Garrett would make some crack about how M&M's were better than Snickers since he knew Snickers were my absolute favorite snack, but he did not.

He glanced at the candy bars, then at me. The Snickers bar was in the A3 slot and the M&M's were on the other side of the machine, at A9. Garrett pushed the A button, then his finger hovered over the number 3. Snickers? He hated Snickers.

I couldn't help but think of the video he had sent me of the boy giving the girl the chocolate bar for the #CandybarChallenge. Was he going to buy something . . . for me? A shock of hope, strong and unexpected, quickly twisted to dread and guilt. But then he quickly pushed A9 and the M&M's fell with a thud.

"I—" I said.

"Juliana—" he said at the same time.

I didn't know what I was going to say. *I need to tell you something*? Might be the first thing. There was no second.

Kevin came down the hall. He glanced between us both. "Oh, sorry! I didn't mean to—"

"We're not—" I said, just as Garrett said, "It's okay."

There was another beat of silence.

"Well," Kevin said. "Chef Auntie's new Instagram account is fantastic, Juliana. My mom loves it. And so does Auntie Liu."

"I liked the cucumber butterfly you did last week," I said.

Kevin beamed. "Hattie said the same thing."

"Did she?" Garrett flashed me a suspiciously innocent expression. Was Garrett Tsai *matchmaking*? What was going on right now? "Interesting."

"Well, I knew the project was going to be awesome as soon as I found out you were going to be in charge, Juliana," Kevin said. "Garrett is always going on about how great you are."

He was?

Garrett shoved him. "Not that much."

Kevin mouthed the words. *All. The. Time.*

"Really," I said. My smile was uncontainable; it was the size of a universe, exploding.

Garrett's ears were red. "Total lie."

"'All the time,'" I said. "Kevin just said '*all the time*.'" I poked Garrett, and we both stilled as he caught my hand. We stood there for a moment, then he reached over to touch my waist, lightly.

There was a sudden rush: my cells shocked awake, my heart crushing in then exploding out. My lungs flattening as his fingers tightened over my hip. It was like someone had thrown on the switch and everything was *more*: the pressure of his fingertips on the thin fabric of my shirt, the tremble of his other hand around mine, the warmth of him as he leaned in.

Garrett's face was a flip-book of emotions: vulnerability, desire, terror. Hope.

I saw now that our time in New Hampshire had been a precursor to today, the way a pink sky signals the rising of a bright sun. That summer was hands brushed against each other, blushes, the undiluted thrill of time spent by ourselves. Today was the day the light came over the horizon, warm and blinding. I was the only one who knew it couldn't last, since it was based on a lie. But I couldn't bear to move aside. I didn't want to.

"Anyway," Kevin said loudly, "Chef Auntie says they're ready."

"What are?" I asked. Garrett smiled and pulled me toward the kitchen, his hand warm around my wrist. On the countertops were row after row of plain cupcakes.

"So . . . ," I said. "We're opening a cupcake store?"

"This is our last push to get signatures for Old Taipei," he said. "The city council vote is around the corner. We're having an event at Auntie Beth's bookstore to draw in some people and let them know what's going on. She even got a bunch of local Asian American authors to do readings."

I would enjoy the moment, only a little. Didn't I deserve it? Then I would tell him. End everything.

I said, "And we are . . . ?"

Garrett pulled an apron over my head, his fingers lingering on the ties. "We're Team Frosting."

* * *

You know how much frosting you need to cover a hundred and fifty cupcakes? A LOT.

The backs of my hands were smeared with vanilla, I had chocolate streaks on my jeans, and I was pretty sure I had some sprinkles in my hair. But I also hadn't had this much fun in a long time.

Ms. Vivian had brought in some music and cranked it up. It turned out she was pretty handy with design and decided to re-create some cute book covers on the VIPs' desserts. She had entrusted Garrett with some of her precious icing bags, and he was studiously hunched over a plate of cupcakes, delicately squeezing out pink and green frosting. I shouldn't have stared, but I couldn't help it. He was a balance of beautiful lines: his jaw, nose, the shadow of muscle on his forearm.

Garrett finally noticed. "What?" he said. He had a crease in the center of his bottom lip, an alluring shadow, and it was like a flare, snagging my attention.

I grabbed the container of vanilla frosting next to him. "Are you using this one?"

He shook his head, confused, as I started vigorously decorating a new tray. Concentrate on the glaze, Juliana.

Soon we were the only ones remaining in the kitchen; Ms. Vivian had to go to class, and she took the speakers and Kevin with her. The silence should have been awkward, but it wasn't.

Garrett stretched, rubbing the side of his neck. "Remind me again why we didn't just print out flyers?"

"This was not my idea," I said. "I would have done flyers for sure."

Garrett said, "You remember when we took that mooncake workshop? And the teacher got mad at us for talking and made us bake extra for all the teachers?"

I laughed. "Yes."

"This is worse."

I peered at the cupcakes. Ms. Vivian had placed tiny fondant books on the top of each one and Garrett was decorating them with green and pink hearts. They were adorable.

"I like the covers," I said. "Also, that appears to be a romance novel. That's a love cupcake, Garrett."

He snorted. "Which will eventually get eaten or tossed into the trash."

"Hattie loves that book," I said. "And so do Maria and Tammy."

"Are those your friends from school?"

I was surprised he remembered. But he was back to piping again, carefully tracing a green heart.

I said, "Yes. They also believe in love. As do most of the other human beings on the planet."

"Aren't they going out with each other?" he said.

"For almost two years."

"Let me guess. Thanks to you?"

I didn't even try to seem modest. "Yup."

He turned back to the cupcake. "I think you see love every-where."

"Said the person currently making hearts out of icing."

He said, "But what happens if they go to college in separate places? Or they dated too early and want to see other people?

217

Or they meet someone else?"

I poked the side of his head with my fingertip. "What is even going on in there?" I said. "Is that really what you think about all day?"

He didn't respond.

"You really *are* cynical. Who broke your heart, Tsai?"

He flushed but remained silent. Oh, of course—his ex.

I was about to apologize when he said, "I know you heard. Because God forbid our parents ever leave anything about our lives private."

"It's why they have us," I said. "Solely to have something to gossip about."

Garrett sighed. "Go ahead and ask."

"So she . . . um, dumped you?"

"Thanks for the tact, Juliana."

But that wasn't the question I wanted to ask. He said he had loved her—what was that like?

"What happened?" I asked.

Garrett picked up an undecorated cupcake. "She cheated on me with my best friend. Well, ex–best friend. And then she dumped me."

"No." I thought of his webtoon, of a panel I had seen where the main character watches his ship and crew sailing away. There was always something haunting about it, and I now understood why. "That's horrible."

"It wasn't ideal."

"It was . . . sophomore year?" He nodded. "Are you . . . still sad?"

His mouth tightened. "Not really—not like I was right after. It's—" He stopped talking. I sensed I wasn't going to get anything more.

"Well, I heard she was Asian but *not Taiwanese*." That got a small laugh. I personally had nothing against dating people who were not Taiwanese or not Asian. But it was a big bô hó for my mom and her friends. I thought suddenly of Eric and Siobhan. Was that one of the reasons why he was so desperate to win the competition? So he could leave and have the freedom to date who he wanted and have his own life, without interference from his parents?

"At least she was Asian," Garrett said. "So my parents only had a partial heart attack. Do you think they give up at some point? Has anyone actually married someone else from Taiwan?"

We both thought. "Esther Lai," I said. Esther was older than us and had achieved the mythical Harvard Hat Trick: undergrad, medical school, then—get this—a PhD in neuroscience. They were going to make a gold statue of her and erect it in the middle of the athletic club parking lot.

"Leo Chan," he said. Yale undergrad, played violin for the president when he was fifteen. "But he majored in music, which negated all of his achievements and his Taiwanese wife."

True.

"Okay," Garrett said. "Which is worse: a) Ivy but never got married, b) non-Ivy undergrad but married Taiwanese, or c) Ivy undergrad, failed to get into medical school but married Taiwanese?"

I thought a moment. "Clearly a trick question. They're all unacceptable."

He was quiet. "So, what then?" His glance connected to mine. The shadows and lines of his face had become etched within me during that summer and I had never forgotten them. But now, once again, he let me see the emotions he usually kept hidden.

"I don't know," I said.

He was unsmiling, but there was something almost unbearably graceful about the angle of his mouth, the crease in his lip.

I needed to say it then. *I have to tell you something.*

But I couldn't. That wasn't correct. I wouldn't. I knew the answer to his question. *What then?* Then everything ends.

I couldn't bear for it to be today.

After we finished all the cupcakes, Garrett put a hand on mine. "Wait here."

He disappeared in the back, then reappeared with a large white cupcake. It had a single candle in the middle.

"Is it . . . someone's birthday?" I asked. His was in December.

"Yup." He placed it in front of me. "Yours."

Uh. It totally was not. My birthday was in May. "I hate to tell you this, but it's in the spring."

"I know."

"So . . . ?"

Garrett said, "Knowing you, I'll bet your last birthday was full of studying and meetings."

Rude! Also, accurate.

"I had cake." Kind of. My mom had come back late from the office with some cupcakes. Hattie had made me a paper card.

"Just as I thought," he said. "You have not properly celebrated this most important holiday."

"It's not a holiday. Not like Christmas."

"Nope. It's even better." He nudged the plate closer to me. "Your birthday is the one day of the year when you are absolutely not allowed to do anything for anyone else. It's a day all about you."

How is it that, with all the people I saw every day, with all the time I spent with my family and the SBA and my friends, he was the only one who had ever seen me?

"I don't even know what that means," I said.

"I know." His voice was gentle. "But you should."

The pressure of feeling compressed and rearranged me. Nothing I had read about or studied had prepared me for this, the force of being understood.

Garrett held up the bag of M&M's he had bought earlier. He pulled out a few and formed an elegant J with the yellow and red ones. The tenderness in his expression was my undoing. It melted everything, all rationality, practicality, logic. Everything but the guilt.

I took a few blue and green ones and drew a crooked G on the other side. "You deserve a day, too, then."

"I guess I do." Even if I were an artist, I don't think I could ever capture Garrett on paper. He would be a dark shell containing a universe of stars; the puff of warm air when you come in from the snow.

"Think of this as a belated apology." He made an ampersand out of icing, not looking at me. "This doesn't nearly make up for everything, but I hope you'll accept it."

The guilt was acidic. "Don't—" I said.

But Garrett was already pulling out a box of matches from his pocket and lighting the candle. "Happy birthday to us?"

He put a hand on my back. I thought of metal filings around a magnet, how they will leap and surround it. My every nerve was pointed toward him, toward the spread of his warm palm on the fabric of my shirt.

I leaned forward with him. We pursed our lips and exhaled.

The thing I wished for could never come true: a life where I got everything I wanted and everyone was still happy. Where I would be free of guilt from . . . everyone.

But it was too late to avoid disaster. Everything was a whirl; everything had turned. Something was changing in me, and I didn't think I could stop it.

31

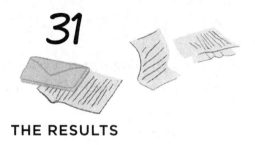

THE RESULTS

AFTER I WENT home, I ran to my room. I couldn't figure out what to do. I was tired; I was unable to sit; I wanted to go outside; I wanted to run; I wanted. I didn't know what I wanted. I knew exactly what I wanted. It was already in ruins.

A text suddenly flashed on my phone. Garrett. He had sent me a photo of a carved radish with enthusiastic toothpick arms and a cute little excited face.

AMY THINKS YOU'RE RAD(ISH)

Carved veggies and a pun. It was like I didn't even know the boy. Before I could stop myself, I texted:

Absolutely radishing.

NICELY DONE, ZHAO.

I stared at the phone. For once, I didn't text back.

A few days later, I logged on to a video call with Garrett. The results of the last round were going to come out at 8:00 p.m.

He appeared on screen, his hair wet and mussed, like he had just taken a shower.

"What's up?" he said. I had my headphones in, so his voice sounded intimate. Close.

"I . . ." I had no idea what to say.

He waited.

"The competition!" I said. "Let's check."

"We're five minutes early."

"You never know!" We peeked. It wasn't up. Four minutes to go.

Garrett rubbed his hair with a towel, and I looked away.

"What's going on?" he said. "You're acting weird."

"Not. Am not." I refreshed the website. Three minutes to go. Why had I suggested doing this on video and not on the phone? But I knew why. It was a tissue-thin pretext to see the angle of his jaw, the shadow of his lip. I wanted to inoculate myself against him, to give myself one last chance to prove that this—whatever this was—was a passing fog. A mist. Instead, it was a force that was almost muscular. A craving.

Behind Garrett were various sketches, and I stared at them as if they could give me a map to what he was thinking, what was happening between us. If anything was happening between us.

He leaned back in his chair, and I absolutely did not stare at the line of his neck, the shadowed dip of his collarbone. "It'll be okay if we don't get in the top ten, you know."

I nodded.

"We'll figure out something."

Except what was really wrong was impossible to reconcile. The unsolvable conundrum.

I reached for the reload button like a spasm. Only this time the page changed. The background was bright blue, and there were some long paragraphs at the top. But that wasn't what caught my attention. At the bottom of the page was an indent. A list.

> MochiBites (solo)
> Team Kraken
> Team SunCloud.

Team SunCloud.
That was us. THAT WAS US.
We were in the top three.

32

WELCOME TO CORPORATE AMERICA

GARRETT YELLED. ON the screen, I saw Amy run into his room.

"What?" she said. "What?" He wrapped her in a huge hug and swung her in a circle.

"It's because we were so bad in the beginning!" I exclaimed. "We totally sucked!"

Amy was running around Garrett's room and dancing.

"You won?" she said.

"No!" I said. "We got into the top three." I scanned the rest of the top ten. I recognized Eric's team name. And Linda and Kelly's, of course. And a few that were solo.

"You won because you sucked?" Amy said.

"*Yes!*"

"No," Garrett said. "We won because we didn't let it stop

us." A genuine smile, breathtaking, broke across his face. "Juliana. *We did it!*"

Garrett and Amy did a goofy dance. Even after we hung up, Garrett kept texting me, little video clips he called the "GIFs of Triumph": a motorcyclist zooming over a canyon, a cheering stadium. I texted him "GIFs of Awesomeness," and then things rapidly devolved to GIFs of We Did Great, We Totally Rule, and We Did Pretty Okay, I Guess.

Finally, after it became way too late, I sleepily received one more message from him.

Hey. I'm proud of us.

I didn't know what to type back.

We were right on track. I had never felt worse.

All the competitors were invited to the Lee Corporation for a tour and the unveiling of the final challenge. It was like Christmas and performing in a piano recital all at once.

It was scheduled for a Tuesday afternoon, which meant we were taking a trip to the city. On the walk over to the building, the wind blew Garrett's hair, tousling it. He had worn a gray suit today with a dark blue tie. I had spent our entire walk trying not to stare at him. But I felt his presence like a vibration, scrambling everything. He walked close to me, and if the wind was blowing really hard, he would occasionally put his arm around my shoulders.

A gust came and Garrett curled around me, his arm shielding my face. He pulled me close until it stopped. He bent his head, his face close to mine, for a second. More. Until I stepped away.

I tucked my briefcase closer to me and tried to focus on the skyscrapers, the tall glass majestic height of them. The rivers of people in suits striding to work. A lot of them were dressed in blue, like me, and were on their phones. Striding forward toward their corporate jobs. But I couldn't help but notice that most of them were clutching the straps of their bags, checking their watches. Not seeing anything around them.

The Lee Corporation had a three-story-high wall of glass in the front of its building. Official-looking revolving doors and an even more impressive security desk. As soon as we walked in, there was a hush, as if to say, *Be respectful. The money is made here.*

We made our way to the far elevator banks. As we waited, Garrett stared at my hair, then tentatively reached over and pushed some of it away from my face.

"The wind," he said.

I had on heels today, so I was taller. I could see, more closely, the crease in his bottom lip, the curl of his hair. How his eyes followed me when I took a tiny step to the side.

Then the elevator rang. I stepped in and—though the rest of the elevator was empty—Garrett stood right next to me. His hand brushed mine. I suddenly thought of a museum display we had gone to years ago, how we had entered a dark room with small flashlights and traced trails of light along the walls. Garrett's touch was a small movement—there then gone—but I could almost feel it etched on my skin. Glowing.

"Do you think we'll be able to do well in the last round?" I was babbling. I couldn't stop myself. I could feel the warmth where his skin had touched mine, like a blush. I had indulged for too long. I needed to shut this down. "I should have done more research on the past challenges."

The doors opened. Garrett put a light hand on the small of my back, and we walked out together. The spot felt warm, feverish. This was only a phase. I had to get hold of myself.

Garrett took me by the shoulders. Led me to a huge plaque that listed all the winners of the Zhao competition. Tucked my hair behind my ear. Then he took a photo.

"What—?"

"Enjoy it, Juliana," he said. "We're here."

He wrapped a warm hand around mine and tugged me toward the pristine glass doors. We were here.

The other competitors came in after us, and they were also carefully dressed and nervous. I waved hi to Linda and Kelly, and they smiled and sat next to us. They seemed awed to be in this room. So was I.

Someone offered us beverages (!) and gave us tote bags filled with a mug, a notebook, and a fancy pen. All had the Lee Corporation logo on it. I tried to imagine a world where I had specially branded items in my office, but all I could think about was Garrett, his knee warm next to mine.

"This suddenly seems real," Linda whispered to me, giddy.

"Right?" Focus on the competition and not on Garrett.

On the other side of the table was another team, who I didn't recognize. They took their seats and set up a matching pair of laptops. Eric was at the far end. Seated a few chairs down from him was Albert. They were not looking at each other. Had they split up during the pivot challenge?

I had asked Siobhan how she was doing, as I had promised Eric. Her heartbreak had been replaced by something more metallic by then, something flintier. She had clearly decided she was done with him. Eric continued to appear miserable.

"What do you think is going to happen?" Kelly said. "An interview?"

The glass doors swung open, and James Lee walked in.

We scrambled to our feet.

"Congratulations to all of you," he said. "Please sit."

Across the table, the laptop team curled their hands over their keyboards like they were ready to speed-type their way to victory.

"I have been greatly impressed with all of your efforts thus far," James said. "Unfortunately, there can be only one winner."

Eric was leaned forward, focused. Like he had nothing left to lose.

"You've hopefully learned a lot about marketing and launching your services. Now it's time to apply your skills to a real-world situation."

This was it!

James said, "The Lee Corporation has recently partnered with a new venue. As a corporate sponsor, our name will be prominently displayed on the outside and within the structure, along with other companies, such as BeneCo, Macrogain, and CompuMerica. We are hopeful that this alliance will bring name recognition for our company and products. The place will be a draw for events and concerts, and as people come to the location, they will become familiar with our name and logo."

The laptop team was taking notes on their computers, and Linda and Kelly were scribbling on their notepads.

James was still talking. "The difficulty we currently face is one that should be familiar to you. Our target audience—young concertgoers—currently do not have brand awareness about the location. We would love to create some prelaunch hype before it officially opens. That's where you come in."

Okay. It was similar to our other challenges, only this time instead of marketing our own service, we would be using our skill sets to advertise a place. No problem.

A boy raised his hand, glaring at the person next to him. "Is it too late to do this on our own? Do we have to work with partners?"

James shook his head. "No. But should you decide to split, you will be judged individually."

Kelly scribbled something on her notepad and turned it toward Linda, who then raised her hand.

"When will we be able to find out more about the place? And can we use our preexisting social media platforms?"

James stood up. "Using your previous audience base is what this challenge is all about. It's about redirecting the influence you have developed over the competition and applying it to an unrelated product. This is a very tricky process, one that will showcase all of your skills. For your final task, you will need to create a proposed marketing plan. You will also advertise the space heavily in your own social media accounts and on your website."

This was it. We could totally win this thing. Okay—our audience base was entirely made up of teenagers, so we should focus on items of interest to them. I wondered what type of building it was. Another convention center? Hotel? Hotels had ballrooms, which we could rent out for prom. I hoped it wasn't going to be something too specialized, like a golf course or winery or something.

As we got up to take a tour of the company, Garrett didn't seem to be paying attention to what the others were doing or trying to get close to James Lee. He was only focused on me.

One of my tote bag straps had fallen down, and Garrett carefully put it back over my shoulder. "Are you ready?"

I nodded.

He looked like he was about to say something more but then we were called away. It was time to see the Lee Corporation up close.

The rest of the company was gorgeous. We saw the executive offices, the fancy break rooms, the copy center. The carpet in the hallways wasn't the nubby industrial kind, like at my mother's building. It was thick, plush.

This in itself might be worth all the hours we had put into the competition. A tour, by James Lee himself!

Our last stop was a large conference room, which had a beautiful wooden table in the center and a wall of windows that overlooked the city. On one side was a large paper map of Esher tacked to a corkboard, with a large red circle around part of it.

"What's that?" I asked James.

"The location for your next challenge."

Linda and Kelly rushed to take a closer peek, and the team next to them started whispering excitedly.

"A sports arena."

I processed the words slowly, a syllable at a time. Sports. A-re-na. Arena.

Arena?

I spun toward the map. The marked area was shaded, and the red edge of the circle bisected Old Taipei.

"But that's Donfield's," I said. "Donfield Inc. It's their project."

"During basketball season, it'll be used for games, of course," James said. "But we'll do the concerts and events on the offseason." He opened a laptop, and the smart board in the front of the room started flashing pictures of the layout and proposed interior. He began talking about the seating capacity and proposed schedules and parking, but I wasn't listening.

"But the arena is not your project." I knew I was repeating myself, but I couldn't help it. "It's Donfield's."

Linda elbowed me. "They're one of the corporate sponsors," she whispered.

"What about Old Taipei? And the people who live there?" I asked. "The businesses?" How was he ignoring this most important thing? Didn't he know what was going to happen?

Linda and Kelly looked like they couldn't believe I kept interrupting him. I almost couldn't believe it myself. And yet, the words kept flying out.

"Old Taipei?" James shut the laptop, started walking toward the door. "The people will need to relocate, of course. The businesses can lease some space in other buildings. Listen, the property owners will get a huge boost to their property value. Even parking spaces are going to go up. We're going to make Esher into a city hub. It's a great opportunity for everyone."

"How is that a great—?" I said.

Linda said loudly, "And the marketing plan? Is it submitted electronically?" She tugged at my sleeve and gave a quick shake of her head.

"It's a great opportunity for *landlords*," Garrett said. He had been quiet through the whole tour, but now his voice was loud. Furious. "The renters will be shut out. They're immigrants and people who don't speak English. They won't be able to afford the higher prices."

"We'll work with the city council to make a solution that is acceptable for everyone. We got approval this morning, so we're good to go." The council had already voted? And they approved the construction?

Garrett was already checking his phone. He stopped scrolling and tilted the screen toward me. James was right.

James propped open the door with his foot, glanced at his watch. "All the details of this last challenge will be on our website for your reference. Additionally, as in past years, you will

234

need to participate in a media campaign for the competition, so please fill out a consent form. My assistant will send it to you."

James gave us all a curt goodbye, then strode down the hall. His assistant swooped in and smoothly ushered all of us out.

Garrett and I stood in the lobby, silent, as the doors to the Lee Corporation swung shut.

33

THE DARKEST OF UNDERBELLIES

I WAVED TO Linda and Kelly as they headed toward the elevators. Then I dragged Garrett down the hall where the others couldn't hear us.

"Did he say—?" I said just as he blurted out, "I had no idea. About sponsorship."

I grabbed his arm. "Do the people in Old Taipei know the Lee Corporation is involved? Or that the city council approved the arena this morning?"

He scrolled through his phone. "I don't think so. The news only came out a little bit ago."

"If they approved it, is that it? It's definitely going forward, then? Can they appeal the decision, or is it final?"

Garrett looked at me soberly. "I don't know."

I grabbed his wrist. "We have to change his mind. Maybe it's not too late."

* * *

We ran back to James Lee's office, and after some of my best persuasion skills, Timothy, his administrative assistant, agreed to give us five extra minutes with him. James stared at us from behind his desk as we burst in.

"Ms. Zhao. Mr. Tsai, is it? How can I help you?" He motioned to Timothy to stay.

"We—" I glanced at Garrett. I didn't know where to begin.

"Is this about the competition?" James said. "I'm only allowed to answer clarifying questions. I can't give any guidance."

"It's not about the AABC," I said. "It's about the arena. Um, we had some thoughts on the proposed location. About the people and businesses in Old Taipei who will be affected if you go forward."

I didn't think James was out to destroy Old Taipei, per se. I thought of him in the conference room, checking his watch. It wasn't that he didn't care what happened to the people. He just assumed everyone could easily relocate. Maybe the same way I would have weeks ago.

Someone had to show him. *We* could show him. If we could convince him there was a real, human impact to the arena, they could pick a different location. Ms. Vivian had told us about different potential spaces, like one next to an abandoned industrial park.

James Lee stopped looking polite. "We've already done this analysis."

Garrett said, "If the arena goes up, there will be businesses that will have to be torn down. Apartments that will vanish."

James held up a hand. "They can find new places to live. Different locations for their stores."

"But it's a community," I said. "It'll be decimated."

He stared at both of us for a hard moment, then sighed. "I know you're young, so you haven't thought about these things yet. Let me show you some stats." He called up some files on his smart board. Anticipated revenue. Increases in foot traffic. A five-year projection for how the space would be revitalized. Analysis of the condition of the buildings and the cost to repair them.

He said, "These are buildings that will eventually need millions of dollars in renovations or will have to be torn down, all within a decade. I'm giving landlords the chance to cash out high."

"But what about the renters?" Garrett asked. "They won't be able to afford their places anymore."

"They'll go somewhere else. They can try some of the cities outside of Esher. They're going to lose those apartments, anyway, either to renovations or demolition."

He said it so easily: *They'll go somewhere else.*

James glanced at Timothy, who pointed at his wrist. "You have to remember this is a corporation. It's my duty as its leader to create profit. All the people hired for construction, legal, the sports teams? Everyone who will drive to Esher and shop in the stores? Those are jobs and revenue. The money will pay for libraries, fire departments, free social services. It's not as easy of a question as you might think."

James's phone beeped and a voice came over. He had a call.

"But what about another location?" I said desperately. "For example, there is a big empty space by the industrial park—"

He stood—our cue to leave. "The arena has been approved. We have already analyzed all the potential areas, and I assure you we have picked the optimal spot. Old Taipei is centrally located and is right by a major transport hub. If we go to your industrial park, how are people without cars going to be able to get to the arena?"

We were silent.

"I appreciate your input," he said. "Now—"

"But *Taiwanese* people live there," I said. "They could be your parents. Or mine." Wasn't that what my dad would have cared about?

James's finger was on the speaker phone button, but he didn't push it. "Would you have them live in those conditions? Have you seen the inside of those buildings? I have. Where will the money for the repairs come from?"

I glanced at Garrett. He didn't have an answer, either.

James gave me a hard look. "Everything has a cost. In the end, business is business. And the only way to create any security for yourself is by having money. Your father understood that, all too well. He was the person who taught us the lesson." There was an edge to his words, one I didn't understand. Why was he talking about Dad?

"I don't think he ever would have—" I said.

"He did," he said. "I suggest you search your own family history, Ms. Zhao."

The phone buzzed again.

"You both have a lot of talent," he said, "and I see you want to help others. But how are you going to do that without funds? Without influence? Do you think you're going to be able to do what you want just because? You're going to have to start making choices."

We stumbled out as his call started. What was he saying about Dad? What family history? Eric had said the same thing. What were they talking about?

We slowly headed toward the elevator. I counted how many people were working on this floor. All the cubicles were filled and so were the offices. There were also a lot of support staff. Legal department somewhere. Accountants. All of these were jobs. Jobs that relied on James Lee continuing to create successful projects. He had a point: if they didn't construct the arena, those jobs would be lost. Other people with no income. Either way you went—arena or no arena—someone was losing.

Was this what business really was? Making excruciating decisions in order to make money so some greater good could be achieved? When my mom and her friends talked about success, they only discussed what business school someone went to, what their starting salary was. If their company was big and famous. This was what I was always told was *success*.

But they never talked about the cost of doing business. The things that had to be broken to squeeze the money out. I understood someone had to do it. But for the first time, I thought: Should it be me?

"Is he right?" I hated that I sounded uncertain. Shouldn't I know?

"No," Garrett said. "Absolutely not. We have to fight this."

I let him take my hand. Squeeze it, his grip warm and certain. Then we raced to the cultural center.

It was packed when we arrived. Everyone had clearly heard about the city council's decision; we heard the shouting in Taiwanese and English before we got into the main room. In the front of the room was Ms. Vivian, trying to calm everyone down. Garrett went to go help her.

I spotted Hattie sitting with Kevin at a corner table off to the side. She had out her steno pad and was furiously scribbling notes.

"What are you doing here?" I asked.

She glanced at Kevin. "I had some time after school."

I shot her a Duck Cleaver Glare, and she winced.

"You should go home," I said. "We need to talk to everyone here about some serious stuff."

"I already know what the city council did."

I gave her my best Big Sister look, but she didn't back down. "You should get home before Mom catches you."

Hattie made a face. "I told her I had tennis. And that you were picking me up on the way back home from your SBA meeting. Where you're supposed to be right now, *Juliana*."

We glared at each other, and Kevin said, "Hattie's writing an op-ed about the city council approval and how the arena will impact Old Taipei. People should know about what's going on."

Hattie crossed her arms. "What did Dad always say? If you oppose something, make it expensive for the other side. We have to put pressure on the council by bringing public aware-ness to this issue."

She was right, technically. But I knew Mom would never approve of her going further down the hole toward journalism. Each article she wrote was one step further away from business school or medicine or law.

Hattie pushed her notebook toward me. "Developers wreck-ing Chinatowns and other minority neighborhoods happens all the time—like in Washington, DC, or Philadelphia. I had already prepared an article for the school paper about the arena proposal and the impact it would have on Old Taipei. But I can use the research and tweak it for an op-ed for the city paper."

I flipped through her research, which was carefully tabbed. There were pages of quotes from people she had interviewed, including people on the city council. How had she gotten access to them? She had talked to business owners around Old Taipei, had meticulously detailed the history of the area and what it meant to new immigrants to the country. It was good—really good, actually.

I turned to where she had already started an introduction to her article. The writing was crisp, snappy. Hattie turned away, but I could tell she was sneaking peeks at me while I was reading.

"This is really impressive," I said. Hattie smiled, and the hope in her face crushed something in me. I knew she valued my opinion, but I had never realized how much. I didn't know I had that much influence over her. But of course I did.

But had I been using it responsibly? Guiding her toward

her—not my, not Mom's—best interest?

The chatter grew louder next to us. Chef Auntie strode out of the kitchen with a lid and a wooden spoon, then banged them together. She pointed the spoon at Ms. Vivian.

Ms. Vivian said, in the sudden, pressured quiet, "Don't panic. We have thirty days to appeal the decision. We'll find a lawyer and file the papers." But even she looked worried.

"But if we lose?" someone asked. "What then?"

Ms. Vivian said, "Then it goes forward. There's nothing we can do." The chatter swelled again.

Hattie pulled my arm. "How did you hear about the city council decision? They just announced it. Weren't you at the competition?"

I filled them in about the Lee Corporation's sponsorship and the last challenge for the AABC.

"You have to create a marketing plan for the *arena* as your last challenge?" Hattie said. "What are you going to do, Juju?"

I had no idea.

"You're not going to continue with it, are you?" she said. *"Are you?"*

I didn't know what I was supposed to do. What the right decision was.

When I didn't answer right away, she shook her head. And on her face was the most devastating thing: disappointment.

My mom sprung as soon as we got home.

"Where were you? How did it go?" Mom made a tsk noise: a short, sharp note that never failed to make me tense. It was almost Pavlovian. "Why didn't you wear more makeup? You look tired."

Hattie went upstairs without a word. She had avoided me the rest of the day and hadn't talked to me on the ride home.

"What did they say?" Mom said.

Everything I had found out was still swirling in my head. How could the Lee Corporation do that to Old Taipei?

"There's one more challenge," I said.

Mom was seated at our table with a large bag of raw pea shoots in front of her, carefully separating each bunch and picking out the delicate center. I always thought the outer leaves were also delicious, but she said they were too tough and always threw them away. I pulled a pile of veggies toward me. What was I possibly going to do? About the competition? Garrett? Everything?

"What is it?" she asked. I watched her quickly and efficiently separating the stalks and tendrils, discarding anything that wasn't tender. Pull, pluck, toss. I was a little more merciful and tried to sneak some of the larger leaves into the bowl. But Mom pulled them back out and put them in the compost bin, tsking.

"A marketing thing," I said. If only it were that simple.

Behind her, a Chinese drama played on the television; this one seemed to involve a suspiciously attractive emperor and the bodyguard pretending to be him. I think? My Mandarin really was terrible.

"Why does the emperor need a double?" I asked.

244

"*Ai-ya*, too complicated to explain."

I tried to make my mom watch an American show once. She was utterly baffled, even after we put on the captioning.

"Mom?"

"Hmm?"

What if I win this competition but have to compromise to get there?

What if this is what's necessary to succeed in business and I can't do it?

Is this what Dad had to do? Face these choices?

Behind her was a photo of Dad from the early days of his company. Five young men, their arms slung around each other, bright because the future hadn't shown itself to them yet. Bankruptcy for some. Divorce. And one death.

What was James Lee talking about?

"You know the start-up Dad sent money to?" I asked. "The one Mr. Lee ran? Why did he help them?"

Mom took another bunch of leaves. Pull, pluck, toss. "It was a good thing to do."

A good thing to do. So, were there more important things than making money? Would Dad want me to take this internship—his internship—if it would hurt Old Taipei? And what about Garrett? Would Dad also disapprove of him just because he may never make a high salary? Because of his family?

I wanted to ask her. The questions were like hard marbles on my tongue waiting to be spit out. If I had the bravery, like the people who had written us letters, I would. But I still could not. It would be like hiring a skywriter to advertise that I had *doubts about this most important thing.* For my mom, having uncertainty was a crime in itself. Even looking for answers could lead to only one thing: more problems.

That night, Garrett video-called me. He was wearing dark-framed glasses and his hair was mussed.

"The Lee Corporation is definitely a part of this," he said. "They've been keeping their name off the project publicly so far, but they are one of the primary sponsors."

I had done the same thing, double-checking the facts as if maybe this whole thing was some imagined nightmare.

Garrett said, "I talked to Kevin—the center is gathering funds to file an appeal. But, Juliana . . . what are *we* going to do? About the internship?"

It was an impossible dilemma. If I kept going in the competition and won, I would be supporting the people who would rip apart Old Taipei. But if I quit—or lost—I would have to bear the disappointment—or disownment—from Mom. The judgment of the community. And the knowledge that I had failed my father.

Garrett suddenly covered his mouth. "Sorry, it's hard to have a serious conversation with you when you have those on. Are those designer bunnies?"

I had completely forgotten that my hair was held back by a puffy pink headband with floppy bunny ears. I ripped it off and stuffed it in a drawer. "Hattie got it for me. I was washing my face."

"Is that what you wear when you give love advice? Like how

wizards have wands or psychics have crystal balls?"

"Ha-ha. There's wisdom in those ears."

"Clearly." He smiled, gazing at me. But then he said, "You know Old Taipei isn't only a bunch of stores. It's a community. You've seen it. You know how everyone takes care of each other. What's going to happen when the whole neighborhood is filled with sports bars and tourists? If everyone is gone?"

I didn't have an answer. Because there wasn't one.

"I can't do it, Juliana," he said. "I'm out."

34

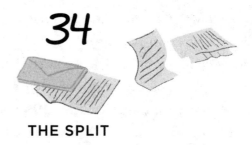

THE SPLIT

IT DIDN'T MATTER that Garrett said it gently. With regret. I'm sure even Mom had some grief when ripping apart our family. All that mattered was that he was willing to do it.

"Even if I continue?" I was too raw to hide it. The vulnerability. "You would still quit?"

"You could support the Lee Corporation? When they're going to wreck Old Taipei?"

The ground was cracking between us, jagged then endless deep. A chasm.

"A lot of other companies are sponsoring the arena. They're not the only one." I knew I was tumbling, desperately grasping for a branch to hold on to. "And even if we drop out, it's not going to change anything." Even I couldn't quite believe that.

"But if we stay, it's like saying what they are doing is okay."

Two separate doors, each leading to a different universe. A different existence.

"What about your scholarship?" I asked.

"I'll work more jobs." He said it lightly, but I knew what it meant for him—juggling multiple work schedules, being exhausted all the time without any hope for a break. "I'm not going to tell you what to do. But you know why I need to quit."

I did. And that was the worst part.

"I can't," I said. "I have to stay."

He could have said, *Then that's it. That's what's important to you so goodbye.* But Garrett was always going past the surface to the heart of things.

"Why?" he asked. There was no sharpness to the question, no challenge. Only this one word, gently floating between us. "Why do you want this internship so badly? I don't think it's because you love the Lee Corporation."

Echoes of James Lee at the networking event: *Why do you want to go to business school? Specifically?*

I specifically didn't want to fail in front of the uncles and aunties. In front of my mother. They had picked the height of the bar for the high jump—they had picked the sport—and I kept running and hurling myself in the air to try and clear it. But I had never asked why. I had never even asked myself if I liked track and field or sports, even. I had just done it.

But underneath every jump was this: a girl who had lost her father.

Garrett was waiting, patiently.

"It's my dad's competition."

I saw everything come together for him, finally, the fragments of me connecting to each other. I had never talked about this with anyone. Even now I couldn't quite look at him directly. I focused instead on the light hitting his face, the shadow next to the small beauty mark by his right eye. "It was the last thing he did, even when he was the sickest. It was his legacy."

I knew Garrett was running through the loops: the competition, my mom, the Linevine, tracing the path of my decisions, how I had gotten here.

"Juliana." The tenderness laced through the syllables made the tears come. "What happens if you don't make it?"

"I have to."

"What if you don't?"

I had been spinning plates for so long. Spin and run and spin, watching the whole system with my heart in my throat.

"Then . . ." I fail him. My mother falls apart again. Our family cracks, irreparably.

"What I mean is," he said, "why does it have to be you? Keeping his memory alive?"

Why did it have to be me? Because it was what was expected. Because I was the last one left when everyone else had a chair and the music stopped. Actually, that wasn't quite true. I think my mom had been doing the same, in her own way, trying to make sure we didn't have a hard life. For him.

"You know why," I said in Taiwanese.

He did. Both of our parents had come here with nothing. They had left everything behind—their families, their language, their dreams. My father spent all his time at his company. Before he had died, I remembered I would sometimes see him on the couch at parties helplessly dozing. My mom had once yearned to become an illustrator, but I had only seen her draw a few times.

What had my parents wanted? They had pushed their own desires so far underneath their sacrifices that they essentially did not exist. I don't think my parents ever had the luxury to ask if they were happy. They asked only if they—and we—were surviving.

There were times when Hattie and I were talking in English or laughing at some pop culture reference my mom didn't understand. She would always get this intensely sad look on her face, like she had given us up, too. She had sacrificed being able to communicate with her own children so we could live well.

After all that, how could I embarrass her in front of the community? Destroy Dad's good name? We carried our parents' hopes and expectations. We carried everything.

That was my answer. Wasn't it? To everything. I had let myself become distracted with Garrett and Old Taipei and the people there, but I couldn't any longer. Like our time together in New Hampshire, all things had to end. We had to get back to the real world. And the reality was that I couldn't have both. I couldn't continue hanging out with Garrett and still keep my mom happy. I couldn't keep our family together like I was supposed to.

"I have to do this competition," I said. "I need to win."

Garrett said, "But what about Old Taipei? What about all

the people we were helping there? Chef Auntie and her restaurant? Uncle Jing and his fortune cookie store?"

If I kept talking to Garrett, he would try and change my mind. He *would* change my mind. Because I could already picture them, the little kids scattered all over town instead of gathering at the center. Auntie Cindy alone in her apartment. Kevin's parents in financial trouble because his mom lost her tutoring location.

And equally as powerful: Garrett. How he had been looking at me lately, with an expression of hopeless surrender. The way his gaze had been hitched to me. He made me want a different life. One I couldn't have. These past few weeks had been magical, but they had also been built on a lie. It wasn't fair to him.

Here was the problem with a highly disciplined brain: it will keep calculating things even if you don't want it to. It will seek solutions.

There was one obvious answer that would solve all these things. It would free Garrett to help Old Taipei and would guarantee that he wouldn't try to change my mind anymore. It would help me honor my dad and keep my family together. It would finally reveal the truth that he deserved to know. And it would end something early before it could hurt us even more.

The only cost would be me.

I looked him in the eye. "I didn't tell my mom I was partners with you."

Garrett staggered as if I had struck him. "What?"

"For the competition. I told her I was doing this with someone from my school." Think of Dad. Think of the family.

252

Think of anything else but the fact that you feel like you are dying, like you are taking a hot blade and carving out your heart. "I did it because she would not have approved of us being partners. You were right about me all along."

I hung up but not before I saw his face, the decimation in it. Then I sobbed.

35

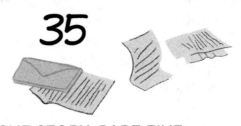

TINY LOVE STORY, PART FIVE

You and I had a summer together. You showed me sketches of things you saw during the day. The twist of a leaf stem. The curve of a back hunched in laughter. The light fingers of a mom on her daughter's hair. I caught myself one afternoon, staring at the whiteness of a flower, surrounded by a field of green. The wisp of a cloud in a beautiful, vast blue.

Until I destroyed us, I thought these daydreams might be enough.

I now understand heartbreak has a color. It is crimson, like blood.

36

Dear Ms. Zhao:

Many congratulations on your accomplishments thus far! I know you have had the opportunity to talk to Mr. Lee and he has detailed the media outreach we would like to do.

Unfortunately, we still have not received your consent form. If you could please complete it and send it back to us at your earliest convenience, we would greatly appreciate it. I have attached another copy for your reference.

We look forward to working with you!

Sincerely,

Timothy Ellis

Assistant to James Lee

37

TIGHTROPE

I HAD READ about heartbreak, of course, and had heard about it. Had seen people, like Eric Lin, wrapped in it, like it was a heavy blanket weighing and muffling everything.

But I had never understood it.

Now I did. It felt like someone had ripped me apart. Like Garrett and I had been entwined and he was torn from me, taking everything with him. I had lived through gutting grief before, but this loss was infected with guilt, the knowledge that I had hurt him.

The house was quiet, so I slipped into Dad's office for answers, to everything.

You are supposed to take shelter under a desk or a doorframe if you are in a room that begins shaking. Something solid that can protect you. But on this day, the one where everything was falling, my shield had cracks. Had I done the right thing?

Would my dad have approved of Garrett? Or would he have sided with Mom? I didn't know. How could I not know?

James Lee had said, *I suggest you search your own family history, Ms. Zhao.* How had he known more than me about my own father?

I started digging through the office, frantically. I started with the file cabinets, yanking out Dad's old papers. The answer to everything had to be in here. To why I had done what I had done. Why I kept hurting everyone even though I didn't mean to.

All of Dad's folders were clearly labeled in his neat handwriting. Three thick ones of our artwork in the front, one for each child. Others with our medical records and preschool progress reports (mine: "Juliana is an unusually focused child and likes to tidy up"). One piece of paper with a sketch of a green blob and the words "I luv you Dady."

The second drawer was more of the same. Hattie and I knew the legend of Dad's business; it had been a tale we had heard since we were children. How Mom and Dad had been struggling before Dad had his patent idea. How he and his team had finished it and sold it to IBM for a comfortable sum, all while he was weak from the chemo. How, as soon as the money came in, he had funneled his portion of the earnings into starting the AABC. Didn't that mean the competition was his intended legacy?

And if it was and I quit it, what did that say about me?

But there were no answers here. I scanned the room. The closet. I tugged open the doors and riffled through the boxes of his old books and notes. Then, when I was searching the top shelf, I found them. A collection of file folders inside a slim box.

There were two labeled "PATENT" and "AA FOUNDA-TION." I read them carefully. There was a balance sheet for Mom and Dad's company, dated before he had sold the patent. I read over the numbers once, twice. Mom and Dad hadn't just been struggling. They had been on the verge of bankruptcy. My mom had never told us.

In another folder, there was an old letter with a familiar letterhead: the Lee Corporation. It was an offer from James Lee's father to partner with Dad to manufacture and distribute the electronic payment system. His patent. But the letter was more than that; it was personal, telling him how he, too, was on the verge of insolvency. Describing how they could join together and save both companies. How their friendship—and their families' friendship—went back to their days in Taiwan.

There was another letter from Dad asking for more details. Another letter from James Lee's father, with a thick file attached, a proposed business plan.

Then . . . nothing. The rest of the file was empty.

I sat on the ground, the papers on the floor around me. I knew how this story ended. Dad had not saved them. The patent was his idea, and he was in charge of the team he had hired to develop the software. He could have easily partnered with his friend's company. Instead he had sold the patent to IBM. And taken the paycheck.

James had said, *The only way to create any security for yourself is by having money. Your father understood that, all too well. He was the person who taught us the lesson.*

Dad had turned his back on his friend. When it was time to choose between helping his friend or making a lot of money, my father chose money. Did it matter if, later on, he left them a generous amount in his will that allowed them to get back on their feet? That he started the AABC and left it to his friend?

All of it happened after his portion of the money came in, months later. During that time, had the Lee family lost all their finances? Suffered?

I had designed my whole life around Dad's, following his path the best I could. I had given up parties in order to study, held my tongue to keep the peace, taken care of Hattie without complaint. I had spent years trying to decipher his last wishes, had thought it was to keep our family together no matter what. Thought it was to uphold his name, his honor.

I put the file down. But the answer had been here all along, in these papers. Those hadn't been his priorities at all. I just hadn't understood it. But now that I did, I wished with every part of my being that I did not.

I thought of Garrett's face, the shattered expression. How I had not chosen him, like Dad had not chosen Mr. Lee's start-up. Maybe I was more like my father than I thought. For once, that brought me no comfort.

That night, my mom poked her head into my room.

"Did you have dinner?"

I had not. Losing Garrett had hollowed me out. Finding out about Dad's patent had numbed whatever remained. I could only process one line, over and over:

The only way to create any security for yourself is by having money.

Dad sold his patent to IBM instead of helping Mr. Lee. That's how we kept the house after he died, how we paid for our school and extracurricular activities and cars. How we were going to pay for my college. My damned Ivy League degree. He had chosen the payout above everything else.

I knew Mom went to work every day at what remained of Dad's company, even though we were not entirely dependent on the income. After Dad sold his patent, their company had been in the process of transitioning into accounting and tax software, and under my mom's leadership as CEO, they had successfully done it. It was less lucrative but more steady. But without Dad's payout, we certainly wouldn't be living the way we were living now. We would have had to move to a different neighborhood, would have seen Mom even less. And there would be more days of her crying when she thought we couldn't see her.

Had Dad traded his friendship for our comfortable life? Would he have wanted me to do the same? I was haunted by him but also by this alternative life where he had lived. Would I have been able to make different choices? Be with who I wanted to? Or would it have been the same?

"Did you eat?" Mom asked.

I said yes, even though it was a lie.

"You keeping your grades up?"

"Yes."

Mom scanned me, like she was checking off a list. Healthy,

okay! School—on track. College applications, almost done. Great, next. But what she didn't see: heartbreak. How it was piercing every cell, bursting them.

"Mom?"

She turned to me, but I knew her mind was already gone, lost to lists and phone calls and emails that needed to be returned.

I had done everything by myself for so long. I had helped Hattie, chosen my own classes, set my own schedule. Never made a fuss. I had never had any guidance, only pressure to *get things done*. To produce results. And I always had.

But now, I was at the bottom. I thought of all those people emailing us questions, sending their vulnerabilities out into the ether with nothing but faith that an answer would return. That they would get direction. I thought Dad would always lead my way. But that compass had broken. I was, in all ways, lost.

"How did Dad decide to sell his patent?" I needed to know the truth about this, at least. I had to find out who he was. To face it, even if it was ugly. "What happened with him and Mr. Lee, before?"

Other parents, like Maria's mom, might have immediately picked up on the randomness of this question. Would have seen my expression and known something was wrong. Would have asked what was going on. But my mom was not like other parents.

"Nothing." She straightened up the sweater hanging on my chair. "He left Mr. Lee a lot of money. And the AABC."

I wondered if she would tell me even if he had done something

261

terrible. If she would ever crack the golden memory we had of him. If she could bear to do it herself. Or even—worse yet—if she thought what he had done was totally fine. Necessary.

Was a compromise okay? And if so, when? If I won the competition and got into Yale and later did things to help the world, would it be bad? A net benefit for society so it was acceptable? How about if I won the competition, went to Yale, and worked for a few years making a lot of money so I would have more money to donate later? What about then? What if I started a large corporation, then created a nonprofit wing to give back? If I . . . became James Lee?

Mom started leaving.

"What if . . ." Courage, Juliana. I knew the internship was supposed to be the launching pad to everything my mom had ever wanted: Yale, Harvard Business. Security. But what if it came at a price? Like Old Taipei? Garrett? This was the hard question I had to be brave enough to ask.

My mom was wearing her worn robe, which she refused to replace. She never spent money on herself beyond what was necessary. She used everything she had—every effort, every cent—on catapulting our family into the upper echelon. Creating safety and security. She put all of her chips on three spots: me, Hattie, and Bella, and prayed every day that our numbers would be called as the winners.

But the memory of Bella cradling her pregnant stomach kept haunting me. *All you care about is your* status. *What about what's really important?*

Dear Sunny and Cloudy: What is the good life? Is it worth it?

"Why won't you call Bella?" I said.

"What?"

"It's been so long," I said. "Can't you take the first step?"

Mom was already turning. The discussion was over. "She's made her choices."

"What choice, Mom?" I was desperate to know what options Mom thought she had. I had assumed it was an easy thing for Bella to do, leaving us. But my lens had cracked over these last weeks, and everything was now a kaleidoscope. A memory came to me now, of Bella's last visit, her packing her things and sobbing. Coming to my room and Hattie's, pressing her old favorite stuffed animals into our hands. Hugging us so tightly. At the time, did she know Mom would cut us off from her, too? That we would be part of her penalty? She must have. "She had a *baby*. What was she supposed to do?"

I had to understand what happened. Now that I, too, had given up something. I needed to know what the end point was. When it would be enough.

"She should never have been in that situation in the first place." Mom said it like she was discussing how hydrogen and oxygen make water or how fire can burn wood. Something factual and inarguable.

"She fell in love, Mom. She had a child."

"You don't understand."

"So tell me."

"If I call her now, it's like saying what she did was okay.

That I approve of her throwing away all of her work, all of her education."

"She's not throwing away anything," I said. "And why does it even matter? It's her decision to make."

I shouldn't keep pressing. I should drop it, but I couldn't. All the things roiling within me—the internship, Dad's patent, Garrett—these were all branches from the same tree. And I felt like they all had their roots with Bella.

"So you think, what? That I should stand by while she makes these mistakes?" Mom said. "She has a baby. She is not married. She has no job and dropped out of medical school. And if this Wesley leaves her, what does she have? You tell me."

"She has her choices, Mom. She has her own life. And she should have us, no matter what."

"We didn't come here so you and Hattie and Bella would have a hard time. I didn't give up everything for that," she shouted. "And you think you shouldn't have to think about others? About your community? Who helped us after Wàigōng and Wàipó died? Who watched you when we had to fly back to Taiwan for Yéye's funeral? We don't have anyone else here. We only have each other."

I did remember how Auntie Liu had come every day after Dad had died, how she had cooked and cleaned for us when we were all drowning in grief.

"But why do you care what they think?" I asked. "More than your family?"

"This *is* for our family. You think you are separate? You think Bella is separate?" my mom said. "You are a reflection of

264

us. Your choices are the family's choices. Your mistakes are the family's mistakes. If you are blessed with a family, that's what comes with it."

"That makes zero sense. I am an individual. If Hattie, what, commits murder, then somehow it's my fault?" We were the old riddle about the three people describing different parts of an elephant not realizing that they were talking about the same animal. Mom was the trunk and I was the tail, and we couldn't understand each other at all.

"Yes." My mom wasn't kidding. "It's your responsibility."

"That's totally messed up!" I said. "And not all of your friends think this way. When Betty Yu wanted to work in Hollywood, Auntie said she was proud of her for being brave. And when Michael Chu married someone from the Netherlands, his parents had no problem with it."

My mom pulled her robe tighter around herself, retied it with a crisp knot.

"Your life has been so easy," Mom said. "Nice house, classes, college all paid for." I saw the ever-present grief under the surface, the undertow. "I promised your dad that you would have a good life. Better than ours."

"But—"

But the discussion was over. "Don't you dare be like your sister."

I had done everything she had asked me to. But Hattie wasn't talking to me. I had lost Garrett. And our family was still broken. I wasn't anywhere close to happy. Close to the good life.

Mom looked away.

"Don't you *miss her?*" I said. "I do."

For the first time, I saw my mother crack. She bowed her head, and I saw all the lines of her age, all of her decisions and hopes, all she had to do by herself after Dad died.

Then she strode out, slamming the door behind her.

38

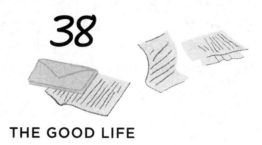

THE GOOD LIFE

I GRABBED MY phone.

There were a few texts from Maria and Tammy. I was tempted to write them back and tell them what happened with my mom. But I didn't. They would support me, but this wasn't the world they lived in. They had their own issues and concerns—equally as important, of course—but I wouldn't know where to begin with explaining mine. If I even could. Everything was too snarled, confusing.

There were a few more messages from some people in the SBA asking about the fundraiser. For the first time, I realized we weren't really close even though I spent a lot of time with them. I never wanted to share my problems since I was worried that would shatter my image. Just as my mom had taught me. But that meant no one was close enough to call to talk about *this*.

Hattie was still mad at me. I had tried to speak to her in the kitchen, but she gave me her own version of the Duck Cleaver Glare. Later on, she shoved articles under my door about Old Taipei and stories about other communities where similar things had happened. She was definitely out.

I was alone.

I wandered over to my computer, listlessly scrolling through the blog. The advice column. Our email account, which was filled with unread messages. Even though that part of the competition was over, people were still contacting us, especially after the #CandybarChallenge.

My best friend and I like the same person. Help!

My boyfriend's parents don't approve of me. So we're dating in secret. Should I be putting up with this?

My girlfriend's religious but I'm not. Now she wants to break up. What should I do?

There they were, question after question, a chorus of voices, all asking us for answers. For certainty. But mine had snapped.

I thought of the tent in Hattie's room. I wanted the days of snuggling with my sisters in the warm yellow light while the smells of browning garlic and onions and ginger floated upstairs. I wanted the days when I didn't even know what it was to think of the future. Where every minute was just a thing that passed, popping like a happy bubble.

I wanted the days when I had certainty, when my parents' word was the truth. *Always wash your hands with soap and count to ten before rinsing. Brush your hair every night or you will get tangles. Don't eat wild mushrooms off the ground.*

We listened. Our lives were better, our hair never had to get hacked due to a huge, unfixable knot, and we never had to go to the hospital for accidental food poisoning. We had no reason to doubt. We didn't even know what doubt was.

If this was adulthood, could I give it back?

I wore my parents' faces on my own. I shouldered their dreams and fears and aspirations. I endured their friends' scrutiny and whispers, the community's opinions, the weight of being measured against a bar that was just a little out of reach. But though my pack was heavy, I carried nothing for myself.

39

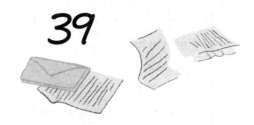

Dear Sunny (and Cloudy),

What happened to Cloudy? Where are his answers?

Signed,

Wondering in the Windy City

Dear Sunny and Cloudy,

No offense, but your answers lately have kind of sucked.
I like your website but thought you should know.

Signed,

Honesty over Modesty

40

PLAYING WITH FIRE

I FOUND MYSELF at Auntie Beth's bookstore after school. I stood outside the window, watching the people inside. I knew from Hattie's socials that they were holding an organizational meeting here today to coordinate a protest against the arena. I didn't know what I was doing here. I knew exactly what I was doing.

Auntie Beth was passing Auntie Cindy a book on knitting and a small bag of yarn. Chef Auntie was at a table, painting some sandwich boards and signs with a group of little kids. Uncle Jing—well, he was scowling, per usual, but he did help this older auntie with a walker sit down in a stuffed chair. He got her a cup of tea. Then he continued scowling.

"Juju?" Hattie was in the doorway of the store. She stepped out, closing it behind her. "What are you doing here?"

"I . . ." I couldn't think of an excuse.

Hattie had a huge stack of books in her arms, a collection of her favorite romances.

"What are those?" I asked.

"What, now you care?" But she wasn't as edgy as I had expected. I knew I looked terrible. I hadn't slept in days, and I missed Garrett with a force that was almost annihilating. I peeked behind her into the store. But he wasn't there.

"Hattie, I—"

She looked away. Then Ms. Vivian came out. "Juliana!" She pulled me inside.

I awkwardly stood in the front. Everyone must know by now about the Lee Corporation and how they were sponsoring the arena. How I was continuing in the AABC. I waited for the whispers, the shunning. The dropping feeling of shame, the sink of it, was almost unbearable. This was a huge mistake.

"I'm sorry," I said. "I can't . . . I can't help you today."

I turned, but Ms. Vivian put her hand on my arm. "It's okay," she said.

No, it's not. "It's . . . the competition. I can't."

Hattie grabbed Kevin, who had wandered over, and stomped off.

"I heard." Ms. Vivian seemed like she was debating whether or not to speak. "It's your dad's, right? Didn't he start it?"

"Yes."

"There are some things that have no easy answers." She smiled sadly.

I had heard that Kevin's dad grew up in a wealthy family in Taiwan and had come to America for his graduate studies. His mom was also Taiwanese but came to America when she was young and was raised in New York. They eventually got married, even though his dad's parents opposed it and disinherited him. They ended up staying in America and made their own way. But they had never been very financially successful, and things had been even worse since his father's business had gone bankrupt.

My mom would have said that Kevin's parents had made a mistake, that they shouldn't have gotten married. But I thought of Kevin and his mom, how close they were. I once saw Kevin's dad give his shoulder a squeeze like, *I am proud of you for just existing.* It had stuck in my memory since it was so unusual. Their family had none of the suppressed resentment or secrets that the other Taiwanese kids seemed to have with their own parents. I knew Ms. Vivian loved teaching, even if it didn't bring in a high salary.

I cradled my dad's jade key chain in my hands, felt the coldness of it. The edges.

She said, "Your sister used to come to the cultural center a lot, did you know that?"

"Hattie?" I said.

"No, Bella."

What? I knew she had disappeared for stretches of time after she went to college, when the fighting was bad. I had no idea she had gone there.

"She used to teach English to the little kids. But I think she wanted a place where she could think."

I could understand that. At points, Mom and Bella couldn't

even be in the same room together.

"I know your mom—and a lot of the parents—have certain . . . beliefs. And our generation, we feel like it's an either-or. We're in between; we have one culture we're taught and another we have to live in. So it feels like we have to choose. But we have the gift—or curse—of being able to see all sides. We can see the best and the shortcomings of both. Do you know what I mean?"

I felt like she was trying to give me a blueprint, a bag of tools, but I didn't quite understand how to use them. I shook my head.

"These are hard choices, Juliana," she said. "They are. But it's okay to be uncertain. You'll never get grief about not knowing or taking time to figure things out. At least not from me."

I hugged her then, tight, and her arms came around me. Bella used to hug us like this, like she could squeeze all the bad out. So had my dad. Was this what family was? Not being responsible for other's mistakes or controlling them? Maybe it was being there for the people you loved, always. Even when things were tough. Especially when they were tough.

Ms. Vivian wiped my face, then gave my shoulder a squeeze. She pushed me toward Hattie. "Talk to your sister. I think you have things to say."

I found her in the back staff room, decorating a sandwich board for the protest.

"Hattie," I said.

She stared at me. Then she said, "You look like shit."

"Language."

"Okay, crap. Wait, you know what? I'm sixteen. You look like *shit*."

I took the seat next to her.

"Why aren't you talking to Garrett? He looks worse than you."

He did? The claws of guilt, sharp, tightened.

"I—" I couldn't talk about him without tears.

Hattie colored furiously on a sign that read, "DOWN WITH THE LEE CORPORATION!"

She snapped, "I don't understand you. You've spent so much time at the cultural center and in Old Taipei. You know what this arena will do. How can you continue with the competition?"

Hattie was like my mom, where she wanted to talk about all crimes all at once. But then she saw my face, and her anger seemed to dissolve. "You really do look awful."

I hung my head. I didn't know where to begin. How my life had become such a mess.

Hattie waited. I had never openly talked about things with her before, but everything in me was swirling, and she was one of the few—if not the only person—who could understand.

"I lied to Mom," I said. "I said Louis Park was my partner for the competition."

Hattie stopped coloring, her marker over the sign. "What?"

I pressed my hands to my eyes, wanting the pressure and the darkness. I wanted to fall into the void, to pretend everything else didn't exist. I wanted to be in a box, sinking into the blessedly cold and empty sea. "And I told Garrett, a few days ago."

Hattie's eyes widened. "Spill everything. Right now."

And so I did. From the beginning. Garrett and I working on the competition together. How we had gotten closer during the challenges. How we had become friends in New Hampshire two summers ago. Hattie could already guess what Mom had said about him and his family at the end of camp, but I told her anyway. She became more and more serious as I talked, and I knew she was thinking of Bella. What had happened with her.

"Is that why you cut him off?" she asked. "Because Mom would have disapproved?"

"He had a right to know what I did." I picked up the black marker. Traced thick lines on the outside of the letters. "I know I hurt him. But it's better for everyone if I stop it now. Whatever *it* is."

Hattie fiddled with the markers on the table, absently arranging them by color. She may want to forge her own path, but there were still some ways we were alike.

"I know you put everyone else in the family first, including me," she said. "But you don't always have to."

Didn't I?

Hattie seemed to be considering her words carefully. "Is giving up Garrett and Old Taipei what you really want? Ignore me and Mom," she said. "What do *you* want? We'll be fine."

Would she? Hattie was and always would be my mèi mei. The one I should take care of. But I thought of Hattie's fight for Old Taipei, her meticulous notes for her article, how much she had done on her own. How she would have to be on her own next year without me.

Hattie still looked so much like her younger self, with her rounded cheeks and hair that stuck up a little in the back. But maybe I needed to do for her what my mom hadn't done for me. I needed to see her for what she was now. An individual.

"Hattie?" I said.

She fiddled with her markers.

"I know I'm sometimes too . . ." Bossy? Overbearing? Like Mom? ". . . much. You've done a lot on your own these past few weeks." It wasn't just the article. Hattie had prepped everything for school and tennis and her lessons on her own. Maybe she hadn't really needed me. Maybe she hadn't for a while. "I'm sorry."

Hattie hugged me. And I felt, finally, that one thing was back to its proper place. She said, "Think about it. Okay, Juju? Think about what *you* want."

And there it was. The most profound question, from my baby sister.

I picked up a few of the markers. Helped her color in part of her sign. And let my mind wander. Dream.

After we finished the sandwich board, Hattie left to show the others what we had made. I stayed in the room because I was too tired to move. Outside, I could hear some laughing and cheering. Ms. Vivian must have gotten a bullhorn from somewhere, and I could hear her chanting, "LET'S GO, LET'S GO!"

I put my arms on the table, put my forehead on them. It was blessedly dark.

What did I want?

Hattie's question tore through me. Not *What does Mom want?* Not *What would have made Dad happy?* Not *What was I supposed to do?*

What did *I* want?

The images came first, before I could form them into words: the hugs from the people in the cultural center as I walked in. The feeling of belonging as I helped the little kids with their projects. Garrett, head tilted, looking at me and trying to hold in a smile. A singular candle on a birthday cake, for the one person who never got a day to herself.

The wrap of my father's hand around mine as we walked into the store, before I knew the future would take him from me. My dad's warm hug when things were tangled, knowing he could be the brush pulling through the knots, helping to straighten everything out.

My dad. I wanted my dad, even if he hadn't been who I thought he was. Even when I didn't know what it meant to love him, knowing what he had done to Mr. Lee and his family. I would still give up everything to see him again.

The burst of grief over everything that had happened during this past week was too much. I started crying. All the boxes I had pushed out to sea—all the things I had not wanted to think about or feel—were shooting to the surface and bursting open, and I no longer had the energy to keep them down.

I felt a light hand on my shoulder. I thought it was Hattie.

But when I lifted my head, I saw Garrett. Rumpled, unsmiling, unforgiving. But here.

Hattie was right. He did look terrible; he had dark shadows under his eyes and his black hair was mussed. My brain—my logical, linear mind—knew he was rightfully furious and disappointed with me. But the rest of me was an instrument with only one chord: *Garrett* and *Garrett* and *Garrett*.

I wiped my face. "What are you doing here?"

He shoved his hands into his pockets. "I came to help and Kevin's mom told me she saw you go back here."

He still came to see me, even though he was mad? But I knew from the way he was standing, stiff, that nothing had been resolved between us. Nor should it have been, not after what I had done.

He asked, "Why are you crying?"

The one person I wanted to talk to the most—him—was the one person I had no right to speak to anymore. But I couldn't help it. "I've messed everything up."

He didn't say anything, but he didn't leave, either.

I had nothing to lose. No way to make this worse, so I might as well be honest. Let him see all of it, my terrible self.

I said, "I tried my best to make everyone happy. I helped Hattie, I listened to my mom, I tried to win the AABC for my dad."

"But?" It was a word with no inflection, giving no clue as to what he was thinking.

"But I screwed things up with Hattie—she thinks I'm trying to control her life. My mom still has no idea that Mrs. Lin was the one behind Eric dumping me, and the competition . . . is going to hurt Old Taipei. I don't know what the right thing to do is anymore. The more I try, the more I wreck everything."

Garrett had the cold beauty of a statue, revealing nothing.

I stared at the table, at the chipped particleboard on the edges. "And I ruined everything with you."

This was the part where I had to be honest. I hadn't understood what love was, before. I had thought it was sparks and attraction. But the foundation to a real connection was this: raw truth. Even if it hurt.

"I told myself that I lied because my mom would give you a hard time," I said. "But it was because I was scared, and it was easier not to."

Even if we became strangers later, there was a part of me that would always know Garrett—the bits of his past he had told me, the things he liked. The way he looked at the world. But I had lost the parts of him that he would give to others: his affection, the gift of his attention, the secret corners of his personality that he let only a few people see. That thought, more than anything, made me start crying again. Because I had those parts and had squandered them. "It took me too long to understand that my mom was wrong. She judged you and your family, and I had, too. I don't expect you to forgive me, but I am sorry."

Garrett's expression didn't change. But there was a slight tic along the side of his jaw, the barest movement. "What were you scared of?" he said, finally.

"What happened to Bella."

The emotions were all held in the corners of his mouth:

scorn, incredulity, and something unnamed. Softer. "That your mom would cut you off?"

I nodded.

"But couldn't anything make her do that? Not just . . . me?"

And there was the heart of it. How quickly he had realized what had taken me so long to figure out.

If everything would lead to pain, to disownment, then what? How do you decide if you should move forward or not?

Things always seemed so clear to my mom. So simple. "My mom always told us to take the safe route," I said. I didn't know if I was talking to him or myself. What I was trying to figure out. "That's what she did. She studied hard, took the highest paying job even though it wasn't in a field she liked, always tried to excel. Saved a lot of money, just in case."

Garrett stared at me, soberly.

"But even with all that . . ." And there it was, in front of me: the truth. Horrifying and undeniable. ". . . still the most terrible thing happened."

It was as shocking as it was indisputable.

Risk—devastation—is always there, whether you want it or not. You can't plan around it, avoid it with hard work, or control it.

Our family had ended when I was eleven. We had shattered in a cold hospital room on an ordinary Friday, in the space of a stopped breath. But in all this time, over all the years since Dad died, we had ignored one very important fact.

"We survived," I said slowly.

Something flickered across Garrett's face.

The worst thing happened, and we still lived.

I had wanted to avoid pain; we both did. Garrett, heartbreak; me, tearing my family apart. But we were both asking the impossible. No matter what you do, you can't get around pain.

And if it was unavoidable, then what were we doing?

There is a cost to not taking chances, to giving up what you could have done. There is something lost. This I now understood.

I dared to reach across, put my hand on top of Garrett's. He jumped.

"I'm so sorry," I said. "For everything."

I almost saw it, a crack in his expression. But he said nothing as I packed up my things and left him in the room, alone.

I dashed out of the store. I needed to see my mom.

41

Dear Ms. Zhao,

This is a follow-up to my prior email. As you may recall, certain paperwork must be filled out so we can begin our media campaign for the Asian Americans in Business Competition. If you could return the completed consent form back to our office at your earliest convenience, we would greatly appreciate it.

Sincerely,

Timothy Ellis

Assistant to James Lee

42

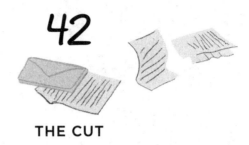

THE CUT

I READ THE email and printed out the consent form. Held it like the bomb it was. Sometimes the truth comes from a hidden file. A secret spilled. Or it can come from something else.

My mom was at the table, and I carefully slid the unsigned paper in front of her. Then I explained the whole thing: the last challenge, what it would do to Old Taipei, what I had learned from the people in the cultural center. Why the form was still blank.

Mom was surrounded by a bunch of receipts and her laptop. She looked like I had suddenly started breaking out into an a cappella version of "The Sound of Music."

"What?" she said. "Too fast, Juliana. I don't understand." I switched to Taiwanese and explained again. Her expression sharpened, re-formed into the Duck Cleaver Glare.

"I thought you said the last one was a marketing challenge," she said.

I needed to have the courage to speak. Garrett may never see it, but I was going to be brave. "It *is*. But for an arena that will destroy Old Taipei. All the businesses are going to be driven out of the neighborhood. The venue is going to bring in a lot of new restaurants and sports bars. The neighborhood will be destroyed."

"It's so old there," she said. "Do you know how many people have invested in the Lee Corporation?"

People? Or her friends? It was obviously the latter. And before I could stop it, I felt it: the smallness of disappointment. That what she cared about was my opposition of the community.

"When was the last time you went to Old Taipei?" I said. "The people who live and work there are just trying to survive."

"That's America," she said. "You think it was so easy when Daddy started his business? We had to move, you remember? Because it was cheaper to have the company here."

"But how can we not help? Some of those people have lived there for years. Decades. This is their community. Their family. It's like you and your friends."

"They can make a new one. It's not your worry."

I had always been told what to do, what was important, what was best. Until the AABC, it had never occurred to me that there were other options. Or that things I had always been told could be more nuanced, or wrong.

285

But they were.

The more questions I asked, the further I could feel myself drifting. Hiding things from my mom, swimming away. I was supposed to be the anchor, the dock. I didn't want my mom to be like Auntie Cindy, alone in her old age, wrapped in loneliness. I had already lost two family members. I didn't want Mom to be next.

But maybe pain *was* inevitable. If it wasn't Old Taipei, it would be the college I wanted to go to, the city I wanted to live in. The boy I wanted to be with.

Mom said, "Don't throw everything away, like your sister." She grabbed a pen and pushed it toward me.

I normally would have thrown myself over the iridescent anger that I was feeling. But I, for once, didn't want to smooth things out.

"Why." I was trying not to shout—I was trying to remember Dad's advice to hold the calm, but I couldn't help it. Most of my life had been spent trying not to drown in the huge wake of Bella's choices. But she had been terrified and alone and forced to make impossible decisions. She had only been a few years older than I was now, holding the weight of another life in her hands. Something she had to protect. "Why do you always say that?"

"Because she had everything and wasted it," she said.

"It wasn't a waste," I said. "Maybe there are some things more important than internships and college applications."

"No. There aren't. This is your future."

"Is it? Is it the end of everything if I don't win the competition?

If I don't get into Yale? If I . . . date someone who isn't going to be a doctor or engineer?"

The form was right there. I could have signed it, ended this conversation. But I wanted to know if she would do it. If she would say it.

"You shouldn't have to ask," Mom snapped. I saw the one thing I never expected: fear. I had heard her calls at work, had sat in meetings where people were condescending toward her because she was an Asian woman, one who spoke with an accent. But the one thing that could never be denied was her impeccable résumé, her degrees from National Taiwan University and Stanford. I knew she had come from a poverty I could not imagine, one I had the privilege of never experiencing.

Mom thought I was balanced on a point, that a push in one direction or another would cause me to topple forever, back into the dark abyss of her own childhood.

"I won't allow you to ruin everything," Mom said. "I promised your father . . ."

Had promised him what? That we would marry rich Taiwanese boys and get Ivy League degrees? We would win his competition? No matter the cost?

"You quit this competition, and I will not forgive you." Mom didn't have to say the words: *You'll be out of this family.*

It was years after she had said the same thing to Bella, and I saw now, with older eyes, the details I had missed under the anger. The panic. The desperation. This was the last card in her hand, the one she thought she had no option but to play.

Mom walked away, her steps precise, cold.

It was the moment I had both been dreading and preparing for. There was a part of me that had held on to a small fragment of hope. I had always been the good child. I had always followed the rules. She could never do it to me.

But she had.

It was more devastating than I could have imagined.

43

IF I COULD write a letter to myself, I would ask this:

> Dear Sunny and Cloudy:
>
> A person I love is forcing me into an impossible choice. I
> know why they did it, but I'm a mess. What do I do?
>
> Signed,
>
> Broken

44

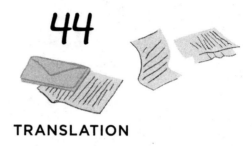

TRANSLATION

I NOW KNEW what Mom was capable of. What she could do, to me.

I thought about what Ms. Vivian had said, about how we were raised by one culture but living in another. If I took my situation and examined it in American light, the answer would have been clear: love is not conditional, and it should be freely given and expressed. Things that infringed on your personal autonomy were not to be tolerated. This was not love, in America. She did not love me.

But for my mom and her friends, love was more complicated. My mom had always taught us to uphold our family and our name. Parents saw it as their duty to fix their kids, to pressure them to be the best they could be. That, to them, was love.

I don't know if it was this way with all Asian families or even with all Taiwanese ones. But it was true of my parents and their friends, so it was therefore true for us, too. They told us the sky was pink, and even though we saw blue, there was always a tiny part of us that would forever be looking for the shades of rose.

What would my father say? *Love is keeping our family together.*

My mom would say, *I will cut you off if you don't do as I ask. Love is keeping you safe from what I judge to be bad decisions, no matter what.*

My American friends would say, *That's manipulation.*

My mom's friends would say, *How do you show love to your parents? You respect their wisdom.*

Bella would say, *You can't control me.*

But what would *I* say?

In the olden days, they used to torture people by tying a horse to each appendage and then sending the four off in different directions. At some point, the body can't keep itself together; the pressure was too much.

Bella had sliced off her own limbs, left them behind so the rest of her could survive. I could do the same but for our family: I could abandon Old Taipei and what I knew was right.

But what if there were things—people—I couldn't give up? At what age can you stop saying, *It was because my parents told me so*, and take responsibility for your actions? When do you have to finally admit that your choices are who you are?

I didn't think there was a set timeline, but I had the sinking feeling it was right around this moment. Now.

I pounded on Hattie's door.

She opened it immediately and pulled me in.

"What's going *on*?" she asked. "Mom never yells at you."

I sat on the edge of her bed, staring at the little crooked seams of the tent, the mismatched and worn fabric. I thought of this little toy Hattie used to have, a sphere made of different pieces. If you pulled out one, the whole structure separated and you were left with a handful of crooked pieces that had to be fitted together again. My heart felt like that, with the parts all scattered, each with a different name: Garrett, Mom, Dad, Bella.

But now I had an ally. My sister.

I told her about what Mom had said, what she wanted me to do. About my visit with James Lee and what he had said about Old Taipei and the arena. And then about Dad's patent. I still couldn't make sense of it. That had been the constant undercurrent, discordant. When I got to the last part, about how Dad had picked IBM over his friends, Hattie rolled her eyes.

"How did you not know that?" she said. "Haven't you been in his office?"

"Were you snooping in his stuff?"

"Weren't *you* snooping?"

Fine. Fair point.

"But you missed one huge piece," Hattie said. "Didn't you see the date? When he first started trying to finalize the patent and sell it to IBM?"

I shook my head.

"It was in January 2018."

What? Dad had died that December. January was when he had first gone to the doctor. When he was first diagnosed.

When he knew he would no longer be around to take care of us.

Everything was whirling. "So, did he . . . did he sell his patent to IBM because of us?"

"I don't know," she said. "But doesn't it make sense? Why else would he do it? Remember how sick he was? But he kept working all those late nights?"

I had blocked all that. It was too painful.

How could a daughter not know her own father? Shouldn't I understand, at a cellular level, who he was? What he wanted and why he did what he did?

But the truth was empty, and silent.

"I don't know what to do," I said.

In Hattie's face, I saw her six-year-old one, small and young.

"I can't continue the competition, Hattie," I said. "I know that now. But if I don't—"

"—she'll cut you off." She stared at me, her eyes huge. "Are you asking me for advice, Juju? Me?"

I nodded.

"She's not going to change," she said finally. "It's like we don't even see the world with the same colors. All the things that she thinks are important . . . aren't. Not to me."

"So I should finish the competition?"

Hattie gazed at the ceiling, as if asking for a ray of patience to be beamed at her from the skies. "No. It's your life. Mom is trying to control you, like she controls everything. But be honest: you don't want to help the Lee Corporation. I can tell. You just don't want to disappoint Mom."

And there it was: what no one else—not even I—had dared to say. But it wasn't the Lee Corporation. It wasn't Yale. It was that the competition was Dad's. It was something of his, and if I could get it, if I could reach it, I could—

—I could bring him back.

That's what this—what all of this—had been about, really. Every late night, every grade, every step I took toward business school and his alma mater and winning this competition. I was trying to resurrect all the pieces of him and put him back together.

I was crying, and Hattie looked at me, panicked.

"It's his," I said, and Hattie understood immediately. "How can I quit?"

"It *was* his," Hattie said. She suddenly hugged me, her arms tight. She was almost my height now. "But it's *not him*, Juju."

So much had fallen in the past few weeks. My beliefs about what was important, how things were valued, how I was valued. But this last bit of truth was the last block supporting the entire structure, the keystone. And now everything was tumbling.

"So, what do I do?" My voice was small.

"Say no, Juju," Hattie said. "For the first time in your life, say no."

I didn't know she had been watching me so closely, but of course she had. The same way I had been analyzing my mom, the way I had always longed to study my dad. Maybe that's also what family was.

I didn't have to win the competition. I laid this sentence out like a ribbon on a frozen lake and then stepped on it, carefully.

I didn't have to go to Yale. Another step.

I could make my own choices. I waited. I didn't fall in the water.

I could ask for what I want.

I could *ask for what I want.*

Everything was in rubble at my feet, but I could still stand. Pick up a board and try to put it up again. Nail it to another and another until I could, perhaps, create something new.

But there was one thing I had to do first: I had to repair our family. Repair all of us.

I said, "I'm sorry I kept trying to do everything for you."

Hattie used to wear my old clothes, would sneak into my room to steal my earrings and necklaces. My mom used to take pictures of us in the same clothes in the same parts of the house and then hang them side by side. But now Hattie was wearing entirely unfamiliar sweaters and dangly earrings that I would have only worn in a dire emergency. She had put some temporary hair dye on the tips of her hair and wore chipped, sparkly blue nail polish.

I had heard about how helpful she had been at the cultural center, how she was always the first to volunteer. Chef Auntie herself had come to rely on her. And at Auntie Beth's bookstore? Hattie had come up with an idea to pair romance books with the #LocalLove blogs and advertise them in the front.

"I'm trying to be better." I squeezed her hand.

"Really?"

"Yes," I said. "I'm going to let you do things on your own

from now on. To make mistakes."

Hattie smiled. "Let's not be absurd."

"I said 'try.'"

"Okay. I have a quiz tomorrow and haven't studied *at all*. What are you going to do? This is a test."

I twitched.

"It's the *last grade before the midterm*, Juju."

I could almost feel the hives blooming.

"*And* I left my textbook at school."

Oh my God.

Hattie smiled angelically.

"Good . . . luck . . . ," I managed to say. "It's . . . *your* . . . test. . . ."

She beamed. "It wasn't so hard, was it?"

"You have no idea," I said.

"I do," she said. "That's why I love you."

I couldn't help but think of next year, when I wouldn't see her every day. No more breakfasts in the morning, chats while we brushed our teeth. "I'm going to miss you when I'm at college."

Hattie stared at the ground. "I'll be fine. Really. It's time for *you*, Juju."

Another thing I couldn't fix. No matter what happened, our family would still be in pieces. Me at some unknown university, Hattie at home but probably mostly with friends, and Mom even more alone than she was now.

"Hattie?" I said. "Even if Mom is mad at me—don't leave her by herself after I go, okay?"

She crossed her arms. "I'm not going to stop helping Old Taipei. And the protest. If she cuts you off, she cuts me off, too."

"I don't think that's what Dad would have wanted." He had given up his last lucid days working feverishly on the patent, on its sale. So we could survive without him. "Family was important to him." That much, at least, I knew.

Hattie said, "Tell Mom. She's the one making everything difficult."

"Just . . . try. For me. Okay?"

Hattie had an identical jade key chain hanging from her purse, only hers was in the shape of a mouse, since she was born in the Year of the Rat. She did the same thing I did; she held it in her palm, as if it could give her answers.

She looked me in the eye. "You do what you want with the internship—*and Garrett*—and I'll consider it."

It wasn't a guarantee, but it was a chance. I was learning, slowly, that might be enough.

45

MESSAGES

THAT NIGHT, FOR the first time in ages, I dreamed of my father.

It was a memory from when I was eight, during a time, I now knew, when we were on the brink of poverty. Bella, Hattie, and I had wanted these fancy canopy beds like we had seen at Mary Wu's house. Our parents had said no.

"But why?" we asked.

In my dream, my father looked almost unbearably sad, as if all of his cells were saturated and bloated with grief. He hugged us for a long moment. Glanced at the picture we had helpfully ripped out of the catalogue and ran a finger over the price. Multiplied it by three.

Buy the canopies and put us further into debt? Or say no to us and bear our unhappiness?

My mom would have said no, like it was a ridiculous thought.

And she did. But my father was different. He put the picture on the fridge for a week, gazing at it as he opened the door. Finally, he bundled us up in the car and took us for a drive.

There was a thrift store down the street from where we used to live, and he led us, hand in hand, to the bedding section. Let us pick out our favorite patterns—purple bunnies for Hattie, red and pink umbrellas for Bella, and blue and gold polka dots for me. Then he came home and started sewing. Attached a two-dollar hook to our ceiling and made us a new tent over what would eventually become Hattie's bed. Our own canopy.

In the real world, the tent was makeshift and slightly crooked. We adored it. In my dream, though, it became a thing of magic. All of us could fit in it, easily, even Mom, and it was filled with cozy blankets and stuffies. Stars sparkled from the ceiling.

Mom was laughing at this sock puppet she had found, and Bella was snuggled against her. Dad had Hattie in his lap, and she was trying to tell him, very seriously, about the differences between horses and lambs.

But then he slowly stopped smiling.

"Dad?" I said. No one else seemed to notice. "Dad!"

He faced me, and there it was: the knowledge of his own death. Hattie tugged on his arm, and Bella, giggling, tried to put a stuffed monkey around his neck. He closed his eyes, briefly, then leaned toward us.

"Are you happy, girls?"

We nodded. He kissed each of our foreheads, lingering.

Then he disappeared.

46

LUNAR NEW YEAR

I WOKE UP grasping, as if I could pull those wisps of my father and hold him to me. To make him stay. But, like in the dream, he faded.

I got dressed slowly as the images wrapped around my mind. What did they mean? Why now?

Mom yelled at us from downstairs. It was the first day of Lunar New Year. It was also the day of the protest. The folks in Old Taipei had scheduled it for tonight, since they thought they would get more press due to the holiday. Same day. Two universes.

Mom had gotten up before the sun rose and had been cooking. She was going all out, using Wàipó's recipes and our best serving plates. She was determined to make an entrance.

Today's celebration was going to be huge, full of all the uncles and aunties. We used to have it at a local community college, but it had since moved to the Esher Convention Center. When we finally arrived, everyone was dressed up and mingling. The competition results weren't out yet, but I knew the aunties and uncles would be asking about it. Mom could say I made it to the top ten, at least. But she didn't know I was going to quit.

When we arrived, Garrett was across the room, facing the door. His gaze followed me as I put the glass container full of dumplings on the potluck table, and it did not waver as I walked toward him. He was not smiling.

"I told my mom about Old Taipei and how the arena is going to hurt the neighborhood." I didn't bother with hello, because neither of us cared about that. "I'm going to withdraw from the competition."

He looked shocked. "Are you sure?"

I nodded. For once, I was. Emily Yao came up to me and pulled me away, but when I glanced back, Garrett was still staring at me. Emily pulled me into a seat next to her and started telling me about her latest updates with Lewis.

Around us were all the people I recognized from our childhood: Hattie's BFF Mandy. Emily. Lewis. I knew a lot of us had the same problems with our parents, but we seldom talked about it. I had heard through Hattie that a lot of them were keeping things from their folks as well: Mandy wanted to take a gap year before college, and David Chan wanted to go to school on the West Coast, even though his mom had expressly forbidden it.

We were all forced to hide ourselves, slide under these husks of respectability. Mom was terrified she would be cut off from everyone. Uncle Wu got laid off and didn't want everyone to know, so he was working two jobs to keep up his finances. Auntie Shih had a brother who had been in trouble with the law. She never talked about him.

Our world was full of secrets. But did they have to be?

Off to the side, I saw Eric arguing with Mrs. Lin. At school, he had been sitting alone at lunch these past few weeks, staring at Siobhan Collins. She had gotten rid of the little tiger attached to her backpack—the mirror of the one he had—and had started to hang out with other people, like Marty from the lacrosse team.

I wasn't close enough to hear what they were saying, but Mrs. Lin was unleashing the Asian Mom Death Glare. It was the twin laser beams of *DO NOT EMBARRASS ME IN FRONT OF EVERYONE RIGHT NOW* and *YOU ARE SO GOING TO GET IT WHEN WE GET HOME.*

I could almost see the layers and years of fury between Eric and his mother. The anger had made the love between them turn into ash. It was like I could see into the future, a horrible vision of loss and anger and bitterness.

Mom had made things into a binary choice: continue in the competition or choose my family. I knew she had done that because she thought it was the only way to push us toward what she believed to be good decisions. Maybe it was the way her own parents had treated her.

I couldn't help but think of Bella, alone, cradling her daughter, Maddie. Knowing what would be ahead for her either way she went. But in reality, didn't Bella only have one option? In order to protect her child from the silent scorn, the stares, and the judgment, she had to leave. All of us.

It's what Dad's negotiation book would have called a lose-lose situation. And now I was facing the same dilemma. No matter which path I chose, the outcome was inevitable: pain. Grief.

Either I lost my mom, or I lost . . . me.

But for the first time, I realized the real problem was the setup. That's what my dream had been telling me. We were trapped in a false dichotomy and had missed the fact that there could be other options. One where everyone could win. Like making a canopy bed but only using materials we could afford.

Wasn't that what my father had done? He hadn't gambled on the start-up, but he hadn't abandoned his friend, either. He picked a third option, one with the best chance of success. Had he chosen the start-up and it failed, then they both would have lost. By picking the large payout, then helping his friend, Dad had made his own solution. It was a painful one, with both negative and positive consequences. But it had saved both of them.

So what was my solution?

Mrs. Lin spotted Mom and some of the other aunties and dragged Eric over to them. They spoke for a while, Eric silently standing next to them.

"The competition is almost over." My mom's voice floated over to us.

"Yes," said Mrs. Lin. "Such a good experience."

"So nice," Mom said. "They are all doing so well."

I saw Garrett flinch, though he tried to hide it.

And the first thing I had to fix was not the competition. It was something infinitely more delicate and precious.

I started to walk over to my mom, but Garrett grabbed my wrist. "Don't, Juliana," he said. "It's okay."

It was not. Garrett Tsai, born in the middle of two academic prodigies, always left to fend for himself. The only other girl he had loved had run off with his best friend. Had anyone ever chosen him? Been in his corner, always?

From now on, that person was going to be me. He may never forgive me, but Garrett deserved to know there was at least one person in the world who would always look out for him.

"I'm going to fix this," I said.

I ran to my mom and made polite small talk with her and the aunties before discreetly pulling her into an empty hallway.

My mom was confused. "Juliana."

"I heard you talking about the AABC." I jumped off a high dive once when I was a child, going from concrete under my feet to nothing but space and blue below. I remembered what it was like to fall through the air, the fear choking you. "There's something you should know. I didn't partner with Louis. I did the whole competition with Garrett Tsai."

My mom looked like I had just told her I had given birth to a live chicken.

"What?" she said. She glanced around, but the hallway was still empty. She lowered her voice. *"What?"*

"So many of the things our team did well—the web design, the graphics—were him. He—"

My mom hadn't heard a word. "What about Louis Park? There were three of you on the team?"

"Louis wants to be a zoologist," I said. "He was never in the competition."

My mom let out a string of Mandarin, all of which added up to: *Are you kidding me right now?*

"How could you do this to me?" she hissed.

"It wasn't about you," I said. "Eric split up with me. I needed a partner, and Garrett agreed to help me. And he turned out to be the best choice."

My mom pursed her lips. "Go get Hattie. We're going home. You will drop him and then win the last round by yourself."

"I'm quitting the competition," I said. "I can't help to destroy Old Taipei."

My mom looked like she wanted to drive straight to a chicken farm and start cooking. "*No.* I forbid it."

But we both realized that she couldn't stop me. When Hattie and I were younger, she used to put us in time-out or take away our toys. But I was now seventeen years old. I was going to be on my own next year. The threat of disownment was the sword she had always held over my head. The ultimate punishment. And for so many years, it had worked. But here's the thing about punishment: sometimes the idea of it is scarier than the thing itself. I knew my friends wouldn't leave me. And neither would Hattie.

My mom cutting me off would be devastating. But would it be worse than this half-life where I hid things from her and we were strangers anyway?

"I don't want to lie to you, Mom," I said. "And I don't want to lose you like Bella did. I love you too much."

Those little words were something our family never said, and setting them loose now had the same effect as a grenade. My mom's eyes filled, but she held it in.

"You don't want that?" she said. "Then don't quit. And drop the Tsai boy."

"I know what you're worried about," I said. "You want a good life for me, and you don't want me to suffer. But that comes in many ways. Not just financial."

Mom clutched her purse. For the first time, she looked uncertain.

I said, "Maybe I don't get into Yale. Or any Ivy League school. But all the things I learned—all the things *you* taught me, Mom, will make sure that I'm fine."

My mom was still, her fingers tight over her purse strap.

It was true. Ironically, the very things she had drilled into me were now the things that would set me free. That was how to solve the unsolvable conundrum. How to get out of the dilemma. I had to show Mom there were ways outside of the system to achieve what she wanted.

"No, Juliana," she said. "You will not throw away this competition. Think about your father."

But that's the thing: I was. I really was.

"You had better finish it and win," she said, then started walking away. Like I would automatically follow.

"Why did he do it?" I called.

She stopped.

"Dad," I said. "Why did he work every weekend and late every night? Even when he was sick? Why did he finish and sell that patent even though he was in the middle of chemo?" This was what I had been trying to figure out all along. "He wanted the money so we could have some breathing room. The space to make *choices*. It was his last gift. I know we're incredibly privileged and lucky. But what are we doing with his sacrifice? Do you think he'd be at peace with you working all the time? With us being strangers? With you not knowing Maddie? With you and Hattie fighting all the time?"

Mom bowed her head.

I thought of everything I had done to try to follow in my dad's footsteps. To understand someone who had been taken from me. But I didn't need an internship or college campus or competition to do that. I knew who he was.

Are you happy, girls?

"Is this how you want things to be?" I asked. "Bella's not coming back. And Hattie and I are going to be forced to leave, too, eventually, if things don't change. Do you think those were his last wishes? How he wanted us to . . . go on without him?"

Mom looked stricken.

"You keep trying to appease the aunties and uncles. But are those your real friends?" I had to tell her. "Do you know why Eric dropped me? It was because Mrs. Lin told him to. She didn't want him to get close to our family. Would Dad want to see you trying so hard to get her and everyone else's approval? Shouldn't they accept you for who you are? I know he did. He loved you, no matter what."

Mom's face was wet now, but she didn't wipe away her tears.

"And so do we," I said. "But we're just asking that you do the same for us."

Her hand was curled, and she pressed it against her chest, as if to keep any more emotion from leaking out.

She had sacrificed so much for us, had done so much each day to keep us fed and healthy. But this might be one of the few—maybe the only—times she had stopped and listened to what I was saying with her full attention.

She pulled out a tissue from her purse and pressed it to her cheeks, eyes. For a second, I hoped that she might acknowledge what I had said. Or start a conversation. But she walked away, without a word.

47

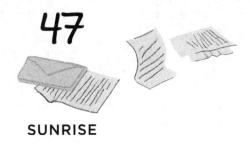

SUNRISE

I WATCHED HER head down the hallway toward the bathroom, then vanish inside. A few minutes later, Garrett walked out of the ballroom.

"Juliana?" He glanced around the halls, at the aunties and uncles wandering to and from the restrooms. "Are you okay?"

When I didn't respond, he led me to an empty room so we could talk in private.

I finally said, "I told her everything." I was still in shock. But I felt something loosening, getting lighter. Finally, the box was open and all the secrets were out.

"Everything?"

"Like I should have from the beginning." I reached for his hand, squeezed it. "I'm so sorry. For what I did."

He smiled, but it was wistful. Full of regret. "I made mistakes, too."

We had both been trapped in the Linevine, tangled in judgments and fear and everything else we had been taught. Maybe what had happened to us was inevitable; after all, that was what the system was designed to create. To perpetuate. Until we were able to free ourselves of it.

"So, what now?" I asked.

Everything unspoken pulsed between us. Garrett looked exhilarated. Terrified. He hesitated, then slowly laced his fingers with mine. "Are you really okay?"

"Yes. No." And suddenly, I was back with him on a riverbank, watching the sun arrive. Bringing a new day. I remembered how close our hands had been to each other, how the inch between being together and apart seemed almost insurmountable. And maybe it was. Look how long it had taken us to get here, where he could cross the distance and clasp his hand with mine. "But that's fine. It doesn't have to be perfect."

He smiled. "Are you, Juliana Zhao, starting to tolerate messiness? Uncertainty?"

I nodded.

He took a step closer. His palm slid across my lower back and tugged me toward him. He was waiting for me to lean back, to run, but I was not moving. I was not even breathing. He hooked a gentle hand behind my neck and pressed his mouth to mine.

Every cell exploded in color; every part of me that had been ragged with heartbreak was now infused with light. I wrapped my arms around his neck, and his arm tightened around my waist. I was finally able to thread my fingers through his hair, the strands tangling.

He pulled away and *smile* didn't even cover it. It was warm, overwhelming adoration.

So, this was what it was like to be loved by Garrett Tsai. How had I never guessed?

Garrett said, "Are you sure?"

I knew the words were important to him, so I said, clearly, "I choose you."

He looked floored. Then he touched a fingertip to my lower lip, leaned in, and kissed me again, his thumbs cradling my cheeks.

And I let it all go then, all the boxes I had tried to hold down, all the plates I had been spinning in the air, all the expectations I had been carrying. I let them all go and allowed myself to be in the moment. With him.

48

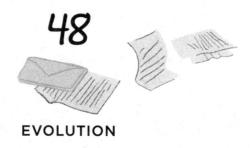

EVOLUTION

WE SURVIVED THE Lunar New Year variety show or what Hattie called the Talent Show Death March. Piano recitals, wushu demonstrations, fashion shows. And after the whole thing was done—after all the sticky rice was eaten, all the Lunar New Year cake was gobbled, and all the piano concertos were played—it was finally time to go home.

As we wandered out to our cars, I ran ahead and pulled on Mom's arm. She had refused to look or talk to me during the rest of the evening, except for one pointed glance when she saw Garrett and me sitting side by side in the back of the auditorium.

"I'm getting a ride with Garrett," I said.

She paused but didn't forbid it. I knew we'd have a talk later. That was a good thing. A new thing.

I checked my watch. The protest was still going on. I could

have gone straight there. She wouldn't find out until it was too late. But I didn't want to hide things—myself—from her. Not anymore.

"I'm going to the protest."

Garrett waited by his car, patiently.

Mom stiffened. We both smiled politely at some aunties and uncles passing by and waited until they were out of earshot. Then Eric, face tight, strode out of the building, his mom trailing behind. I could see, but he could not, her sadness as she tried to keep up with him. The longing. My mom saw it, too, her eyes tracking Mrs. Lin as she hurried behind her son.

Mom walked to her car without answering me. But she didn't demand that I come with her or try to stop me. She just left.

And now I, too, knew the imbalance of being set adrift on an uncertain ocean. But I wasn't defenseless. I had all the tools she had given to me over the years: perseverance, intelligence, optimism, resourcefulness. I would use them to build my own future.

For me. For all of us.

49

Dear Mr. Lee:

I sincerely appreciate the experiences provided by the Asian Americans in Business Competition. However, for reasons we have previously discussed, I must respectfully withdraw.

Sincerely,

Juliana Zhao

50

PROTEST PARTY

BY THE TIME Garrett and I got to Old Taipei, the protest was already in high gear. The uncles and aunties were holding signs and shouting. Uncle Jing had a bullhorn and was chanting something in Mandarin. And, if I was not mistaken, Chef Auntie was next to him in a matching shirt. They were handing out special chocolate-covered fortune cookies; on the back of each fortune was trivia about Old Taipei.

I squeezed Garrett's hand. He had been in constant physical contact with me since we had arrived, touching my hand, hair, sleeve. As if he was checking if I was real.

"Is that *couplewear*?" I said. "As in, are they a *couple*? As I had predicted?"

"Unbelievable." He fussed with my scarf, wrapping it warmly around my neck.

"What can I say?" I said. "The Zhao magic is still there."

He wrapped an arm around my waist and pressed his mouth to mine. "So it is."

The kids from the cultural center let out a loud *ooooh*, and we laughed. All the aunties and uncles from the cultural center were behind them, and so were Kevin and Ms. Vivian, who practically clapped when she saw us holding hands.

Cars were honking as they passed, and I spotted some local media trucks on the side. Auntie Beth and Auntie Cindy came running up to us and pressed signs into our hands. And we joined the group, yelling, cheering, and fighting for what we believed in.

My mom might never forgive me. But the people here would love me anyway. And I would love her and wait until we could come together again.

Epilogue

SIX MONTHS LATER

I HAD SOME pretty bad ideas in the past. But by far the worst was agreeing to let Hattie drive. In a two-minute span, she hit a curb backing out of our driveway, didn't stop for a stop sign until the middle of the intersection, and ran a red when she tried to speed through a yellow light.

"OMG, Hattie, I'm not going to live to see college."

"This is great!" she said, and turned the music up. In the back seat, both Kevin and Garrett seemed a little queasy.

"We're only going to the bookstore, right?" Kevin said.

"Yes, but I need to practice getting on the highway." Hattie changed lanes. "Here we go!"

"NO!" we all yelled, but it was too late.

She finally arrived in Old Taipei and quickly parallel parked. About a foot away from the curb, but whatever. We all climbed out of the car, then Garrett leaned against the side.

"She's getting better," he said weakly.

Kevin was still a bit green. Hattie grabbed his hand and skipped into the store with him. Garrett and I stayed outside for a moment, just us.

Down the street, a few people were taking pictures in front of Uncle Jing's newly repainted giant fortune cookie. There were signs for his new flavors: matcha, ube, sesame. I guess Chef Auntie had been working her magic.

Hattie and I had sent Bella a message a few weeks ago, and she had taken a little bit of time to respond at first. I understood. It had been years, and she didn't know if we would support or judge her. And Maddie. But we kept trying, and she finally sent us one, then two pictures of Maddie, Wesley, and their cozy home in San Francisco.

My phone beeped. It was Hattie. She had taken a snapshot of me and Garrett through the bookstore window; I was looking at Uncle Jing's store and he was looking at me.

Hattie: It's you and your BOYFRIEND.

I sent a candid picture I had taken of Hattie and Kevin, one where she was midsentence and making a ridiculous face. I waited. Three seconds later, I heard the yelp through the door.

I showed my screen to Garrett and he laughed. In the weeks since the protest, we had been spending all of our time together. Mom didn't stop me from seeing him, but she didn't encourage it, either. She had said nothing when the news that I had quit the competition tore through the Linevine. But then Ms. Vivian had posted about the impact of the arena on Old Taipei and how proud she was that we were helping the Taiwanese community. Better yet, she wrote an article for the *Taipei Times* about how the daughter of Jùnhóng Zhao, founder of the Asian Americans in Business Competition, was continuing his legacy of helping the community by defending Old Taipei. Ms. Vivian, too, knew a little bit about threading the needle between cultures.

The appeal was still being decided, but we had been talking with the owners of Dynasty Mall to offer leased retail space at a discount, just in case. And researching which corporations might be interested in sponsoring a new cultural center in that area. The protest had gotten a lot of press, and the city must have been eager to shed the negative publicity. Maybe we could leverage that to have the city council approve a permit to build new rent-controlled apartments by Dynasty Mall. To re-create Old Taipei in a different part of the city, even if we lost our appeal.

I started researching an area of business called social entrepreneurship, which focused on getting corporations to use their money and influence to help communities and the world. As I learned more, it was like a sudden turn of a lens; everything snapped into focus. I thought about the things that had actually brought me joy over the past few months: volunteering at the cultural center, helping Old Taipei, playing with the little kids and teaching them English. Even matchmaking was connecting people, bringing them together. Ms. Vivian got me an interview with a friend of hers, and she recommended some other schools for me to apply to: Berkeley, Northwestern, Duke. Her old alma mater, NYU.

(You may be wondering what happened with the competition and my colleges. Linda and Kelly handily won the competition and already had plans to get investors for their service. Eric lost but got into Dartmouth and, last I heard, graduated early and moved to New Hampshire. I got rejected from Yale and wait-listed at Harvard. But I did get into NYU, with a full merit scholarship. NYU, which not only had a stellar social entrepreneurship program but was also only a few hours away from one Rhode Island School of Design, future alma mater of a certain Mr. Garrett Tsai.)

(My mom wanted me to write to Harvard so I could get off the wait list. But Garrett and I visited New York with Hattie and Kevin one weekend, and we kind of loved it. The magic of a city.)

There was a tap on the window. Hattie was inside the store, holding up some knitted animals. Auntie Beth had convinced Auntie Cindy to sell her items at her store, and they were proving to be surprisingly popular.

For Maddie? she mouthed.

I gave a thumbs-up to the penguin and turtle, a thumbs-down to the shark.

My mom still hadn't come around, but I continued to tell her about everything: the plans for social entrepreneurship, NYU. Reaching out to Bella. I left a picture of Maddie on the fridge. The next morning, it was gone. I found it a few days later, next to Mom's nightstand. She was hanging out with Auntie Liu more and less with the Linevine. The other day, she even left a note that she was going to play mah-jongg with Auntie Liu,

Chef Auntie, and their friends.

In the end, I was heading toward what I thought my mom really wanted—a fulfilling and meaningful life. It might not look like the one she had planned, but it would be a good one, nonetheless.

Are you happy?

Yes, Dad.

Garrett kissed me, then reached for my hand and held it tightly.

"You ready?" he said.

I nodded.

I was. For anything.

Acknowledgments

THEY SAY THAT drafting the second book is often harder than the first. I have found this to be absolutely true. THANK YOU to my brilliant editor, Jen Ung, for all your guidance and wisdom during the quadrillion (bazillion) revisions of this story, for your patience and encouragement, and for making this book what it is today. It's been an absolute honor to work with you.

To my agent, Alex Slater: Thank you for always being in my corner and providing so much support over the years. You are truly the Best Agent Ever™!

This is a book about parents and their children, and I am so thrilled that it will be launching on my mom's birthday. Mom and Dad, thank you for always believing in me, for always being there, and for your patience during my teenage years. ☺ I am so grateful that we now have a better understanding of each other's perspectives. I know how much you sacrificed and what hardships you endured so Charles and I could have a better life. I love you! (Linevine: the parents in this book are not based on my actual parents, truly! Don't call them!)

Speaking of Charles—you are on the dedication page but also get a mention here since you are awesome. One day we'll actually have a fight. Until then, I am lucky to be called your sister.

I am eternally thankful to the following people: my husband George's wonderful parents, Ariana, Camillia, Chris, Keralena, Kienan, Ivan, Phoebe, Rachel, and Sophia.

To C.H. Huang and P.J. Park: This writing journey would have been impossible without you both. Thank you for your feedback, your advice, the stellar snacks, and your in-depth conversations about the latest K-dramas and C-dramas.

Thank you as well to the following individuals, whose support means the world to me: Jenny B; Henny Bhushan; Lisa C; Mike D; Nicola DeRobertis-Theye; Susan Upton Douglass; Chris H; Pallavi Jagasia; Matthew Kovach; Sher Lee; Dr. Anne Lyman; Captain Jason McLaughlin; Yasmin Moorman; Susan Murphy; Amy S; Salvatore Scibona; Sharon Song; Daniel Sorbello; Angela Su; Brian Su; Emily Su; Thomasina Su; Leslie Sullivan; Carolyn Wang; CAPT S.W. Wong, JAGC, USN; Pearlin Yang; and Lee Ming Yeh.

To all the fellow writers in the 2023 Debuts group and in the Class of 2k23 books: thank you for helping me to survive debut year!

Thank you to the amazing people at Quill Tree and Harper-Collins, who all were a part of making this book what it is: Rosemary Brosnan, David Curtis, Danielle McClelland, Suzanne Murphy, Jean McGinley, Audrey Diestelkamp, Abby Dommert, Patty Rosati, Tara Feehan, Laura Raps, and Kerry

Moynagh and the Harper sales team. Special thanks to Jon Howard, Dan Janeck, and Robin Roy for making sure that this book was both grammatically correct and internally consistent. Sorry about all those commas! And thank you to Laura Mock and Debs Lim for the adorable cover and artwork!

To my dearest husband, George: You are the original blueprint for the ideal romantic lead. Thank you for making everything magical and for going on this wonderous life journey with me.

To Sophia and Ariana: yes, you finally got on the dedication page. ☺ I know you wanted pages and pages in this acknowledgments section, but I will just say the most important thing here: I love you.